About the author

James Warden was a teacher for forty years and retired in 2006. He now enjoys his retirement as much as he enjoyed his time in the education service and is catching up on those things which he left undone and ought to have done – in particular, his writing. He writes every morning between nine o'clock and noon, for thirty-six weeks of the year.

He is fortunate enough to be able to act in several Norwich theatres – the Maddermarket, the Sewell Barn and, with the Great Hall Players, at the Assembly House – and this experience informs his writing. His stage adaptation of Laurie Lee's *As I Walked Out One Midsummer Morning* was performed at the Sewell Barn Theatre in November 2009. His original play, *Letters from a Boy in the Trenches*, which was based on the letters of a WW1 soldier, was performed in Marchington, Staffordshire in 2015.

James is married – for the second time – and lives in Norfolk. He and his wife travel as much as possible. They have visited Italy (where they were married in 2002) several times, Canada, Bermuda, Egypt, India, the Czech Republic, New England, Poland, Slovenia, Antarctica, the Falkland Islands, Alaska, the Galapagos Islands, Australia and Switzerland. In 2018, they travelled across the USA on Route 66. They have also taken several holidays in various Mediterranean resorts – the basis for his first novel, *Three Women of a Certain Age*, which was published in July 2010, and *Bingham Goes to Cannes*, to be published in 2024.

During his years in education, he wrote about twenty play scripts for children. These included the one that formed the basis for his children's story, *The Great Gobbler and his Home Baking Factory at the North Pole*, which he wrote in 1982 and published in December 2010.

He has three sons by his first marriage, and they inspired two of his novels – *The Vampire's Homecoming*, which was published in 2011, and *The One-eyed Dwarf*, published in 2012. With them and his first wife, he also travelled to the southern states of North America, France, Germany (West and East), Estonia and what was Czechoslovakia.

i

Writing by James Warden

Stories of Our Time
Three Women of a Certain Age (2010)
The Age of Wisdom (2015))
Swinging in the Sixties (2016)

'Tales of Mystery and Imagination'
The Vampire's Homecoming (2011)
The First Rendlesham Incident (2017)

Stories for Children
The Great Gobbler and his Home-Baking Factory
at the North Pole (2010)
The One-eyed Dwarf (2012)

Biography
The Boy in the Photograph: Bill Pieri's autobiography (2014)
A Child of the Fifties: autobiography of my childhood (2017)

Plays
As I Walked Out One Midsummer Morning
*(Adapted with the permission of Laurie Lee's estate and performed
at the Sewell Barn Theatre in Norwich in November 2009.)*
Letters from a Boy in the Trenches
*(Adapted from the letters home of Sydney Harrison and performed
by the Marchington Amateur Dramatic Society in November 2015.)*

The Bingham Detective Stories
Bingham's First Case (2018)
Bingham and the Runaway Wife (2019)
Bingham Seeks an Odd Couple
(To be published in 2020)
Bingham Pursues a Minister's Clerk
(To be published in 2021)
Bingham and the Traveller's Daughter
(To be published in 2022)
Bingham Along the Stuart Highway
(To be published in 2023)
Bingham Goes to Cannes
(To be published in 2024)
Bingham and the Lost Years
(To be published in 2025)

The Search
For
Edwin Drood

by

James Warden

Grosvenor House
Publishing Limited

This book is published by
Grosvenor House Publishing Ltd
Link House
140 The Broadway, Tolworth, Surrey, KT6 7HT.
www.grosvenorhousepublishing.co.uk

A CIP record for this book
is available from the British Library

ISBN 978-1-83975-151-6

With thanks to Charles Dickens
who has given me, and will continue to give me,
years of pleasurable reading,
and, particular thanks, with
regard to this novel
for
The Mystery of Edwin Drood
The Life and Adventures of Nicholas Nickleby
Our Mutual Friend
and his
Journalism 1834 - 1870

Contents

Chapter 1	The Disappearance of Edwin Drood	1
Chapter 2	Neville Landless Loses His Temper	10
Chapter 3	Rosa Budd Remembers a Shadow on a Sundial	19
Chapter 4	Mr Tarter Ties a Knot	28
Chapter 5	Mr Grewgious Unbends Only Slightly	36
Chapter 6	John Jasper Reiterates His Determination	45
Chapter 7	The Rev Septimus Crisparkle Revisits the Weir	58
Chapter 8	Mr Durdles Shakes His Keys	72
Chapter 9	Mr Datchery is Unsettled	83
Chapter 10	Helena Landless Displays Her Unusual Powers	94
Chapter 11	Princess Puffer Smokes a Pipe	105
Chapter 12	Samuel Warden Ponders *the Gritty State of Things* Past	113
Chapter 13	Samuel Warden Takes on a Deputy	129
Chapter 14	Mr Durdles Shakes Off Some Stony Dust	139
Chapter 15	Helena Landless Under Many Circumstances	149
Chapter16	The Fall of Mr Datchery	156

Chapter 17   John Jasper Takes the Train   173
Chapter 18   Mr Grewgious Takes a Walk   186
Chapter 19   Helena Landless Accepts a Challenge 193
Chapter 20   A Visit to the Theatre   206

Chapter 21   A Cry is Heard   218
Chapter 22   John Jasper Gets His Man   232
Chapter 23   Samuel Warden Attends a Wedding   243

Author's End Note and Acknowledgments   251
Map of Cloisterham from DS Warden's Notebook   255

Chapter 1

The Disappearance of Edwin Drood

Samuel Warden had taken his usual route to work that morning, knowing the day held something more than the commonplace. Intuition was not a tool of the trade in the new Detective Police, but it was a faculty he had inherited from his mother and one on which he relied at times without admitting the fact to his brother officers, especially his superior officer, Detective Inspector Charles Field, who sat watching him from across the broad, leather-topped desk.

They were a newly-formed branch of the Metropolitan Police and looked upon themselves as going about their business in a workmanlike manner, calmly and steadily pursuing their quarries using the deductive method, clue by clue from small beginnings to the final resolution of whatever crime represented their challenge of the time.

Each of the eight sergeants working under Inspector Field had their own specialisms. Samuel Warden had two: country people and the London markets. He had taken naturally to the latter when operating as a beat officer and the former was supposed to spring naturally from his having been born in a village near the town of Ipswich in the county of Suffolk. Watching Inspector Field preparing to speak, he wondered which of these might call upon his skills that day.

Field was a burly man and the possessor of moist eyes, making him appear older than his forty-two years. This mark of aged wisdom was helped by a husky voice and a deliberate manner, one aspect of which was a tendency to tap his nose with a fat forefinger, something he was doing at that moment, while thinking.

"Does Cloisterham mean anything to you, Sam?"

"It's a small town on the Medway, isn't it, sir?"

"Cast your mind back six months to last Christmas time."

"There was a spot of bother there – the disappearance of a young man called Drood. Nothing ever came of it, as I remember."

"And nothing has come of it to this day. The local boys have turned nothing up, no body, no sudden re-appearance of Mr Edwin Drood elsewhere – as you say, nothing. Nought but a complete void. Which is where we come in, Sam. I want you to go down to Cloisterham and find Mr Edwin Drood, whether he be dead or alive."

Samuel Warden had been forewarned. A message reached him at home that very morning suggesting he should 'settle his immediate affairs' and arrive at the detectives' headquarters, Great Scotland Yard, just off Trafalgar Square, ready for 'a few days in the country'. Anywhere outside the immediate metropolis was 'in the country', as far as Inspector Field was concerned.

Samuel had even packed a bag before setting out on his regular three mile walk from where he lived in Camberwell to Westminster. It was a walk that settled his mind to the work of the day, cold and desolate though it was an hour before sunrise. Once over Vauxhall Bridge and in the 'city proper', beyond the coarse grass and the rank weeds of the marshes around Millbank, his mind took on a calmness that prepared him for the various classes of criminals he might face: the thieves, the prostitutes, the swindlers, the swell mob, the pimps, the sneaks, the robbers, the pickpockets, the smugglers, the coiners, the river pirates, the forgers, the embezzlers, the magsmen, and others of their kind each took their allotted place in some quiet corner of his mind as he strolled along.

It was, perhaps, his childhood in the countryside that inclined him to enjoy the noiseless times, and with the buildings closely shut and the busy crowds absent Samuel found such moments on his early morning walk.

Samuel was born in the village of Wherstead, the son of a railwayman who also cultivated an allotment situated in the nearby town already mentioned. Samuel had, as a young man, followed in his father's footsteps, but the lure of the great city called out to him and he applied to join the Metropolitan Police in the autumn of 1841, much to his mother's dismay. The education he had received at the village school, together with a sharp brain, proved enough to meet the literacy requirements necessary and he began work as a police constable. He was 23 years old.

Samuel was attached to E division, which included the area around Covent Garden and the labyrinth of alleyways and passages that comprised Seven Dials. It was here he learned the tricks of his trade and where he gained his stripes, a world away from his quiet, Suffolk village.

In a place where the shops specialized in the purchase of cast-off clothes, old kitchen ware, pet birds and dead rabbits, where entertainment comprised dingy public houses and gin shops, where lane after lane of houses displayed only broken windows, it was, perhaps, not surprising that the main activities were idling against shop fronts, lounging on corners or the most convenient post, pitching in with any squabble, gossiping idly, tormenting one's neighbours and beating one's wife.

Samuel quickly became known for his swift intervention when trouble seemed to be brewing. Although of slight build, he was fast on his feet and quiet in his manner. A word from him would stay a husband's hand, move a troublemaker on, quell a drunk or separate two harpies intent on scratching each other's eyes out. He never raised his voice but, rather, interposed his presence between the combatants.

It was in this way, by gaining the trust of the dirty men, the squalid women and the reeking children that his attention was drawn to a solitary man, a stranger noted for living a life of seclusion, emerging from his back attic to purchase only half-pints of coffee, penny loaves and the occasional pen with "a ha'porth of ink". Samuel obliged him into conversation on one such excursion and noticed that his jacket sleeves were burned with acid. The next time the stranger left his room, Samuel forced the door and found pamphlets and posters advocating political terrorism among the acids and glycerine he supposed to be for bomb making. When the man returned, Samuel was waiting for him and requested his company on the way to E division police station in Bow Street.

His perspicacity attracted the attention of Sir Richard Mayne and he was introduced to Inspector Field of the Detective Police. Five years after joining the Metropolitan Police as a uniformed officer, Samuel Warden became a member of an elite force of men dedicated to the tracking of criminals across the metropolis and beyond, when the need arose. Free, now, to roam, Samuel Warden soon familiarised himself with the entire metropolis, sometimes appearing as himself, sometimes in disguise as a shoemaker, a cabinet maker, a costermonger, a race-track tout, an opium user and, once, as a statue.

He was drawn, especially, to the various markets – Covent Garden, Billingsgate, Smithfield, Hungerford and the scores of smaller ones such as Lumber Court in Seven Dials – where crime was rife, especially with the likes of pickpockets and sharpers.

It was in Covent Garden that he struck up a friendship with Sarah Rowse, who was selling produce from her nursery garden in Camberwell. A widow, living alone in one of the terraced houses in the village, she welcomed the extra money a lodger would bring and invited Samuel to join her, an arrangement that suited them both nicely: he was now earning good money and would lend a hand with her vegetables and fruit when off-duty, she kept a clean house and was a first-class cook.

Moreover, he enjoyed getting away from the city, the relative quiet of Camberwell and the peace of his walk to work each morning. Occasionally he would come across a late-night reveller, one of the homeless crouched in a doorway or a uniformed officer on his beat, hoping for, and expecting, a peaceful end to his tour of duty; but usually the streets were deserted, the drinking places closed, the coach stands waiting their first arrival.

On that morning, in the hot summer of 1847, upstairs windows were open, and he heard the slumberous murmurings of those wrestling with sleep. Tiredness was everywhere: in the horse pulling the market cart, in the boy opening the shutters of a public house, in his mother setting up the tables in readiness for a street breakfast, in a woman toiling past him, a heavy basket of fruit on her head, in the labourer on his way to work, his dinner tied up in a handkerchief.

In was in this quiet, reflective state that Samuel Warden reached his own place of work and sat facing Inspector Field, who – having given his nose a final tap with the forefinger of his right hand – proceeded to lay out the case of Edwin Drood's disappearance, as far as it was known.

"The last time Edwin Drood was seen alive and well was at his uncle's house on Christmas Eve. He had gone there to share dinner with his uncle and a young man called Neville Landless, who we will come to in due course.

Previously that day, Mr Drood visited a jeweller in Cloisterham to have his watch wound and set. The jeweller told us that he'd try to persuade him to buy a signet ring, *as many young gentlemen were inclined to do with the date of their wedding day inscribed inside*; but that Mr Drood had declined, explaining that the only jewellery he allowed himself were his watch and chain, which were his father's, and his shirt-pin. Evidently, this fact had already been confirmed by the boy's uncle, John Jasper, when he had dropped in for a watch glass only a few days before. Our jeweller had tried his salesmanship on the uncle, also, suggesting that *should he wish to make a present to a gentleman a ring would be most acceptable.* The uncle explained that the only jewellery his one relative wore was a watch and chain and his shirt pin. You will see the significance of these articles of jewellery as we proceed, Sam.

Mr Landless – according to his sister, Helena, and the Rev Crisparkle, his, shall we say, mentor – had spent the day preparing himself for a walking break over the Christmas period. His preparations included putting his room in order and packing a knapsack with a few articles of clothing – stout shoes and socks among them. He'd bought the knapsack a few days before from a shop in the High Street and, at the same time, had purchased a heavy walking stick – a very heavy walking stick, not to say *much too heavy*, according to Mr Crisparkle.

Neville Landless then visited his sister at the Nuns' House, a seminary for young ladies run by a Miss Twinkleton. According to the local constabulary, Miss Landless was not the easiest person to interview. She was – shall we say – a trifle touchy, but she confirmed her brother's intention to start out on his walk early the next morning – that is, Christmas Day. He felt that in his present state of mind, *unsettled and unhappy and unsettling and interfering with other people*, he was best out of the way at such a festive time."

Inspector Field checked a report before him as he quoted the young woman's words.

"He planned to be away for a fortnight and promised to write to her every alternate day. Miss Landless did add that her brother had expressed a disinclination to be going to the dinner with Mr Drood and his uncle, but she wouldn't be drawn on why this was so. She did say that she stood looking after him as he made his way along the street, that he passed the Gate House – that's Mr Jasper's home – twice, apparently *reluctant to enter,* but she saw him hurry in when the cathedral clock struck one quarter.

Mr Jasper had spent his day about his cathedral duties. He is a Lay Precentor: he conducts the choir and directs the services – from a musical perspective, of course. He was, according to Mr Crisparkle, *in beautiful voice.* The Minor Canon felt that he had *never sung difficult music with such skill and harmony as he did in that day's anthem."*

Again, Inspector Field consulted the report on his desk.

"This despite the fact Mr Jasper had *been unwell and his throat a little tender, so that he was obliged to wear a large black scarf to protect his throat, even with his ecclesiastical robes.* Mr Jasper had been trying a new medicine for an ailment of his. (I suppose it pays a choirmaster to look after his voice, Sam.) He seemed in very good spirits.

He had also visited a Mr Sapsea, who is the mayor of Cloisterham. Mr Sapsea confirmed that Mr Jasper was looking forward to his dinner with the two young men and said that the meal was to *make up their differences.* He was unable to explain what these differences might have been, but he had a very dim view of Mr Landless who he described as *un-English.*

It was, according to our friends in Cloisterham, rather a rough night, weather-wise: chimneys being toppled, shutters being rattled, people being swept off their feet, roofs being on the pavement by morning. You get the picture, Sam? It may or may not be relevant, as you will see in due course.

The following morning – this being Christmas Day, you understand – Mr Jasper turns up at our Minor Canon's house asking if he has seen Mr Drood. Mr Jasper is in an excitable state, judging by the fact he is only half-dressed. He explains that his nephew had not returned home the previous evening having been down to the river to look at the storm with Mr Landless. Mr Crisparkle explains that Mr Landless did return home and had already set off on his walking tour that morning as planned.

Later in the day, Mr Landless is apprehended and brought back to Cloisterham by a group of men led by the local omnibus driver, a man by the name of Joe, where he makes a voluntary statement before Mr Sapsea. He said that Mr Drood returned to the Gate House after their visit to the river and explained that the blood seen on his clothes and walking stick was a result of his having put up a fight when apprehended. The mayor suggests issuing a warrant for the young man's committal, but Mr Crisparkle undertakes to keep him at home and produce him when necessary.

The following morning – Boxing Day, Sam – the river is dragged, all day and late into the night. Nothing is found on that day or the next, despite an apparently very thorough search: the river itself, the banks, the shore, the creeks, the causeways.

Now we come to an interesting discovery by our Minor Canon. For whatever reason – and this is not made clear in the report – Mr Crisparkle decides to take a walk to Cloisterham Weir the night after Boxing Day. This weir is two miles above the spot where the young men purportedly came to watch the storm. No search had been made here because it was supposed that should Mr Drood have had the misfortune to fall into the river he would, quite rightly, have been washed downstream from the spot they visited. While at the weir, Mr Crisparkle has a funny feeling, what he describes as *a strange idea that something unusual hung about the place.* I quote his exact words. For an intuitive man like yourself, Sam, that might be significant."

Inspector Field looked at his sergeant and smiled, as much as if to say, 'you thought I didn't know, didn't you?'

"So strong was this feeling that he returned to the weir the next morning and took a swim in the icy waters. And what did he find caught by its chain in the timbers of the weir? A gold watch engraved with the initials E D! Nothing daunted, our intrepid ecclesiastical gentleman takes another dive and comes up, not with a body but a shirt pin. Mr Landless was detained, pending enquiries.

The Cloisterham constabulary are to be congratulated on their next move, which was to consult the jeweller to which

Mr Drood had taken his watch on Christmas Eve. The watch had stopped, and it was the jeweller's opinion it had never been re-wound, meaning that the watch and Mr Drood had parted company not long after he left Mr Jasper's on that day.

On the strength of this evidence, Mr Landless was re-detained, and the search continued into December 28th. Nothing more was found – no body which would have proved the young man was dead, and so Mr Landless was released.

And that, Sam, is as much as we know."

"It's a very thorough report, sir. May I retain it?"

"Of course. Thanks to our excellent postal service making several deliveries a day, I have been in touch with the Cloisterham boys to clarify a few points and enlarge on others; and the incident was well-covered at the time in the local papers, which I also have for you."

"Thank you, sir."

"There's no need to thank me. Thank the missing young man's uncle. It was he who brought them, following his letter asking us to look into the case."

"John Jasper asked us to look into his nephew's disappearance?"

"None other, and in a very emotional letter."

Inspector Field drew the same from the file on his desk.

"Here we are …He ends with these words."

I swear … that I never will relax in my search. That I will fasten the crime of the murder of my dear dead boy upon the murderer. And that I devote myself to his destruction.

Chapter 2

Neville Landless Loses His Temper

Samuel Warden sat for almost two hours in Inspector Field's office reading through the very detailed newspaper cuttings, the report from the Cloisterham constabulary and their answers to the inspector's letters of enquiry. It was his custom to familiarize himself with the circumstances surrounding any investigation before he began his pursuit of the truth. By the time he rose from his chair, he had a clear mental picture of those places in Cloisterham where the events of the previous Christmas Eve had occurred and as precise a knowledge as was possible of the movements of those involved.

"Would I be right in supposing that Mr Landless was obliged to leave Cloisterham, sir," he asked Inspector Field, when he was able to track his senior officer down following the latter's briefing to his other officers and his organizing the circulation of that day's route paper to neighbouring divisions by uniformed constables on foot or horseback.

"Indeed, you would, Sam, and – one might say – *with a blight upon his name and fame*, 'cursed from the earth … a fugitive and a vagabond'. After the events of last Christmas, Cloisterham *knew Neville Landless no more,* but we do, thanks to a few enquiries I set in motion with our Mr Jasper. Mr Landless resides in Staple Inn, and seldom leaves his rooms except by night."

"Holborn?"

"Your old stomping ground, Sam. Good luck, my boy."

Once again on the street, Samuel Warden made his way along the Strand and Chancery Lane to High Holborn. The city had now come to life and the quietness of his early morning walk was replaced by the continuous, splintering growl of omnibuses, coaches, wagons, bells and conversations held, always, at the tops of voices. Sam was only too pleased to veer off into Staple Inn, one of London's sanctuaries for the legal profession where the cluster of buildings – comprising a dining hall, a chapel, a library and chambers for the residents – ensured peace and quiet, a place where views might be exchanged, and discourses held with a chance of them being heard.

Had Inspector Field seen Neville Landless's 'rooms', he might have dropped the plural, since it suggested an expansiveness not apparent in the reality. Certainly, there were 'rooms' in the sense of there being more than one, but they were cramped places, little more than small attics or large cupboards with sloping ceilings that bore down upon the head of the occupant as he sat at a little table containing several piles of books.

Samuel Warden knocked but entered without being beckoned, turning the latch swiftly and silently.

"Who the Devil are you, sir, may I ask?" said Neville Landless, rising abruptly from his studies and turning his dark, gypsy eyes on the detective as Samuel looked around the young man's habitation, taking in at a glance an inventory of the room and its contents.

He noted the ugliness of the place: the rust, the fusty woodwork and the walls where the smoke from a small fireplace had left its mark over the years. Then, his gaze fell upon the young man, now standing facing him in a manner both defensive and aggressive.

"I am Detective Sergeant Samuel Warden of the Detective Police, Mr Landless, and I am seeking to throw any light possible on the circumstances surrounding the disappearance, last Christmas Eve, of Mr Edwin Drood. I am hoping – I am anticipating – that you may be able to help me with my search."

Samuel spoke slowly and deliberately, both to calm the situation he had deliberately provoked by entering the young man's rooms uninvited and to establish that he was in command.

"I am tired of hearing that name. It wears me down beyond belief."

"Come, now, Mr Neville, chin up (as they say) and best foot forward. Do your studies go well?"

"As well as can be expected under the circumstances."

"What would you be studying for, sir?"

"The law. I need a profession and my advice points in that direction."

"Your father's advice?"

"I have no father. My friend, the Rev Crisparkle, guides my steps."

"Do you see much of him, Mr Neville?"

"Every few weeks. His cathedral duties call upon much of his time."

"Of course, of course."

During their brief exchange, Samuel noticed that the young man had not stopped clenching an unclenching both his hands. There was temper there, an almost over-riding anger that seemed desperate for relief and deepened the hue of his dark skin.

"You're not from this neck of the woods, are you, sir?"

"Ceylon. My sister and I come from Ceylon."

"Your sister, Helena, resides with a Miss Twinkleton, I believe?"

"It is now the summer recess, sir. My sister lives here with me for a time."

"She must be very welcome company, Mr Neville?"

"She is, indeed, sir ... We are twins, you see, and very close."

"I understand that is always the case with twins. Peas in a pod, so to speak?"

"There is *a complete understanding between my sister and me*, sir. *Though no spoken word may have passed between us she very well knows I am speaking to you* at this moment."

"That is an enviable quality for anyone to possess, Mr Neville," replied Samuel, thinking how useful such a gift might be in his own work and among his own kind. "Are you similar in temperament, Mr Neville?"

"Indeed not, sir! She has come out of the disadvantages of our miserable life much better than I. *Whereas it cowed me, nothing ever subdued her. We ran away from home – if one can call it by that name – four times in six years and the flight was always of her planning and leading. Each time she dressed as a boy and showed the courage of a man. I lost the pocket-knife with which she was to have cut her hair and she tried to tear it out, bite it off.* Where I am revengeful, she is resourceful; where I am false and mean, she is open and kind."

"Tell me how you come to be here, Mr Neville," said Samuel, eager now that he had the young man talking to pursue his quarry: his quarry being the Truth.

"I was driven from Cloisterham, sir. I will never forget the last time I walked down those streets – *the averted eyes, the better sort of people silently giving me too much room to pass, that I might not touch them or come near them. Even here I cannot go about in daylight. I cannot persuade myself that the eyes of even the stream of strangers I pass in this vast city look at me without suspicion. I feel marked and tainted.*"

"As well you might, sir," replied Samuel, injecting a note of sympathy into his voice, "I understand you were on a walking tour when apprehended?"

"Eight of them accosted me, and none would say why."

"And yet you are of slight build, Mr Neville. I would have thought one man could have brought you in, had he gone about his work in an orderly manner," Samuel replied, remembering the times he had taken burly drunks into custody with a firm hand and an even firmer look in his eye, "Were they, perhaps, expecting you to resist arrest?"

"They had no reason to do so."

"You returned to Mr Crisparkle's house after your evening with Mr Drood and his uncle, and set out early on Christmas morning?"

"I was eager to be on my way."

"And yet the evening went well?"

"Tolerably, in such company."

"I am given to believe, sir, that you were *unsettled and unhappy and unsettling and interfering with other people*," said Samuel, referring to his notebook, "Why was that?"

The colour rose again in Neville's face, his eyes brightened, and his fists clenched.

"You are well informed, sir!"

"It's my business to be, Mr Neville, if I am to get to the bottom of this matter, which must be as much in your interests as mine ...," replied Samuel, leaving the sentence ending, 'if you are innocent', for Neville Landless to complete, himself. "Were there differences between yourself and Mr Drood?"

"There were, sir."

"And the meal at Mr Jasper's on Christmas Eve was intended to iron out the creases?"

"Yes."

"And were they ironed smooth?"

"The evening went without mishap. Mr Drood and I parted on good terms after our visit to the river to watch the storm."

"Was that your idea or his, sir?"

"It came up in conversation. I forget who suggested we should take the walk."

"You were both amicable, your differences resolved?"

"I have said!"

"Come on, Mr Neville, you know you want to tell me. Your present despair will not be unravelled by way of a miracle: only the facts will unclench those fists and lift that fever from your eyes. In my time in the force, I have seen many a face brightened, many a cloud lifted from a troubled brow by the simple expedient of reaching out for the Truth."

"You are persistent, sir."

"Indeed, I am, and will be even more so in due course if you remain obdurate. What were the differences between yourself and Mr Edwin Drood?"

"*He goaded me, sir.*"

"Go on, Mr Neville."

Neville Landless looked at Samuel Warden as though he had expected a reprimand. When none came, he seemed relieved

"*I cannot say whether or no he meant it at first, but he did it.*"

Samuel smiled.

"*He certainly meant it at last.*"

Samuel smiled again.

"On a previous occasion, I tried to congratulate him on his betrothal to Miss Bud, something Mr Crisparkle had mentioned to me. I supposed him to be proud of it."

"As any right-thinking person would, Mr Neville."

"He took objection to my good wishes in the most offensive manner, implying that while his life was too busy for such 'chattering' mine clearly was not. I pointed out that I was merely trying to be civil and he told me the best way of doing that was to mind my own business …"

"Go on, Mr Neville – better out than in, as my mother would say."

"I told him that from where I came he would be *called to account* for such a remark. He looked me up and down, sir, with such disdain I …could have *cut him down.*"

"Ah! But you didn't?"

"I have told you – we later parted on good terms."

"After your Christmas Eve dinner at Mr Jaspers?"

"Yes. Mr Jasper had overheard our disagreement. He came up as we spoke and reminded Mr Drood of his obligations as host – me being the stranger in Cloisterham. He was determined there should be 'good understanding' between us, and he invited us back to his Gate House. Mr Drood was leaving the next day and his uncle felt a stirrup cup to be in order."

"And you were happy to go?" said Samuel, injecting the irony in the question.

Neville Landless looked at the detective as if he thought Samuel Warden read minds.

"No, sir, I was not! Mr Drood seemed to brush off our argument as if it were of no account. Indeed, he seemed remarkably cool, whereas I was red hot."

"And what happened at Mr Jasper's home on that occasion?"

"There was a painting of Mr Drood's fiancée on the wall. I said I thought it a poor likeness, not knowing that Mr Drood was the artist."

"And he took offence?"

"Far from it! He yawned and passed the painting off as a joke, saying he would do better one day, referring to Miss Bud as 'Pussy'. His air of indifference was infuriating."

"He leaned back in his chair and clasped his hands behind his head?" suggested Samuel.

Again, Neville Landless looked at the detective with amazement.

"He did, sir."

"To provoke you?"

"He suggested that he might paint a portrait of my sister, having first ascertained that I could not paint. I told hm he would never obtain my sister's consent. Damn him!"

Neville Landless, who had until that moment remained sitting at table, which served as his desk, suddenly stood and walked over to the garret window and looked out over the rooftops. Watching him, Samuel realized how drawn was the young man, confined as he was and hemmed in on all sides by suspicion. Without turning around, Neville Landless continued:

"Mr Jasper mixed us our drinks and we toasted Mr Drood. His uncle then praised him, commenting on the life he had to look forward to: stirring work, excitement and domestic ease. And all the while he sat lounging in that chair, his hands clasped behind his head, taking it all for granted. His uncle actually said, '*See how little he heeds it all!*'

He then went on to say how it contrasted with his lot and mine ... I could not help myself, sir. I could not help remarking that it might have been better for Mr Drood had he known some hardships. He might then have been more sensible of his good fortune, which *was not necessarily the result of his own merits.*

"You upbraided him?"

"I did, and he reminded me that earlier that evening I had said that in my part of the world he would have been called to account for his incivility. I told him that his *conceit was beyond endurance*, that he was not *some rare and precious prize but a common boaster.*

At the window, Neville Landless's hands clenched and unclenched; at one point, Samuel though he might bring them up and grind them through the sill.

"Mr Drood replied that I might know a *common black boaster* when I saw him but that I was *no judge of white men* ... I threw the dregs of my glass into his face, sir, and the goblet would have followed had not Mr Jasper grasped my arm. We struggled, sir, chairs were overturned, and I threw the goblet into the grate ... I remember leaving the house and standing in the cold night air. My head was a whirl, although I had had but the one drink. I recall the graveyard and thinking of my sister and then I was at Mr Crisparkle's house and he opened the door to me."

"Sit down, Mr Neville sir, and calm yourself. I thank you for your frankness," said Samuel.

The detective sat for some time saying nothing, much to the consternation of Neville Landless, who turned back to his books but, unable to concentrate, twisted and turned in his chair. Dealing with the criminal classes, Samuel had learned that silence was an effective weapon. It unsettled the guilty: hands entwined themselves, faces twitched, the culprit could not sit still. Eventually, Neville Landless rose and went to the door.

"I have studies to complete, sir. If I can be of no more help to you then perhaps you would care to leave."

"Tell me about your life in Ceylon, Mr Neville."

"I don't see what that has to do with my present pre-dicament."

"It may have everything to do with it – or nothing, Mr Neville. At this stage in my investigation, I cannot tell. You and your sister ran away four times, you say – from whom?"

"Our stepfather. Our mother died when we were young and left us in his care. I use the word in its loosest sense, you understand. He did not care. He begrudged us food to eat or clothes to wear. He *stinted on our education, liberty, money, dress, the very necessaries of life, the commonest pleasures of childhood, the commonest possessions of youth. He was a cruel brute ... It was as well he died when he did, or I might have killed him.*"

"Neville, you should not talk so. It does you no good to dwell on the past."

The young woman must have had the lightest of steps because neither the detective nor her brother had heard her footfall, despite the creaking stairs she had to climb to his room.

Helena Landless – Samuel realized she could be no other because of the resemblance to her brother – stood in the doorway, a basket of produce from the local market over one arm. He thought he had never seen such a beautiful young woman; she possessed the looks he always associated with India: dark skin surrounding vivid white eyes with their brown centre, slender of body, lithe in her movements.

As he stood to greet her, the word 'defiant' came to mind, but whereas Neville's defiance manifested itself in anger, hers possessed an undoubted serenity. Samuel explained who he was and as he spoke, Helena's eyes never left his face, nor did her gaze falter.

"If you believe my brother to be guilty of this crime, Mr Warden, you need to speak with Miss Bud."

"Crime, Miss Landless? I do not recall mentioning a crime. Disappearance is not a crime, unless you have reason to suppose otherwise."

Chapter 3

Rosa Bud Remembers a Shadow on a Sundial

Helena Landless's insistence was a match for Samuel Warden's persistence and soon the two of them were crossing Holborn from Staple Inn to Furnival's Inn; he determined to speak with the young lady who seemed to be at least one cause of the dispute between the two young men, she determined to protect her friend from intrusion.

The news that Rosa Bud had arrived in London only a few days before could only be good as far as the detective was concerned. He knew his way would eventually lead to Cloisterham where his intuition told him the mystery of Edwin Drood's disappearance would be resolved, but meeting Rosa Bud prior to his journey there would arm him with more of what he wanted: clues, the unravelling of which, step by careful step, would lead him to his man, dead or alive as Inspector Field had expressed the matter.

"Rosa is to leave here this evening," explained Helena, "when she takes up residence in Southampton Street with Miss Twinkleton."

"Miss Twinkleton has a house off Bloomsbury Square?"

"She comes to London in the recess and makes herself available for interviews with metropolitan parents; but on this occasion she is to be with Rosa by request."

"By the request of whom?"

"Mr Grewgious, Rosa's guardian."

Grewgious! The name rang a bell for Samuel but for the moment he could not recall when or where they might have met, if ever.

"Rosa has had a terrifying experience, Mr Warden. You are to treat her with consideration."

"No other manner would cross my mind, Miss Landless."

"My brother was shaken when I arrived home. I knew. It was why I hurried back."

They spoke at the tops of their voices – there was no other way of being heard – but what they said was borne off by the noise of the city. Elbowing the clusters of people aside, darting between carriages and ducking under the heads of horses they eventually came to Furnival's Inn and several sets of stairs much like those leading to Neville's rooms, only more frequently swept of dust, and a room that was airy, clean and comfortable.

Rosa Bud was a surprise to Samuel Warden, and he was unsure why this was so. Had he expected a demure young woman, alone in the world, at the mercy of the kindness of strangers? He had, perhaps because of the name she bore, perhaps because of the nickname her fiancé had given her; but the gaze with which she favoured him said otherwise. There was steel in the eyes, a quiet determination he did not miss.

After Helen Landless had made the necessary introductions, Samuel took the young woman's hands in his and spoke softly to her.

"Miss Bud, I understand you have been through rather an ordeal, and so please excuse my intrusion, but I would be grateful for your help. If, however, you would rather I returned at a more convenient time, please say so."

"No time could be more convenient than the present, Mr Warden, if anything I might have to tell leads to finding Eddy. Do you think it possible he might still be alive?"

"It is too soon for a detective to have an opinion, Miss Rosa. I know some of the circumstances of his disappearance and I have spoken with Miss Helena's brother, but that is all. I understand that he was your fiancé?"

"We were betrothed to one another as children; I was seven and Eddy eleven. Mr Drood, who was an engineer, and my father, a university man, were friends. Mr Drood was a great comfort to my father after my mother died in a boating accident. Mr Drood was a widower, you see, and so he and my father thought Eddy and I would be safer together should anything happen to them. As it was, my father died on the first anniversary of my mother's death and so we came to be as we were."

Samuel sat motionless, his outstretched arm resting on the side table where he had placed his hat. He had sat thus many times, in many different places, waiting, while some wretch poured out the circumstances that had led him, or her, to a life of crime. He would then take them into custody and let the law takes it irrevocable course. Orphans, alone in the world, with no one to care for them and nowhere to go. In that sense, at least, Rosa Bud had been fortunate.

"And, so, you went to live at Miss Twinkleton's?"

"Yes. I have known no other home since I was seven, but I have been happy there. I have been thoroughly spoiled and have become *a giddy, little creature.*"

"I think not," said Samuel, quietly, Go on."

"Eddy came to think of me that way. I was always 'Pussy' to him, and he came to accept that our marriage was inevitable, something meant to be, unstoppable like a river in its course, and so he never questioned it."

"But you did?" said Samuel, his tone matching hers, urging her on.

"Yes. It was the day before he disappeared, Mr Warden. I never thought I may never see him again when we walked by the river that night ... I never looked upon him again ..."

Rosa's struggle in telling her story was so apparent that Samuel almost forgot himself and was about to excuse her from saying more, when Helena Landless leaned forward, put her arm about the distraught young woman and drew her close. She looked out of her dark eyes at Samuel, but there was no anger in them, only understanding and relief.

"I had thought about it for a long time," Rosa continued, "I had hinted to Mr Grewgious, my guardian, that I was not settled in my mind. He didn't understand me, but he said we should consider our circumstances seriously and so I made up my mind to speak to Eddy when he came to see me at Christmas. I said that we must be courageous and see ourselves as brother and sister from that day on, never again as husband and wife.

I knew this had been in his mind, too, but I was so, so, sorry to be the one to say it. We were not right for each other, you see, not right in that way. We had not chosen to be betrothed, had we? But we liked each other; we parted liking each other."

"I'm sure you did, Miss Rosa."

"I think, if I had not spoken to Eddy, he would have spoken to me. He said Mr Grewgious had talked with him when he was in London. He was so worried that his uncle, Mr Jasper, would be upset. Poor Eddy, his mind was in a turmoil."

"And you do not know, of course, whether he spoke to Mr Jasper."

"Oh yes, I do. We agreed that I should write to Mr Grewgious and that he, our trustee, should speak with Eddy's uncle when he came down at Christmas."

"Your Eddy did not want to tell him, himself?"

"He said he was a little afraid of Jack. Eddy always called his uncle 'Jack'. They were much the same age, you know. Eddy coming up to his majority and his uncle only twenty-six himself."

"Why should he be afraid of him?"

"I don't know that he was. It was just Eddy's way of speaking."

"But, nevertheless, he didn't want tell him himself?"

"His uncle was very fond of Eddy and was prone to fits, Eddy said. He was afraid the news of our decision not to become husband and wife might bring one on. He said he thought Mr Grewgious could *talk Jack's thoughts into shape*."

"I see."

Samuel Warden's work had made him a keen observer of even the slightest changes in human behaviour: reactions were always the acutest indicators. Although intent on what Rosa was saying, he had noticed the frown that scared Helena Landless's brow when her friend talked of John Jasper. He made a mental note to speak with her, later.

"And so, you went your separate ways?"

"Eddy planned to leave England as soon as the arrangements could be made. He was to go to Egypt, where there is work for engineers. I was to stay at Miss Twinkleton's, at least until Helena left, and, of course, I had to tell the other girls. I was to ask Miss Twinkleton to break it to them."

"And now you have joined your friend sooner than you expected?"

"Yes."

"Would you care to tell me why?"

Rosa Bud looked up at her friend, at the dark Ceylonese face and eyes and knew she did not have to say a word if she did not want to do so; but the very calm, the very silent anger in those eyes gave her the confidence she needed at that moment. She looked at the detective, a man almost twice her age: still young in worldly terms but old to her eyes, old and knowing.

"After everyone had left for the summer recess, when I was alone in the house, Mr Jasper came to call. He asked to see me. I was annoyed with the maid for telling him I was at home. Mrs Tisher – that's Miss Twinkleton's companion – was on leave, and Miss Twinkleton had joined some of her friends on a picnic. She had taken a veal pie, you see."

Whether the nature of the pie held some significance, Samuel doubted, but made a mental note, just in case.

"I said I would see him in the garden: the windows of the house overlook the garden. I didn't want to be in the house with him. It had been a hot day and the sun shone, and so I collected my garden hat and went to meet him. He was leaning on the sundial and I sat on the seat beside it. He was still in mourning, all in black … all in black.

He started by asking when I would resume my musical studies with him. When I said never and did not wish to be questioned about my decision he said that *we must sometimes act in opposition to our wishes* – those were his exact words – and that I *must do so now or do more harm to others* than I could ever put right. He then called me *Dearest Rosa! Charming Rosa!* He had never spoken to me in such terms before. I tried to stand – I did stand – but his look threatened so much I dare not fly from him. *Sit down*, he said, *sit down my beloved.*"

The young woman's hand flew to her mouth and she rose from the small settee where she sat with her friend close to her. Rosa crossed to an internal doorway that must have led, Samuel guessed, to her bedroom; and then, as though returning from an imaginary flight, she hurried back to her seat. She looked at Samuel, half-apologetically, half-defiantly.

"*I loved you madly*, he said. He used the phrase, over and over again: even when he – meaning Eddy – was to have me for wife, even when he strove to make him more devoted to me, even when he was given my portrait, which he worshipped in torment; in the work of his days, in the misery of his nights, wherever he wandered, through Paradise or Hell … His words were horrible, Mr Warden, horrible and his look was demonic while his composure, to all who might have witnessed his outburst, was calm. That only made what he was saying more hideous.

He pretended that he had kept his desire secret in loyalty to Eddy, but I told him this was not true, that he had always pursued me whenever I was forced to endure his company, that he was false to his nephew, daily and hourly, and that he made my life a living hell, afraid to tell Eddy of my fears."

"There is no need to go on, my darling," said Helena Landless.

"Yes, yes there is. I must, I must for I have this dreadful suspicion."

Tears rose to her eyes and she trembled, her face aflame with fury and embarrassment.

"He said he would have my anger and my hatred, that he didn't want my love. *Give me yourself and your enchanting scorn*, he said, *and that will be enough for me.* And then he stretched out his hand towards the porch of the house, inviting me to leave him, knowing I could do no such thing. And then he threatened me."

"Threatened you?" asked Samuel, "Miss Rosa, are you able to remember his exact words. They are so important."

"Remember them! I shall never forget them. He said, *I have made my confession that my love is mad. It is so mad that had the ties between me and my dear lost boy been one silken thread less strong, I might have swept even him from your side when you favoured him ... I mean to show you how mad my love is ... It was hawked through the late enquiries that young Landless ... was a rival to my boy ... an expiable offence in my eyes ... I have devoted myself to the murderer's destruction, be he who he might ... circumstances may accumulate so strongly even against an innocent man that directed, sharpened ... they may slay him ... Young Landless stands in deadly peril ... you do care for your bosom friend's good name ... Then remove the shadow of the gallows from her, dear one ... I am the worst of men ... My love for you is above all other love, and my truth to you is above all other truth ...*"

Rosa broke off again and ran for the door that led to the stairs, the stairs that would take her down and away from Furnival's Inn and across the city. *She put her hands to her temples* and looked wildly about her.

"Enough now! Enough!" cried Helena Landless.

"No, no, I must finish, Helena. *Not a word of this to anyone or it will bring down the blow, as certainly as night follows day ... If you were to cast me off now – but you will not – you would never be rid of me. No one should come between us. I would pursue you to the death.* Those were his last words, as he raised his hat and left."

Rosa Bud buried her face in her friend's bosom and clung to Helena Landless, whose *wild black hair fell down protectingly over the childish form.*

For a while all three sat in silence: Rosa relieved that she had now spoken her innermost fears to a stranger who seemed, at least to her, to be a kind man; Samuel pondering on so much that had been left unsaid; Helena brooding over her friend's distress and irritated by the detective's persistence. A clock ticked; its steady sounds echoed in the hollowness of the walls. Tick, tick, click, click it paced out the minutes as they sat. It was Samuel who broke the silence.

"You said a moment ago, Miss Rosa, that you had a 'dreadful suspicion'. What was that?"

"Mr Jasper was so absorbed in his nephew and is now so absorbed in the pursuit of the enquiry as to how he came by his death – if he is dead – that it seems inconceivable he should have been responsible for Edwin's murder and yet ... yet I have that suspicion. Is it wicked of me to harbour such a baseless thought? What do you think, Mr Warden?"

"In my line of work, Miss Rosa, we soon learn the error of being too quick to jump to conclusions. It is usually the case that things are not what they seem to be. Mr Jasper's behaviour towards you, as described by you, is not the behaviour of a gentleman, but that does not make him a murderer. We must proceed with caution.

You say that Mr Jasper spoke of Mr Landless as being 'a rival to my boy'. What did he mean by that? Has Mr Landless made overtures to you in any ... "

"Never!" cried Helena Landless, rising from the settee.

"Has he, Miss Rosa?"

"Mr Landless has never *in any way addressed himself to me.*"

"But?"

"His feelings – his supposed feelings – for me were *well known far and wide.*"

"And so, in this way Mr Jasper would have heard of them?"

"Yes, but I have a *full belief in Helena's brother's innocence.*"

"Of course," said Samuel, "Miss Rosa, I would like a word with Miss Landless, but you have been through enough today and I suggest, therefore, that, once you have composed yourself, she and I should leave you in peace. I thank you for the confidences you have shared with me. They will, no doubt, prove invaluable."

He rose as he spoke, taking his hat from the table and balancing it in his hands. Helena Landless's eyes had never left him since her outburst and now blazed with anger.

"If you will leave us alone for a while," she said.

"That was my intention, Miss Helena. I will wait below. There is no rush. See to your friend in your own good time."

Samuel left quietly and quickly, having given a slight bow to the young women. He was eager to be alone with his thoughts and made for the private garden around which the buildings of Furnival's Inn were situated. There he sat and waited.

It seemed to him that Rosa's loathing of John Jasper included a loathing of herself. Was she ashamed to acknowledge that Jasper's motive for killing his nephew, had he done so, would be his love for her? Did she fancy she had been responsible for kindling this demonic passion in the man? There was always a fine line between love and hate; they were the two sides of a very thin coin, in Samuel's experience. Was there just a chance that she had once been in love with her music master – however fleetingly – and had encouraged him? She was, after all, little more than a child: seventeen is no age and young women are then very vulnerable. Was the hate she showed for him, now, a balancing act for the love she might once have inspired?

The smoke was gathering around John Jasper if Rosa Bud's story was to be taken at its face value, but Samuel Warden was not one to believe there was no smoke without fire. He had met many people – usually women – who were adept at creating such an illusion.

Chapter 4

Lt Tartar Ties a Knot

Samuel Warden was expecting a warm reception from Helena Landless without there being a great deal of warmth, and he was not disappointed. She sat beside him on the narrow bench that was situated within the low, privet hedge that surrounded the little garden, but with as decent a distance between them as was commensurate with good manners.

"Thank you for joining me, Miss Landless," he said, dropping the more familiar 'Miss Helena' as though by instinct, "If you are able to place a few bricks in the unfinished wall of information I have received from your brother and Miss Rosa, I should be grateful."

She looked at him and the expression in her eyes told all the reservations Helena Landless felt, those of loyalty to the brother and the friend she loved. Love between women was not new in Samuel Warden's world: their loyalty to each other, as a sex, was something he had found in those considered the lowest of their class, the women of the streets. Sometimes, he knew, it was the one comfort many of them had in a world set so much against them.

"Where did you first meet Miss Rosa."

"When we arrived in Cloisterham with the man appointed as our guardian, Mr Honeythunder, a man as loud as his name suggests and as mean as his name does not. When our stepfather died, we were handed over to this man for no better reason than that he was an acquaintance of his."

"Mr Honeythunder, the philanthropist?"

2 8

"You have heard of him?"

"He has offices in the Strand, referred to, I believe, as the Haven of Philanthropy."

Helena Landless smiled, and Samuel knew he was winning her over: philanthropists of a biblical persuasion, being prone to piety and humbug, were clearly no more a favourite of hers than his.

"Are you able to recall your first conversation with Miss Rosa? What was she engaged upon when you met?"

"It was at a little gathering in the Rev Crisparkle's house. His mother invited us there when we first arrived. Our guardian left after the meal – rather hurriedly hastened to the omnibus by Neville and Mr Crisparkle – and we gathered around the piano in the drawing room. Rosa was to sing for us ... Mr Jasper was to accompany her on the piano. He did so without striking the notes, but by watching her lips intently and hinting the key-note ... Rosa stopped suddenly and cried out '*I can't bear this! I'm frightened! Take me away!*' I caught her up and laid her on the sofa. Mr Drood suggested that his uncle was *such a conscientious master* he had frightened her, but it wasn't that – it was more than fear. I watched him all the while. My eyes never left his face."

"And you felt the fear?"

"*Not under any circumstances*," returned Helena.

"Did you have a chance to speak with Miss Rosa about this?"

"We shared a room at Miss Twinkleton's, and Rosa spoke to me of him that very night. Do you understand the unspoken power that some people have over others, Mr Warden?"

"Oh yes."

"She said he forced his thoughts upon her without saying a word. His eyes never left her whenever she was taking a lesson with him. His thoughts were in the sounds of the music. He pursued and commanded her even when she was away from him. She never felt safe from his ... his desire for her ..."

"Go on, Miss Helena."

"Rosa said that on that night, she felt he had kissed her."

"And she felt ashamed?"

A *gleam of fire slumbered in her dark gypsy eyes* as Helena turned them on Samuel.

"Ashamed," she replied, "and hurt and terrified."

"Don't leave, Miss Helena," said Samuel, as the young woman rose from the bench and made for the gateway of Furnival's Inn, "You do your friend no good by running from what she has said. I will pursue you. I will know the Truth, and better here, where no one overhears us, than your brother's chambers."

Helena Landless stopped dead in her tracks and spun round. Her brother's anger was in her eyes but whatever it was that was *tigerish in her blood* was immediately subdued and she returned to the bench they shared.

"When we spoke, earlier, in Miss Rosa's rooms, I asked her whether your brother had ever made overtures to her. Do you remember?"

"Indeed, I do!"

"And you said 'Never!' and you said it emphatically, Miss Helena."

Helena Landless looked at Samuel Warden, the expression of defiance he had come to expect very present in her eyes.

"I am always suspicious of emphasis, Miss Helena."

"My brother never declared his feelings for Rosa."

"I never suggested he did, Miss Helena, but those feelings were present were they not, and you knew about them. We do not come to the Truth by skirting round it. When did your brother tell you of them?"

"We were walking, one night, by the river. It was a wild night and cold. The wind was driving in off the water. We came across Mr Crisparkle. He was concerned that Neville should make some kind of apology to Mr Drood, who was to return to Cloisterham at Christmas.

During the course of our conversation, Neville had occasion to confess that he admired Rosa. Mr Crisparkle said that

Neville's *admiration was outrageously misplaced*. He made him promise on the most solemn of pledges that he would never mention this to anyone, that it would forever remain a secret within his own heart. He went on to say that he was surprised I had not checked Neville in what he called his *irrational and culpable fancy*."

"Had you?"

"I tried, but to no avail. Mr Crisparkle pointed out that we were twins and had *come into this world with the same dispositions*. Could I not help my brother overcome the same passions in him as I had overcome in myself? He said I possessed the greatest wisdom of all – the wisdom of Love."

"As no doubt you do, Miss Helena, as no doubt you do. Your brother's 'admiration' for Miss Rosa was one of the reasons he had no wish to attend the dinner on Christmas Eve arranged by Mr Jasper?"

"Yes."

"The other being his instinctive dislike of Mr Drood?"

"Yes."

Samuel Warden looked into the dark eyes and saw no doubt. Was he to believe that these two young men, one fiery and the other insolent, walked down to the Medway to view the storm quite amicable in each other's company? He wondered what Mr Jasper did to reconcile these two opposing spirits.

"Your brother did not know on that occasion that the engagement between Miss Rosa and Mr Edwin had been called off?"

"No."

"You did not know?"

"No, Rosa had not taken me into her confidence."

"How strange, since she and you were so close."

"We had not spoken of Mr Drood, since my brother's declaration of his feelings for Rosa."

"A pity," said Samuel, quietly.

"Yes," replied Helena, and had she not been so well brought up, the young woman might have placed her head on his shoulder in gratitude.

They sat together for a while, both exhausted by the game of question and answer they had been obliged to play, neither keen to make the next move, which was to return Helena to her brother's rooms: she because she feared more questions, he content to sit in the company of one so beautiful.

In point of fact, Samuel had but time for one question for Neville Landless when they arrived from the dirt and noise of Holborn.

"Miss Bud was not mentioned at all on Christmas Eve," he said, "Strange, because her portrait still hung over the chimneypiece, and yet we all avoided mention of her name."

"As you say, Mr Neville, strange – and yet not so strange, since she was the cause of your previous disagreement ..."

How much more Samuel might have teased from the Helena's brother he was not to know because at that moment another man appeared at the window of Neville's chambers. The man, a stranger to Samuel but clearly not to Neville and his sister, *was a handsome gentleman with a young face, but with an older figure in its robustness and its breadth of shoulder: say a man of eight-and-twenty, or at the utmost thirty ... extremely sunburnt ... broad temples, bright blue eyes, clustering brown hair, and laughing teeth.* The look of surprise on his face when he saw Samuel was matched by the detective's own.

"Just checking the lines, sir, all taut and trim here," he said, and was about to disappear across the rooftop when Neville, a smile on his face, the first Samuel had seen, called out to him.

"Mr Tartar, please, do come in!"

At which the newcomer eased himself in through the garret window and landed neatly on the floor.

"Mr Neville's neighbour, sir," he said, addressing himself to Samuel, *"corresponding set, next door.* One-time First Lieutenant, Royal Navy, now retired. And you, sir, if I'm not much mistaken are a policeman. Am I right? I can usually tell a man by the cut of his jib."

"Quite right," replied Samuel, taken aback despite himself.

"Mr Neville has kindly allowed me to extend my garden across the rooftop to his own window: *a few lines and stays for the scarlet runners, some boxes for the mignonettes and wallflowers along the guttering, all shipshape, spick and span.*"

"Mr Tartar has obliged us by making himself useful in other ways, too, Mr Warden," said Helena, also smiling for the first time since she and Samuel had met. "He has agreed that Rosa might use his room to talk with me unseen. We converse across the rooftops."

"Unseen by whom?"

"By Mr Jasper."

"Mr Jasper is here in London?"

"He stalks my brother, Mr Warden. He allows him no rest."

"More than six months after Mr Drood's disappearance he comes to London to watch your brother's movements?"

"Yes, sir, that is the case."

"He lacks nothing if not persistence – and patience."

"Patience?" asked Helena.

"I have in mind what Miss Rosa told us only a short while since."

Helena Landless frowned the deep frown Samuel had noticed when they first met, a frown that knitted her brow and deepened the anger in her face.

Samuel turned to Neville Landless.

"You are aware of the reason Miss Rosa gave for her flight from Cloisterham?"

"Of course!"

"I have some catching up to do, you see, and my perspective is, not surprisingly perhaps, somewhat different to yours ... So, I am to understand that Miss Rosa crosses Holborn with Mr Grewgious and goes to Lt Tartar's rooms from where she speaks with Miss Helena, who converses with her from Mr Neville's room?"

"Sometimes, I fetch the young lady myself, sir. Mr Grewgious thought it more natural that way."

Samuel looked at the naval officer and thought he detected a blush, unusual in a man, especially a man of Lt Tartar's stamp, but it was there, more in the eyes than the face.

"You have made Miss Rosa's acquaintance since she arrived in London," asked Samuel, emphasizing the 'since'.

"You've hit it, sir, square between the eyes."

"Might we repair to your chambers, Lt Tartar? I do like to gain a sense of place."

"Follow me, sir!"

And without another word, the sailor nipped out through Neville's window and settled himself along the lines of scarlet runners, offering his hand to Samuel who was edging himself over the sill of the window, his eyes fixed on the fall he would suffer if he slipped on the tiles of the roof.

"This way, sir, and we'll go below."

Lt Tartar's chambers were the neatest, the cleanest, and the best-ordered chambers Samuel had ever seen. *The floors were scrubbed ... every inch of brass-work was polished till it shone like a brazen mirror. No speck, nor spot, nor spatter soiled the purity of any of his household goods ... Everything had quarters of its own assigned to it; his books ... his brushes ... his boots ... his clothes ... His gleaming little service of plate was arranged on the sideboard ... No man of war was ever kept more spick and span from careless touch ...* Well, almost the 'best-ordered': the neatness, the tidiness and the cleanliness reminded him very much of the home he shared with Sarah Rowse, the widow with whom he lodged in Camberwell.

When he looked up, the sailor's eyes were upon him, and Samuel wondered what Rosa Bud made of those eyes, those *far-seeing blue eyes* that no doubt *watched the world without flinching*.

"You have come to know Miss Rosa well in a very short time?"

"Too true, sir. Why, on the day after she arrived, I took her and Mr Grewgious up the river, *the weather being delicious and the tide serving*. I have a yacht at Greenhithe – that's about twenty miles from London Bridge, and so we had a fair day out, the tide taking us one way and, very thoughtfully, bringing us back the other."

"And Miss Rosa tried her hand at rowing, no doubt?"

"We had a good time, sir, and lessons were learned," replied the sailor with a smile.

Samuel had wanted to see Lt Tartar in his own quarters: a person's home had much to say about them. He liked what he saw, and he liked what he heard. Anyone other than a policeman might have taken that at face value; and even Samuel, as they shook hands *with great heartiness,* could not doubt the evidence of his eyes. However!

"I have not eaten since breakfast," he said, "If you would care to join me, they do a very nice steak and oyster at the Cheshire Cheese in Fleet Street, a fifteen-minute stroll from here."

He wanted to know more about this man before he approached Rosa's guardian, Mr Grewgious, and the best time for such a visit, he decided, was after the work of the day was done and with a good meal to bolster him. He had remembered how it was he and the lawyer first met.

Chapter 5

Mr Grewgious Unbends Only Slightly

The meal was not a disappointment, and nor was the naval officer's company. Settled nicely and privately in one of the booths in one of the many side-rooms and attended by a waiter Samuel knew from previous visits, they set to with a will. On the waiter's recommendation – and Samuel's policy was always to trust the waiter who had, after all, a greater knowledge of what was going on in the kitchen than the customer – they forsook the idea of steak and oysters and plumped, instead, for roast leg of pork, a salad with four heads of celery standing pyramidically, mashed turnips spooned over a large flat plate to the height of a quarter of an inch, beautifully ladled with parsley and butter, and a side dish of chicken; all washed down with copious amounts of ale. The ever-attentive waiter was as ready as they were to round off the meal, but they waved aside the apple pies and custard in favour of a Swiss cheese, a slice of butter and a few watercresses served on a change of plates and cutlery. A piping hot Turkish coffee served to complete their repast.

The two men strolled back to Holborn, a trust built between them, tentative on Samuel Warden's side, anything but on Lt Tartar's. Expecting them to part at the doorway of Staple Inn, the naval officer extended his hand for a vigorous shake, which the detective reciprocated.

"After you," he said.

"You have further business with Mr Landless tonight?" asked Lt Tartar, "I do think he has been through enough today. He told me he had undergone some mental distress. His health has been affected."

"You're very thoughtful, Mr Tartar, but have no fear. It is Mr Grewgious I must see before I leave."

"In that case, sir, may I, once again, bid you goodnight and safe passage."

They mounted the five steps and passed in through the doorway of one of the Inns of Chancery, the sailor to a quiet evening with his books, maps and charts, the detective, less enthusiastically, to what he expected to be a fruitless interview with Hiram Grewgious, Edwin's lawyer and Rosa's guardian.

Mr Grewgious opened the door of his chambers on Samuel's first tap and eyed his visitor up and down before standing aside to beckon him in: his eye had been on the front of Staple's and he had seen the detective approach.

"I have been expecting you," he said, dryly.

"Nothing much escapes your eyes, does it, Mr Grewgious, Solicitor," answered the detective, stating the lawyer's profession as though it were a title, "and nothing much passes your lips, if my memory serves me correctly. Allow me to introduce myself – Detective Sergeant Samuel Warden of ..."

"... the Detective Police. I know who you are, Sergeant Warden, although I must confess, my memory serves me ill regarding our previous meeting."

"May I?" asked the detective, as he placed his hat a small side-table, "And if I could beg a seat, sir, it would make the occasion more sociable."

His eyes had scoured the room as soon as he stepped by the solicitor and had missed nothing. He could see that Mr Grewgious had been sitting by the fire, writing, a glass of red wine to hand.

There was no luxury in the room. Even its comforts were limited to being dry and warm (uncomfortably so on a summer's evening) *and having a snug though faded fireside ... its private life was confined to the hearth, and an easy chair, and an old-fashioned occasional round table that was brought out upon the rug after business hours.* Samuel remembered from his previous visit that one of the *outer rooms was the clerk's; Mr Grewgious's sleeping-room was across the common stair; and he held some not empty cellarage at the bottom of the common stair. Many accounts and account-books, many files of correspondence, and several strong boxes, garnished Mr Grewgious's room ... conscientious and precise was their orderly arrangement.* It was a request to open one of those strong boxes that had first brought Samuel to these chambers.

The solicitor pulled another chair from somewhere at the side of the room and nodded Samuel to it with as off-hand a manner as he could contrive.

"Would you care for a glass of wine, Detective?"

"If it's all the same to you, sir, a glass of whisky would be more greatly appreciated. I have dined with Lt Tartar this evening and we supped well on the local ale. I never mix the grape and the grain if it can be avoided. I seem to remember you invariably take dinner at the hotel in Furnival's Inn, Mr Grewgious, Solicitor. I trust I am not keeping you from your evening meal?"

"It would take more than a detective to accomplish that feat, Sergeant Warden. I dined early this evening. Perhaps we could arrive at the purpose of your visit – hmm? But first, satisfy my curiosity – where and when have we met before?" asked Mr Grewgious, reaching into a small cupboard to the side of the fireplace and extracting a bottle of whisky from which he poured a measured amount into a glass that he placed before the detective who had taken the proffered seat and was making himself comfortable across the hearth from the solicitor.

"Cast your mind back two years, Mr Grewgious. In the district of Marylebone, a gentleman was in quest of a lady's maid and advertised in 'The Times' newspaper, and at the same time answered a number of advertisements by anonymous persons. The next day his house was thronged by people anxious to obtain the situation. After they had left, a number of items of considerable value were missing. He contacted the police.

We keep our eyes on situations such as this, sir, as you might imagine, and it was but a few days before we apprehended a lady in the Edgeware Road, as having been guilty of the felony. Her apprehension led to the discovery that she had been pursuing a system of robberies of this description over various parts of the metropolis."

"Yes, I remember, now. You were the police officer on the case, were you not, Sergeant? The gentleman was my client and had lodged with me a list of his valuable acquisitions. You needed the list."

"That is correct, Mr Grewgious, Solicitor, and – after some persuasion – you agreed to open one of your many strong boxes and provide said list."

"I remember. It was a sad case, was it not?"

"Indeed, it was, sir."

"The young lady received three years' penal servitude in ..."

"... in Millbank Penitentiary, sir."

"And committed suicide after serving three months?"

"Yes, sir."

Samuel remembered the solicitor's reaction when Samuel had returned to report the outcome of the case, but he said nothing. The old man, crusty as a dry loaf, had clearly doubted the wisdom of his client answering advertisements by anonymous persons; and Samuel had concluded that he considered it to be encouraging crime and bringing the harsh penalty of the law to bear on a woman whose only other means of earning a living was on the streets. He looked Mr Grewgious up and down.

Mr Grewgious *was an arid, sandy man ... He had a scanty flat crop of hair ... The little play of feature that his face presented, was cut deep into it, in a few hard curves ... he had certain notches in his forehead ... With too greater length of throat at his upper end, and too much ankle-bone at his lower;*

with an awkward and hesitating manner; with a shambling walk, and with what is called near-sight ... Mr Grewgious still had some strange capacity in him of making on the whole an agreeable impression.

"You had a clerk, as I remember, sir – a Mr Bazzard: *pale, puffy-faced, dark-haired person of thirty, big dark eyes that lacked lustre.*"

"That is correct, Detective," replied Mr Grewgious, hiding a discreet smile, "I regret to say that Mr Bazzard is *off duty here, altogether, just at present.*"

"He gave me the impression that he would be difficult to replace, sir."

"That would certainly be Mr Bazzard's impression of himself. Mr Bazzard is somewhat misplaced as a solicitor's clerk. He sees himself more as a playwright. Indeed, *he has written a play,* The Thorn of Anxiety, *but nobody will hear, on any account whatever, of bringing it out.*"

"I can see, sir, how that would grind a man down."

"Quite so, but you haven't come here to talk about Mr Bazzard, have you, Detective? You are making enquiries regarding the disappearance of Edwin Drood."

"I am, indeed, Mr Grewgious, and you, I am told, were his lawyer. When did you last speak with Mr Drood?"

"It would have been a week before he disappeared – December 16th, to be exact."

"May I ask the purpose of that meeting?"

"We enjoyed a meal together in my chambers in the company of Mr Bazzard and conducted a small piece of business entrusted to me. That is all I am prepared to disclose, Detective. The nature of the business was a matter of trust between myself, Mr Drood and ... those departed."

"Mr Edwin Drood's parents, perhaps?"

"I did not say anything of the kind, and you would be foolish to assume so."

"And you never saw Mr Drood again?"

"I did not."

40

"But you were in Cloisterham at Christmas time?"

"I was."

"You had been asked to convey information to Mr Jasper that Mr Drood considered would upset him."

"That is so."

"And what was Mr Jasper's reaction upon receiving said information?"

The solicitor looked at the detective, his dry lips pursed, the carved notches on his forehead furrowed even deeper. It was hard to determine whether he was considering sharing what he knew or asking the policeman to leave.

"He was upset, as Mr Edwin supposed?" suggested Samuel.

"He was."

"Being very fond of his nephew?"

"Being very fond of his nephew."

"I believe you remained in Cloisterham during the search for Mr Drood."

"I arrived after it had begun."

"On December 27th?"

"Yes."

"Did you see Miss Rosa?"

"Of course."

"And how was your ward?"

"You *can imagine her condition*, can you not, Detective?"

"And Miss Landless?"

"She was *in defiance of all suspicion* regarding her brother."

"As one would expect ... Mr Jasper, I understand, was engaged with the search for his nephew. How did you find him?"

"You are very persistent, Detective."

"You are the second person to indicate as such, today, Mr Grewgious, Solicitor, and you will find me more so, as time goes by, if I do not receive the answers necessary to my finding Mr Drood."

"You are sure you will find him?"

"I have no doubt of it, sir. You may stake your life upon it. How did you find Mr Jasper – exhausted, perhaps?"

"*Disordered, bedaubed with mud, his clothing torn to rags. He had just dropped into an easy chair* when I arrived at his home."

"And so, you withheld the news entrusted to you."

"I did not say so."

Samuel Warden did not move and, clearly, had no intention of doing so. He sat, quietly, watching the solicitor who returned his composure in equal measure.

"He was, as you must guess, very upset. He collapsed."

"What did he have to say?"

"At that moment, nothing."

"And later?"

"I am a lawyer, Mr Detective – not a man given to speculation. I discharge my duty and that is enough for me and, as an officer of the law, for you. I would *now release you, sir, from the incumbrance of my presence.*"

"I have no wish to intrude upon your presence unwelcome, at this moment, but, be assured, intrude I will when the time comes, and I would not wish to discover that information had been withheld that might have expedited my finding Mr Drood."

Samuel Warden stood and retrieved his hat from the table. At five-foot-eight, he was tall enough for the police force but not as tall as Mr Grewgious, who also rose from his easy chair and whose lean, angular figure looked down upon the other man.

"I bid you good day, Mr Grewgious, Solicitor. I hope to catch the last train to Maidstone tonight and then pick up the omnibus to Cloisterham."

"You are going to Cloisterham, tonight?"

"That is my intention, sir, where Mr Jasper will, I am sure, further my enquiries."

"If you want to speak with Mr Jasper, you could do no better than look out of the window, Mr Detective – if not at this precise moment, then at any other."

"You believe Mr Jasper to be here at Staple Inn?"

"I have seen him, *a slinking individual, looking anything but agreeable.*"

"And what would he be up to here, sir?"

"Why, watching Mr Neville, *haunting and torturing his life.*"

"More than half a year after Mr Edwin disappeared?" asked Samuel, the last paragraph of John Jasper's letter coming to his mind.

"Aye!" replied the solicitor, snappishly, unsettled by having said more, as a lawyer, than he intended, but perhaps less than he intended, as a man.

Samuel Warden smiled and nodded slowly, a habit of his when lost in thought, sifting information, often conflicting information, through the routeways of his mind. He took the solicitor's outstretched hand and shook it warmly, if not gratefully, nevertheless pleased with the small amount he had ground from the grain of such a dry old mill.

It was unfortunate he left when he did. Had he but returned to Camberwell and the comforts of Mrs Rowse, and caught the morning train, he might have furthered his investigation in the metropolis more speedily.

It was after midnight when Mr Grewgious was woken from his slumbers by a frantic banging on the outer door of his chambers. He had sat up late, looking at the stars from his bedroom window, wondering whether he had said too much or too little to the detective, and was still dressed as though for work.

Opening the door, he found Helena Landless clinging to the banister with her free hand, half-dressed in her day clothes, her face white, the wild black hair strewn about her shoulders. Rather prosaically, Mr Grewgious realized she must have run across the quadrangle in that state, a state so unbecoming to a woman of her quality.

"What is it, my dear?"

"It's Neville – he has not returned home."

"Doesn't he walk the city at night, finding the darkness friendly, to tire himself out?"

"Since I came to Staple Inn, he has always returned by midnight, knowing how I worry for him. It is well past that time, now. Besides, *there is a complete understanding between my brother and me, though no spoken word may have passed between us*, and he is gone from me."

Chapter 6

John Jasper Reiterates
His Determination

The omnibus, very obligingly, pulled up in front of the Royal Victoria and Bull Hotel in Cloisterham High Street about the same time as Helena Landless was rushing across the quadrangle at Staples Inn. *In those days, there was no railway to Cloisterham,* but the omnibus did its best to remedy the deficiency.

Samuel Warden had a fondness for omnibuses: it gave him a chance to watch people and hone his perceptions. *The passengers changed as often in the course of one journey as the figures in a kaleidoscope,* and all of them gave scope for observation, food for thought. Besides, the conductors were a detective's equal in their shrewdness and a veritable mine of information when Samuel was on a case.

One, whose acquaintance he had fostered, was instrumental in enabling the detective to collar a young man whose gloves had been found at the scene of a murder. The young man was exceedingly fond of his appearance and the conductor, noting this fact, had dropped into conversation with him on several occasions, hanging on by his leather strap and chatting through the window as the omnibus jogged along. Noticing, one morning, that the young man was without gloves, the conductor had commented on the fact, only to receive a look that merged sheepishness with anger: a look that could mean only one thing to a keen observer. Since the young man always took the same route, from the city to the top of Oxford Street and always alighted at the same spot in the vicinity of Bedford Row, it had taken Samuel only a few days and a number of brandy-and-waters at the local hostelries to locate him, once the conductor had confided his considerations.

The twenty or so miles from Maidstone to Cloisterham gave Samuel a similar chance to gain the confidence of Joe, who was both driver and conductor of the short, squat omnibus serving the cathedral town. It was a warm, summer evening and Samuel had opted to sit not only on the outside but actually on the box. The three-hour journey enabled Samuel to elicit the comings and goings from Cloisterham to Maidstone, and thereafter to London, of the various residents of the town.

He learned of Rosa's flight.

"Caught me just in time, sir, she did – got to the corner of the High Street, where we depart. *'Stop and take me if you please, Joe. I am obliged to go to London,'* she said. And so, of course, I made sure when we got to the railway station that Miss Rosa was safely deposited with her little bag beside her in a suitable carriage."

"As one would expect of a young man such as yourself, Joe," replied Samuel, aware of what the young man saw as a 'suitable' carriage' for a young lady, "Miss Rosa was somewhat distraught, I believe?"

"Distraught, sir! It's unnerving to see a young woman in that state. She made me promise to go around to Miss Twinkleton, when I got back, to assure the good lady that Miss Rosa was seen off safely."

He learned of Neville's capture.

"Fought like the devil, he did, sir. He'd only *the build of a girl to mine and he'd got this weight strapped to his back*, and I *went down with him* – not before that ironwood stick of his had caught me on the head. We *struggled together on the grass* and I called to the others to *let him alone*. We rolled about a bit. It was a *close scuffle* and we were both smeared with blood, but I got my knee to his chest and called to the others to take him *arm-in-arm*. Called us a pack of thieves, he did, and I said to him '*We wouldn't have touched you if you hadn't forced us.*' I recommended him not to talk and said there'd be a friend waiting for him at the high road."

"Who was the friend?"

"There were two – Rev Crisparkle and Mr Jasper. They walked him back to town and we all followed."

"Did you see him again, Joe?"

"I saw him when he left as I saw him when he arrived."

"With his guardian, Mr Honeythunder?"

He learned of Mr Honeythunder's philanthropy.

"More Thunder than Honey by nature, sir, if you take my meaning. Sat where you are, Mr Warden, only **on** me as distinct from **beside** me. '*Tell your master to make this box seat wider,*' he said, '*Take my card*'. '*What's the use of that to me?*' I said. '*Brotherhood,*' he said. '*My mother was contented with myself,*' I replied, '*and so am I. I don't want no brothers.*' '*I am your brother,*' he said. I can tell you, Mr Warden, I was a trifle chafed by his manner. It was a good thing Rev Crisparkle arrived to mollify the matter."

"Does the Rev Crisparkle make use of your services much, Joe?"

He learned of Mr Crisparkle's charity.

"A good deal, sir. He's back and forth when his ecclesiastical duties allow. More so since Mr Landless deprived us of his company."

"You didn't take to Mr Landless?"

"I only met him the twice, sir, as I said – except for the occasion when we took him in, of course – but I'm not partial to ill temper, Mr Warden. We can do without that, can't we: you never know where it might lead."

"It's not an attractive quality in any man, is it, Joe. Do you have many regular passengers from Cloisterham – other than the Rev Crisparkle, I mean?"

He learned of Mr Jasper's brief sojourn's in the metropolis.

"There's Mr Jasper, sir. He's down there, at the moment. Never stays long. Always comes back looking … I don't know

… How shall I put it? Exhilarated but exhausted. He's always in a bit of a dash and so you'd expect his breath to be short, but he's *dazed* – yes, that's the word – dazed at times – there's a *giddiness* about him and a *dimness* in his eyes as though he's about to have a fit – very *shivery* even in this weather."

It was a beautifully warm night as the horses brought them, at last, into Cloisterham High Street and Joe delivered the animals into the care of the ostler who emerged from the deep archway of the Royal Victoria and Bull.

Samuel's immediate impression as he arrived, the street lit under the glow of a summer moon, was that Cloisterham was much like any other provincial town he had seen: there would be the Corn Exchange with the public clock, the Town Hall, the greengrocers and the fishmongers and the bakers, a theatre, the booksellers, the doctor's house. He saw them all holding their own individual sway under the shadow of the cathedral.

In the morning he would take a walk and find those places mentioned in Inspector Field's report; the Nuns' House, where Rosa had spent her life since she was a child of seven years; the Gate House that was John Jasper's home and from where the two young men had stepped out on that fateful Christmas Eve, over half-a-year before.

Samuel rose early, as was his habit, to a magnificent breakfast and an equally magnificent morning. Emerging from his lodging – which the landlord informed him with undisguised pride had once been called, merely, The Bull, a posting house and coach inn, but had been renamed the Royal Victoria and Bull Hotel, in 1836, following an overnight stay by the, then, Princess Victoria, when her journey was delayed by storm damage to the Cloisterham Bridge – Samuel gazed along the winding High Street and pictured Rosa's flight to the corner, near where he now stood, with Joe's omnibus already pulling away.

He breathed in the fresh air and gazed at the blue sky. A flock of starlings passed over, diving down between the houses and swirling away again towards the cathedral that stood behind. The early sun caught the walls of the buildings and burnished them according to their substance: brick glowed red, flint silver, stone flecked greys and yellows, wood a deep brown or bleached white according to its age.

He turned away from the river and made for the Nuns' House. He felt his search should start there but came first to Jasper's Gate House, a stone and flint building with a wooden residence above. There was no light within, and so he supposed the man who had sought his help was still in London. Samuel walked in under the arch and noticed the small door which would open on to the postern stair. Beyond the arch, he came upon an open door through which he glimpsed a dungeon-like room, where a man with a shock of white hair sat over his breakfast, with a pile of writing paper at his elbow.

The Nuns' House was further along the main street of the town, a brick building, once home to those its name suggested but now Miss Twinkleton's Seminary for Young Ladies, a fact made clear by *a resplendent brass plate on the trim gate*: an Elizabethan nunnery, a present-day boarding school. He eased open the gate and made his way to the garden where Rosa was frightened by John Jasper's attentions, and there was the sundial and the little seat where she cowered from him.

He returned to the street and wondered where the young couple, Rosa and Edwin, would have walked from here, when he called upon her. Surely out of the town centre, he thought; and so, made his way up the hill opposite the house. The road brought him to some steps that led into a tree-lined path. There were several seats under the elms, already well in fruit, and Samuel sat and pictured the young people on their final walk together. Where had they gone from here? He took out his leather-bound notebook and checked. Rosa had mentioned the river.

Samuel carried on, beyond the trees, through a gap in the far wall and so to *a quiet place in the shadow of the Cathedral, which the cawing of the rooks, the echoing footsteps of rare passers, the sound of the Cathedral bell, or the roll of the Cathedral organ, seemed to render more quiet than absolute silence.* The name plate on the wall announced this as Minor Canon Corner, and Samuel was pleased to have found where the Rev Crisparkle must live; he would be returning for a word with that gentleman.

The road from here led down, inevitably, to the cathedral, but Samuel did not want to travel that way – not yet; first, he wanted to find that walk by the river, taken by both Rosa and Edwin and Helena and Neville. He bore to his left, passing a cream house, and then made his way downhill on a broad path, sometimes aided by wooden steps, at others left to the mercy of the slope. In this manner, he came to the edge of the Medway, realizing the young people must have found an easier route. Samuel glanced upstream; somewhere there must be the weir where the Minor Canon found Edwin Drood's watch, chain and tie pin.

Samuel gazed into the waters. They seemed peaceful enough on this hot, summer's day, but he knew rivers: he had learned to swim in the Orwell, down along the Freston Shore from Ipswich. There were always undercurrents. He tried to picture that storm-tossed night when the two young men had walked down to where he now stood, and he was troubled. The movement of the waters caught his mood, stirring uneasy reflections, reflections that all tended one way with the current. The sun, rising towards its noontime place in the sky caused the waters to sparkle and flicker, and the sharp shafts of light thrown from the river carried his thoughts in one direction only.

Samuel shuddered. Intuition had its merits, but one had to be careful: it was the deductive process that was to carry him to the Truth and for the moment there was nothing the detective could do but make his way back to the cathedral.

The brightness with which the day started had intensified and Samuel was working up a pleasant enough sweat but looked forward to some relief from the sun. At the public pumps, workmen were cooling themselves, splashing each other and *bubbling and gurgling with their hands to the spouts*. He crossed between the burial grounds and entered along the nave.

Inside the cathedral it was cool – cool and damp. He was pleased for the respite but chastened by the accompanying green patches that garnished every surface: tomb, arch and vault. It was, indeed, a gloomy place: pleased, he thought, to welcome funerals but, surely, raising an objection to baptisms and weddings. He pictured John Jasper's choir and wondered whether their singing lifted the spirits and the mood of the building. Standing between the choir stalls, he felt he had had enough of the place, at least for the time being. It might call him back, but not yet, not on this lovely summer's day.

Samuel Warden had what he wanted now: a first-hand view of the town and the daily peregrinations of those people in whom he must seek the Truth of Edwin Drood's disappearance. He wondered about Cloisterham. It was an agreeable place on a summer's day, a town where a man might raise his family, a respectable place. True, it spoke of *a bygone time … with its hoarse Cathedral-bell, its hoarse rooks … Fragments of old wall … built into many of its houses and gardens* that, today, *blushed with ripening fruit*. It was a place where a man with an *independent position* – a Lay Precentor and a Music Master – might find his *niche in life* or be *cramped by the monotony of his existence*.

As he stood to go, a man brushed past him in a hurry, a folio music book under his arm, making for the chancel. Their eyes met, and Samuel knew immediately that he was in the presence of John Jasper. *He was a dark man … with thick, lustrous, well-arranged black hair and whisker*. Samuel knew him to be twenty-six, just five years older than his nephew, but *he looked older as dark men often do*.

"Mr Jasper?"

The frown with which his comment was greeted must have been of the kind Rosa Bud claimed had been bestowed upon her at the sundial.

"Do I know you?"

His voice was deep and good, his figure, as he turned to face the detective, *good, his manner sombre.*

"I am Sergeant Warden of the Detective Police. You have requested our help in finding your nephew," replied Samuel, stretching out his hand, which the other man took.

"Sergeant Warden, I ... Pray give me but a moment, sir, to retrieve some manuscript from the organ and I will be with you."

It was but a moment, and he took Samuel's arm and led him from the church, turned to his right and made for the Gate House.

"I have just now arrived from London, where I had business of a pressing nature. Come, my house is only a few steps from here."

And so, they *went up the postern stair.*

John Jasper's rooms were, like him, *a little sombre. They were mostly in shadow ... sun seldom touched the grand piano in the recess ... the folio music-books on the stand ... the bookshelves on the wall ... the unfinished picture of a blooming schoolgirl hanging over the chimneypiece.*

"And the young lady is ...?"

"Miss Rosa Bud. *It was done by Ned who made me a present of it.* Miss Bud was my nephew's fiancée. I must offer you a drink, Sergeant Warden – a welcome cup."

"Perhaps a brandy-and-water, sir, would be most welcome."

John Jasper mixed the drinks and ushered his guest into the easy chair, while resting his own back against the empty fireplace. Samuel raised his glass.

"To a successful search, Mr Jasper, and thank you for calling us in."

"To our successful search, Sergeant Warden," replied Mr Jasper, draining his glass, "How much do you know, sergeant? Where shall I begin?"

"It will be best, sir, if you assume I know nothing," replied the detective, eager as always not to put anyone he might interview on their guard, "Perhaps we might begin with the night your nephew disappeared. I understand, he came here for dinner with a Mr Neville Landless."

"There had been differences between them that the meal was intended to heal."

"And did it?"

"They left together, amicably, to watch the storm over the river. I never saw Ned again."

"And you feel that Mr Landless must be in some way involved in his disappearance?"

"Is there another explanation? Neville Landless was the last person to see Ned alive."

"As far as we know, sir."

"You have some other idea?"

"Not at the present time, Mr Jasper. Tell me about these differences."

"I came across them after they left the Nuns' House. They had *both become savage*. I placed my hand on Ned's shoulder and came between them. I said '*Ned, we must have no more of this … Mr Neville is a stranger and you should respect the obligations of hospitality … Let there be nothing amiss*'. And so, we made our way to my bachelor house where I mixed them both a stirrup-cup, and we toasted Ned, wishing him a safe foot *in the stirrup*."

Mr Jasper's eyes did not leave the detective's face as he related his story, covering much the same ground as Neville Landless had already navigated, fists clenched.

"And what divided them for a second time that evening?" asked Samuel.

"They railed at each other, Sergeant Warden. It is difficult for a peace-loving man to pinpoint their moment of departure from cordiality, but it resulted in insults being thrown. Mr Neville referred to Ned as a common boaster and Ned retaliated quite shamefully – later to regret what he had said, openly admitting he had forgotten himself and wishing bygones to be bygones."

John Jasper turned his eyes away from Samuel and looked down into the grate, as though his distress at recalling such a memory had upset him beyond the ability to endure it in the company of another.

"Mr Neville then threw the dregs of his wine at Ned, who leapt from his chair. I entreated him to be still and demanded that Mr Neville give his glass to me, at which point he hurled it into the grate and dashed from the room. I was relieved at his leaving. I feared *he might have laid my dear boy dead at his feet.*"

"Your concern for your nephew is admirable, Mr Jasper."

"*There is ... was such an exceptional attachment between my nephew and me.* I sometimes felt that I am ...was more sensitive for my dear, unfortunate boy than for myself."

"Was it your idea for the reconciliation on Christmas Eve, Mr Jasper?"

For a moment, John Jasper seemed to hesitate, and a very perplexed expression took hold of his face; then, he said, quite abruptly:

"It was an understanding arrived at between the Rev Crisparkle and me."

"Ah yes," replied Samuel, feeling he had mined all that was available for the moment; and wishing to pick up the traces of what the lawyer had told him, he steered the conversation in another direction. "I understand you took part in the immediate searches."

"That is the case."

"Very commendable, Mr Jasper, if you do not mind my saying so. I am sorry nothing appears to have come from your efforts, but they will, sir, they will."

"You seem very sure of the fact, Sergeant Warden."

"You can stake your life on it, Mr Jasper," replied the detective, taking the notebook from his pocket and appearing to consult the contents, "Now, I believe you received a visit from your nephew's lawyer at about that time – a Mr Grewgious. What was his business in Cloisterham?"

"He brought information regarding my ward."

"And what would that information have been, Mr Jasper?"

"Is this pertinent to finding my nephew, sergeant?"

"Who knows, sir."

"He came to tell me that Ned and Miss Bud had broken off their engagement."

"Can you remember his exact words, sir?"

"Are they so important?"

"Words are everything, Mr Jasper."

"He said *After some innocent and generous talk, they agreed … to dissolve their existing, and … their intended, relations, for ever … and ever.*"

The detective's eyes never left John Jasper's face as the uncle struggled to either remember the exact words or to enunciate them.

"Thank you, sir. Why do you think Mr Edwin did not tell you himself?"

"Ned feared my reaction. I had a great affection for my darling boy. *Uncle and Nephew were words prohibited* between us *by common consent and express agreement.* He feared I *would be bitterly disappointed by so wide a departure from his projected life.*"

"And were you, sir?"

Mr Jasper, whose eyes had only left the detective's face once during their conversation, said, quite suddenly, as though arriving at a calculation with which he had struggled.

"It gave me hope. I thought that my dear boy, distressed at his loss of Miss Bud, may have decided to leave human company, to disappear for a while."

"May that not still be the case, Mr Jasper."

"I can no longer believe it to be so."

Samuel, who had drunk nothing since their original toast, drained his glass. He leaned forward in his seat, eager to give the impression that he was weighing possibilities, seeking answers to straightforward questions, although it was not information he sought but a reaction. He found himself on the cusp of an untruth.

"Might I ask, sir, whether Mr Neville had any feelings for Miss Bud?"

"What makes you ask? Who have you been talking with? Be open with me as I have been open with you."

Withholding information was only natural in Samuel's profession; but he needed to gain the trust of all and, therefore, needed to be 'open' with Mr Jasper. He recalled Rosa Bud's actual words *'Mr Landless has never in any way addressed himself to me'* but *'His feelings – his supposed feelings – for me were well known far and wide'*. Yet, the detective did not want to involve the young woman, at least not yet.

"The portrait, sir," he said, looking at Rosa's picture on the wall, "You told me that Mr Landless took some objection towards Mr Edwin's attitude to the painting, and I thought, perhaps ..."

Samuel spread his arms as though his explanation illuminated the room.

"I see," replied John Jasper, "There was some gossip at the time."

"And what was your reaction to the gossip, Mr Jasper?"

"*It was an expiable offence in my eyes.*"

"Naturally, sir ... I can see, Mr Jasper, that my line of questioning is making you uncomfortable, and I have no wish to do that. Perhaps we could proceed on another tack – your visits to London, sir. May I ask what this 'business of a pressing nature' might be?"

"Is this pertinent ..."

"... to finding your nephew? You've asked me that once, Mr Jasper, Guardian, and I repeat my answer 'Who knows, sir?' Would your business be of an ecclesiastical nature?"

"No, not exactly, sergeant."

"Of a personal nature, then, Mr Jasper?"

"Yes, personal!"

For the second time since the start of what had become an interrogation, John Jasper took his eyes from Samuel's face and, for the first time, moved away from the chimneypiece.

"You are a man of the city, are you not, sergeant?"

"I am now, sir. Once, I was a country boy living on the edge of a small town."

"Then you will know how suffocating such a life can be. Despite my devotion to my art, *the cramped monotony of my existence here grinds me away by the grain*. There are times when I yearn for the *whirl and uproar* of the city, *the risk, the change of place*. Can you believe that I sometimes *grow weary of the echoes of my own voice among the arches* of the cathedral?"

"Yes, Mr Jasper, I can well understand your feelings," replied Samuel, and he could, and felt for John Jasper.

"It is then I go to the city, to find those pleasures denied me here by the very *vocation to which I must subdue myself*. You accept, Sergeant Warden, that this is a confidence between us?"

"Of course, Mr Jasper."

There were other areas he wished to pursue with John Jasper: the incident at Miss Twinkleton's around the piano, his recent visit to Rosa in the garden of the Nuns' House, the exact outcome of Mr Grewgious's visit following the fruitless searches for Edwin Drood, the uncle's presence in the vicinity of Staple Inn. They could wait. He had gained the man's confidence, and that was enough, more than he might have hoped would come to pass. Samuel's intuition told him that Mr Jasper's confidence could well be critical in the times ahead.

"You said I might stake my life on you finding my nephew, sergeant. Can I really believe that?"

"Oh yes, Mr Jasper, Guardian."

"I do hope so, for I am pledged never to relax in my search ... I will fasten the crime of the murder of my dear dead boy upon the murderer ... I devote myself to his destruction."

Chapter 7

The Rev Septimus Crisparkle Revisits the Weir

Standing, early the next morning, in the crisp air of a wonderful summer's day, Samuel Warden heaved a sigh as he breathed in deeply. The weather had been glorious, so far, and away from the heat of the metropolis the joys of the season could be savoured more cleanly, more sweetly, than ever. It took Samuel back to his days on his grandfather's and, now, his father's, allotment: the smell of the vegetables and of freshly turned soil.

He relished the memory of those days but did not miss them; the work he was doing now, mainly in London, absorbed him. There were criminals he detested, but there were others of the kind, victims of their circumstances, adrift in a world not of their making.

Normally on a case the seeking came first, but in his search for Edwin Drood the witnesses had come to him, only too ready to share their stories. Already a pattern was emerging, a curious one, full of its own peculiar complexities.

And the town was itself was beginning to take hold of him. He had seen it in the distance as they approached on Joe's omnibus. It had risen from *among the cornfields, pastures, orchards, gardens, woods and river: the bridge, the roofs of ancient houses, the ruins of the abbey, the venerable Cathedral spires.* His walk had heightened his fascination: *the long perspectives of pillars and arches* in the Cathedral, *the earthy smell* of the place, *the stained-glass windows, the carvings on the stalls, the long gleams of light slanting into the crypt, ivy twining around the graves, the bells ringing in the tower.*

He was bound for Minor Canon Corner and the Rev Septimus Crisparkle, who he hoped to find at home; in his experience, the clergy were not early risers. *Red-brick walls toned down in colour by time, strong-rooted ivy, latticed windows and stone-walled gardens* welcomed him to the home of the Minor Canon and his mother. It was she who opened the door to his knock, her eyebrows raised in indignation at her son being disturbed.

"At such an hour? Can the matter not wait?" were her words of greeting to the detective.

"Time and tide, and the ways of the world, ma'am, wait for no man – or woman."

"We are at breakfast."

"In that case, ma'am, I shall be pleased to wait on your doorstep until such time as the reverend gentleman has completed his repast," replied Samuel, giving the old lady a polite bow and turning to lean against the wooden railings that shielded the basement from the pavement and the gaze of passers-by.

"We cannot have you standing there," bristled the old lady, "You must wait in the hall."

Samuel obliged by following her into the cosy, little house and resting his hat and cane upon the stand. She reminded him of his own mother: a pretty old lady *with bright eyes and a trim figure, her face cheerful and calm* despite her frosty welcome, dressed in the *dress of a china shepherdess, dainty in its colours.* Samuel was not oblivious to either her charms or the fact she had not asked his business before gesturing him to enter. He inspired trust in old ladies, whatever they night say to give the opposite impression, and he knew she would be the proverbial mine of information.

"Who have we here, Ma dear," asked a man of about thirty-five years who appeared in the doorway of the breakfast room and stood looking at the detective who was pinned between his mother and the hat-stand.

He approached Samuel, his hand extended, and the detective noticed the joy in the mother's eyes. She was proud of her son, a *fair and rosy* young man, *cheerful, kind, good-natured, social, contented and boy-like.* Samuel read it all in his manner, in his features and in his approach.

"I fear I have disturbed you too early, Rev Crisparkle."

"Indeed no. I have already been for my swim and practiced my boxing. Mother and I were on the point of completing our breakfast ..."

"Sept!"

"... almost completing our breakfast. You will join us, if only for a cup of tea, will you not?"

"I would be delighted – if only for a cup of tea. I am lodged at the Royal Victoria and Bull, and the breakfasts there are mighty ones. Allow me to introduce myself – Detective Sergeant Warden of the Detective Police."

There was a sudden shiver of apprehension from both the Minor Canon and his mother, and the look she gave Samuel suggested she took him to be too gentlemanly for a policeman.

"Nothing to disturb your peace and tranquillity, ma'am – a small matter, only with which I seek your son's assistance and advice," he interjected, adding the last word without meaning it, merely to placate and flatter the China Shepherdess.

"I think it best if we talk in my study, Sergeant Warden. My breakfast was all but finished."

Tea and the remains of the Minor Canon's breakfast followed hard on the heels of the two men taking a seat, eyeing each other and passing a few pleasantries; a period that allowed Samuel to remark:

"You are an only child, sir?"

"Yes, indeed, how did you know?"

"Your mother's manner, Rev Crisparkle, and the lack of family photographs on your windowsill and side-table."

"You don't miss much, sergeant."

"I don't miss anything, sir. It doesn't pay to – not in my line of work."

It was always Samuel's policy to be cheerful and encouraging with those with whom he had dealings while, at the same time, establishing that he was not to be taken as a fool and have his time wasted by evasions.

"The elderly gentleman, sir, I take to be your father," he continued, nodding towards the portrait of a distinguished-looking clergyman on the wall.

"Yes. My mother is long-widowed. Apart from a sister, she has only me. Alas, my *six little brothers before me went out, one by one, as they were born, like six weak little rushlights, as they were lighted* – hence my name, you see, Septimus."

Although the Minor Canon's turn of phrase verged on the jocular there was nothing of the kind in his tone; he might as well have been delivering a sermon form the pulpit or commiserating with a bereaved family.

"I have been asked to find Mister Edwin Drood, Mr Crisparkle, Reverend – that is the purpose of my visit to Cloisterham – and I believe you may be able to assist me in my enquiries. I have already spoken with Mr Neville Landless, his sister Helena, Miss Rosa Bud, Mr Hiram Grewgious and Mr John Jasper – to name those parties most likely to advance my search – and so I have an almost complete picture of those eventful days a full half-year ago when the young man disappeared from the face of the earth. If you would be so kind as to clarify a few details, I would be in your debt, sir."

"I will give you all the help I can, sergeant, but do you think there is any hope of finding Edwin Drood so long after he vanished?"

"Find him we will, Mr Crisparkle, Reverend. Have no doubt about the certainty. I understand, sir, that you have championed the man who was considered most likely to have been implicated in his disappearance?"

"You mean Neville Landless?"

"I do, sir."

"I have absolute faith in Neville's innocence."

"So, I have heard, sir. I would ask you to cast your mind back to the occasion of their first confrontation. I understand that Mr Landless returned to your house having assaulted Mr Drood by throwing the dregs of a glass of wine in his face."

"He did, sergeant."

"He was drunk?"

"He was not sober but assured me he had had very little to drink. He was confused. He said the drink had overcome him *in the strangest and most sudden manner.*"

"As it tends to do, Rev Crisparkle, in those unaccustomed to drinking. Did he express the strength of his feelings towards Mr Drood?" replied the detective, and then continued "Don't hesitate, sir," aware of the clergyman's reluctance to be drawn further.

"He said he would have cut him down if he could."

"Have you witnessed such anger before in your line of work?"

"No, I must confess I have not."

"I understand that it was you, sir, in consultation with Mr Jasper, who suggested the reconciliation on Christmas Eve."

"It was indeed. I was as much concerned to placate Edwin's uncle as to bring the two young men together. Mr Jasper had taken a positively hostile dislike to Neville."

"And when did you and Mr Jasper discuss these arrangements?"

"It would have been in early December. I had met with Miss Landless and her brother along the river. It was a *wild night: the sundown, the wind driving in from the sea.* I was surprised to find then taking their usual walk on such an evening and at that time of year. I received a promise from Neville that he would allow me ..."

"Somewhat reluctantly, Mr Crisparkle, Reverend?" asked Sam, when the clergyman paused.

"Somewhat reluctantly, sergeant, but urged on by his sister. 'Follow your guide now, Neville,' she said, 'and follow him to Heaven.'

"You admire Miss Landless, Reverend?" suggested Sam, and was pleased to see the Minor Canon blush.

"Indeed, I do," replied Mr Crisparkle, adopting his mother's tone.

"Carry on, sir. You received a promise."

"Yes, and I decided to go at once to Jasper. I found him asleep at the Gate House. He was on his couch before the fire and woke with a start ..."

"You entered without knocking, sir?"

"There was no answer to my tap on the door ... I am popular with the Cathedral establishment and knew he would not object."

"I understand, sir. You say he woke with a start?"

"It was most strange. He leapt from the couch in a state between waking and sleeping and called out 'What is the matter? Who did it?'"

"Echo of a famous cry, sir."

"I'm sorry?"

"Macbeth on seeing Banquo's ghost 'Which of you have done this?'"

"Yes, yes, of course,' replied the Minor Canon in a tone suggesting he was none the wiser and, apparently, not a regular visitor to the theatre.

"And how did Mr Drood's uncle respond to your suggestion?"

"Reluctantly. He agreed because of his faith in my judgement and influence over Neville and after some careful thought. He then showed me his diary and an entry he had made following the argument between the two young men."

"Are you able to remember his exact words, sir?"

"Odd phrases – no more. He spoke of his *morbid dread* of *horrible consequences* to his nephew. He spoke of Neville's *demoniacal passion* and *his strength in his fury* and said that twice he had gone into Mr Drood's room to *assure himself that he was sleeping safely, and not lying dead in his blood.* But he did write as promised and three days later brought me his nephew's reply, which accepted his own blame in the argument and wished *that byegone to be a byegone.*"

"When did you first learn of Mr Drood's disappearance?"

"When Jasper came knocking at my door on Christmas morning. It had been a wild night. There were workmen on the Cathedral roof, led by Durdles, checking the damage, and a group of people gathered outside our house, watching, when Jasper, half-dressed, broke through them crying 'Where is my nephew?' and demanding that I call Neville, who had left early on his walk that morning. He announced, loudly, that he had not seen his nephew since he went down to the river with Neville the previous evening. I felt sorry for the man, sergeant. He looked most piteous clinging to the railings outside our home."

"If you would care to complete your breakfast, Mr Crisparkle, Reverend, while I make a few notes in my book, I should be grateful, and if your maid could be persuaded to reheat the tea-urn, so that we might savour a further cup that cheers, it will make a useful morning even more pleasant."

In truth, Samuel wanted time to think. He had an account of Neville Landless's arrest from two independent sources and wanted to assure himself that a further one was unnecessary before moving his interrogation on to the finding of the watch, watch-chain and tiepin at the weir. He was still uneasy about the finding of these objects on December 28th.

After the tea arrived and both men sat refreshed and smiling, he said:

"I understand, sir, that it was you who found Mr Drood's jewellery on your Christmas visit to the Cloisterham weir."

"It was, indeed, sergeant."

"I should like to take a stroll with you in that direction, Mr Crisparkle, if you could oblige me with the time."

"Of course. I do have some matters the Dean wishes me to attend to this morning, sergeant, but if this afternoon would suffice?"

"This afternoon, sir, would be admirable. A pleasant walk on a summer's day rather than a chilly one on a winter's!"

With such pleasantries, the two men parted company: Reverend Crisparkle on a downward path towards the cathedral, Detective Sergeant Warden on an upward one towards the gap in the wall that led to the sheltered place among the elm trees. This was where Rosa Bud and Edwin Drood had taken their last walk and been at their best, the place called the Monk's Vineyard according to the maid at the Royal Victoria and Bull who had served him breakfast that morning.

He still had questions for John Jasper and might come across him incidentally, a mode of approach favoured by Samuel; and there would be others who had met the protagonists in this mysterious case, others who might have caught the odd word or captured the odd look.

He stood in thought before setting out and had not moved from the pavement outside number one, Minor Canon Corner, when the voice of the China Shepherdess called to him. The old lady was dressed for a walk and dressed – thought Samuel – rather hurriedly: the bonnet was not quite straight, and the light cape was at an odd angle on the shoulders.

"Mrs Crisparkle, you are a vision of delight," he said, "Are you off to the High Street? May I accompany you?"

Clearly, this was what the old lady intended and, pleased with her subterfuge, permitted Samuel to take her arm. It was when they reached the tree-lined path where Samuel had pictured the young people on their final walk together that Mrs Crisparkle suggested they should rest awhile on one of the seats under the elms.

"My Septimus is a kind-hearted man, Sergeant Warden, as I expect you have realised."

"Just so, ma'am."

"And kind-hearted people are easily taken in, are they not?"

"Easily, ma'am – too easily."

"His view of Neville Landless is not mine. He thought me too hard on the man," she said, looking up at Samuel as though daring him to deny her opinion.

Samuel did no such thing.

"He arrived at our home the night after his quarrel with Mr Jasper's nephew the worse for mulled wine. He *did great discredit to our house and showed great disrespect to our family.*"

"Where you still up on that occasion or did our son tell you this?"

"It is Sept's *custom to sit up last of the household.* I had already retired. *Had it not been for Mr Jasper well-bred consideration in coming up to me, next day, after the service, in the nave itself, with his gown still on, and expressing his hope that I had not been greatly alarmed or had my rest violently broken, I believe I might never have heard of that disgraceful transaction. He was still pale as gentlemanly ashes at what had taken place in his rooms over-night.*"

"Your son kept it from you for your own *peace and quiet?*"

"Of course. Sept is always considerate where I am concerned, but *I thought ill of Mr Neville then and I think ill of Mr Neville now, and I say that I hope Mr Neville may come to good, but I don't believe he will … I ask you,* Sergeant Warden, *what would he be without his sister.*"

"What would any of us men be without the ladies in our lives, ma'am," replied Samuel, partly to flatter the China Shepherdess, partly thinking of his own mother and his landlady, Sarah Rowse.

The old lady smiled across at him.

"You were relieved, then, ma'am, when Mr Landless left Cloisterham?"

"The Dean saw to that matter, sergeant. He told Sept that *the clergy must keep their hearts warm and their heads cool and hold a judicious middle course.*"

"Unlike your kind-hearted son, the Dean was not in favour of offering sanctuary?"

"He informed Sept that *the days of sanctuary were passed. It was only after he had gone from Cloisterham that Mr Jasper, haggard and red-eyed, resumed his place in the choir.*"

As always with a case, Samuel noticed, wryly, that each of parties concerned saw the circumstances only from their point of view, whereas he, the detective, had the advantage of objectivity; his task was to observe the unwinding of events from everyone's point of view. Until all were focussed, the Truth would not emerge.

He walked Mrs Crisparkle from what had once been a vineyard, passed the Travellers' Twopenny, where the homeless and destitute lodged, and so to the High Street. They emerged at a point almost opposite the Nuns' House, but there was no one there, locked as it was for the summer recess. Here, he bade her goodbye and watched her toddle off towards whatever local shops might take her fancy on what he supposed was a daily itinerary.

The disappearance of the young man must have caused quite a stir at the time, he assumed, but the town had settled down, almost as though nothing amiss had happened. Like many of its kind, Cloisterham was *a drowsy city, so silent that on this summer's day the sunblinds of the shops seemed scarce dare to flap in the south wind.*

He wandered along the one narrow street from which *the yards with their pumps* bore off until he came to the theatre, the Lyceum by name. It was an old building and imposing with a grand portico entrance. Samuel stood watching for a while, glancing up at the three stories, the second of whose windows opened onto small balconies from where theatregoers might sip their interval drinks and watch those in the street below.

He crossed the street and walked into a panelled foyer. A young man in a white shirt and a blue, silk waistcoat with matching trousers close-gartered to his calves greeted him with a smile and explained that their next production was in rehearsal and that he was the male lead. The place looked busy but slightly neglected as though the stage might be kept alive more by enthusiasm than customers. When Samuel asked whether this was so, the young man bristled at first and then acknowledged it to be the case.

"It's not so unsatisfactory at this time of the year but when the cold weather arrives …," he explained, leaving the sentence unfinished.

With a shrug, he disappeared through a door by the box office and Samuel wandered out into the street again. He was not sure why he had entered the theatre. Something had drawn him there; he had a sense of being impelled that he could not explain. It was while he puzzled over this strange influence that John Jasper hailed him. The choirmaster was on his way to the cathedral and in their brief exchange of words expressed delight that the detective had spoken with Rev Crisparkle and was accompanying him to the weir that afternoon.

"The truth may be sought there, Sergeant Warden – a sad truth but a truth that desires to see the light of day."

Samuel wondered whether Mr Jasper had time to share luncheon – his idea being to draw John Jasper back along the street to the Nuns' House, where the story of his love-making to Miss Rosa might be drawn from him – but the choirmaster offered his apologies: the cathedral called.

Samuel enjoyed a luncheon of cold lamb and cold pigeon-pie at the Gordon House Hotel, sitting in the dark-panelled dining room surrounded by portraits of former notables, both local and national, and hunting scenes. Anticipating a long afternoon, he forsook the ale offered and settled for a brandy-and-water.

He was, therefore, in a jovial frame of mind when he joined the Rev Crisparkle in the early afternoon and they made their way to Cloisterham Weir.

The day was at the height of a summer's afternoon when they reached the weir and the two men sheltered from the sun in the shade of the willows that lined the banks. The river, full despite the dry summer, rushed over the weir and tumbled strongly to its lower level. Both men listened to the falling water for a time before speaking, Samuel keen to encourage the clergyman to remember, Septimus Crisparkle drawn back many months. It was he who spoke first.

"I never knew why or how I came to be here," he said, "*I took no heed of the objects I passed. My first consciousness of being here was the sound of the water. No search had been made here*, you see, because *it is a full two miles above the spot where the two young men watched the storm.* All I knew was that *something unusual hung about the place.*"

"This would be the night of December 27th?"

"Yes. The weir haunted my sleep all night and I returned the following morning at sunrise. It was bright and frosty. Something glistened in the water. I removed my clothes and dived in and found Edwin's watch and watch chain among the timbers. I placed them safely on the bank and returned to find his tie-pin in the mud below."

"Hoping to find his body?"

"Yes – expecting, not hoping, sergeant."

"Show me," said Samuel, taking his penknife from his pocket

It was a heavy knife in a silver case, given to him by his father on his thirteenth birthday. The detective walked to the edge of the weir, tossed it into the river and watched the precious object sink out of sight.

The Rev Crisparkle looked at him in amazement before removing his clothes, swimming to the weir, mounting its timbers and diving off. He had swum here many, many times and *knew every hole and corner of its depths.* He surfaced and dived again and again, emerging after his sixth attempt with Samuel's knife clutched in his right hand and a triumphant smile on his face.

"You did not believe me, sergeant?" asked the clergyman as he shook himself dry before replacing his clothes.

"It is my business not to believe anything at face value, Mr Crisparkle, Reverend. I needed to know. You say that you do not know what influence brought you here?"

"That is so."

"Tell me where you were before your night visit to this place. What had happened there? Who were you with?"

"I had gone to visit Mr Jasper and found him in a much-exhausted state ..."

"*Disordered, bedaubed with mud, his clothing torn to rags?*"

"Yes."

"In the company of Mr Hiram Grewgious, Solicitor?"

"Yes."

"Ah – good!"

"Mr Jasper had been entirely involved in the search for his nephew ever since his disappearance on Christmas Day. When I arrived, he was collapsed in his easy chair. The remains of a meal – provided, I imagine, by the good Mrs Tope – were on the table ..."

"Mrs Tope?"

"Her rooms abut Mr Jasper's residence. She provides for him."

"I see. What did either of the gentlemen have to say?"

"Mr Grewgious very little. Mr Jasper a great deal. He was in an exuberant mood. Mr Grewgious had just informed him that Mr Drood and Miss Bud had come to the decision that they would be happier as brother and sister rather than husband and wife. He took *crumbs of comfort in this communication*. There was hope, he felt, that in *finding himself in his new position*, Mr Drood had taken flight. In this way, he would not have *to account for himself to the idle and impertinent*. He went on to say that prior to the communication imparted by Mr Grewgious it had been *impossible to entertain the idea of his nephew voluntarily* leaving Cloisterham *in a manner that would have been so unaccountable, capricious and cruel*, especially to Miss Bud, but that now he began to *believe it possible that he may have disappeared from among us of his own accord and that he may yet be alive and well.*"

"And what was Mr Grewgious's reaction to Mr Jasper's change of thought?"

"He said, merely, that *such a thing might be*.'"

"One moment, if you please," requested Samuel, walking to the edge of the weir, continuing to shake the water from his penknife and holding it up to the sun.

He needed to think, needed to dwell on this turn of events. Hiram Grewgious had been deliberately less than helpful regarding John Jasper's reaction to the news of the broken engagement; indeed, had the detective not known about it from Rosa Bud he thought it unlikely that the solicitor would have mentioned the matter at all.

He had been equally cagey in relation to Edwin Drood's visit to him on December 16th. 'We enjoyed a meal together in my chambers in the company of Mr Bazzard and conducted a small piece of business entrusted to me. That is all I am prepared to disclose, Detective. The nature of the business was a matter of trust between myself, Mr Drood and ... those departed'.

What secrets was the old man was being so close about – and why?

Chapter 8
Mr Durdles Shakes His Keys

The two men parted company, after a convivial walk back to Cloisterham, at the west door of the cathedral, the clergyman making his way along the nave to the quire, leaving the detective to gaze out at the burial ground. He had much to think about and two new names with which to conjure: Mr Durdles and Mrs Tope, the former, perhaps, promising little but the latter, probably, promising much.

It was late afternoon and Samuel wanted to sift through what he had learned from the clergyman before visiting Mrs Tope and, later, hopefully, John Jasper. It was too early for dinner and too late for tea and so the detective walked back through Prior's Gate, which was at one end of Minor Cannon Corner, and so to the cliff path that led down to the esplanade. A soft summer breeze was drifting off the Medway, and he walked slowly, savouring the smell of the water, watching young people strolling along, as Edwin and Rosa would have done on December 23rd of the previous year, having made their decision. 'It was the day before he disappeared … I never thought I may never see him again when we walked by the river that night …'. The young woman's words came back to him, obscuring all else for that moment.

Eventually, he reached Cloisterham Bridge and the north end of the High Street into which he turned and arrived, almost immediately, at the Royal Victoria and Bull and the welcome smell of dinner. His walk had taken the best part of an hour. He felt refreshed and hungry, and his nostrils told him that fish was on the menu. It transpired that the fish was turbot, and this was followed by lamb cutlets and a game bird the waiter informed him was ptarmigan; cheese rounded off the meal nicely and all was helped down with a bottle of Chambertin.

Samuel was feeling quite mellow when he set out for an evening stroll, not with any immediate purpose other than to walk off his meal before chancing to find Mrs Tope at home. He passed under the archway of Mr Jasper's Gate House and, seeing no life apparent, made his way towards the cathedral and the burial ground where he had parted company with the clergyman earlier. 'Chancing to find' was a favourite turn of phrase that amused Samuel because such finds rarely occurred by chance; they only seemed to come that way, and such casualness was all to the good when dealing with the riff-raff of mankind that was his daily lot. 'Time and chance happeneth to them all'; the words from Ecclesiastes came to him, and he failed to understand why this was so.

But chance came his way that evening in the shape of Mr Sapsea, the Mayor of Cloisterham; he came across that gentleman in the Cathedral Close. *When Mr Sapsea had nothing better to do, towards evening, and found the contemplation of his own profundity becoming a little monotonous in spite of the vastness of the subject, he often took an airing ... thereabouts. He liked to pass the churchyard with a swelling air of proprietorship ... and should he meet a stranger* his evening was enhanced tenfold.

Samuel's eye caught the mayor's as the mayor's caught Samuel's. Samuel raised his derby and the mayor bestowed upon Samuel a nod and a smile he knew was bountiful; here was a man who would listen and appreciate and, indeed, *profit by the wisdom of his elders.*

"You are a stranger here, sir," he said, by way of introducing himself.

"I have been in Cloisterham but two days," replied Samuel, eager not to introduce himself too fully, having assessed his man as a pompous know-all: a state of being that indicated a mine of information.

"Allow me to introduce myself. I am Thomas Sapsea, auctioneer, valuer, estate agent of this city – a man of this city and, yet, a man of the world, whose knowledge of the world, extensive as it is, requires others to look up to him as, once, did the lady to your left."

Samuel turned, and finding no lady to his left, looked at Mr Sapsea with a bewildered expression on his face.

"Ethelinda, sir, reverential wife of Mr Thomas Sapsea, Mayor of Cloisterham."

The name rang a bell and Samuel remembered a large monument he had seen previously in the churchyard. He looked again and saw the edifice, supposedly in memory of the mayor's wife; in reality in enhancement of the mayor, since the inscription carried much the same words as those with which he had introduced himself with the added invitation to the stranger that he might ask if he, too, could look up to Mr Sapsea, and if not '*WITH A BLUSH RETIRE*'.

"*You approve, sir,*" asked the mayor, as Samuel read the inscription.

"*Admirable!*' replied Samuel.

"Admirable! – the exact words of my friend, Mr John Jasper, Lay Precentor and Choirmaster of the very cathedral in whose shadow you now stand."

This was not literally true, since they stood at the west side of the cathedral but, the sun setting where it does, it was true that the cathedral might have been said to stand in Mr Sapsea's shadow – a long one, not so much to do with Mr Sapsea's stature as with the late ness of the day.

"You are acquainted with Mr Jasper/" asked Samuel.

"Acquainted, sir – why he has *improved* in my company *since our first meeting when we partook of port, beef, salad, backgammon AND THE EPITAPH! I have been received at the Gate House, sir, with kindred hospitality, Mr Jasper seated at the piano singing, not kickshaw ditties, sir, but ENGLISH NATIONAL SONGS AND AIRS, calls to stand by our guns, calls to duty …*"

"I have met Mr Jasper," said Samuel, keen to stem the mayor's flow without losing it altogether, "but I have yet to hear him sing."

"He is a young man *who is sound, sir, at the core.*"

"I have no doubt of that," replied Samuel.

"An admirer of mine, sir! Why, it was my knowledge of mankind that first stimulated Mr Jasper to take more than a casual interest in *the tombs, vaults, towers and ruins* of our cathedral. It was I who suggested that he might, *as a lover of the picturesque*, write a book upon the subject. It was I who brought *Mr Jasper and Durdles together …*"

"Durdles?" asked Samuel, eager, once more, to divert the current of the mayor's flow.

"Durdles the stonemason, sir."

"The man who directed operations on the cathedral roof after the storm last Christmas Eve?"

"The very man, sir – *stonemason in the way of gravestones, tombs, monuments and as contractor for rough repairs* to the cathedral. A *wonderful workman*. It was I, sir, who recommended him to the Dean. *No man is better known in Cloisterham than Durdles – a character*, sir, and one who I, *with a few skilful touches*, am able *to turn inside out.*"

The image of being turned 'inside out' by the mayor was not an attractive prospect, but meeting with Durdles, a man who seemed to know John Jasper, promised, however slightly, possibilities. It was always the odd insight, often from one in the wings, that illuminated the stage. 'Time and chance happeneth to them all'; the phrase came back once more, but he still failed to grasp its meaning.

"If I might drag myself away from your company, Mr Sapsea – with the prospect, sir, of billowing our acquaintance at a date in the near future," suggested Samuel, "where might I find Mr Durdles?"

The mayor, clearly *nettled* that Samuel should wish to leave his presence, puffed out his chest and drew himself up to his full height before replying, "He abides, sir, in a hole in the city wall, somewhere in the vicinity of the Travellers' Twopenny. I bid you good night."

As the mayor departed, Samuel realised why he had chosen the word 'billowing'; it suited the mayor's style of passage. He also noted that the man had not bothered to ask his name, but that omission suited the detective.

His previous acquaintance with stonemasons – especially those who also filled the roll of sexton and gravedigger, both at his home village of Wherstead and in London itself – suggested to the detective that a flask of refreshment might be in order before he paid his visit to the 'hole in the city wall'. Accordingly, he returned to his lodgings and acquired a bottle of Hollandse before setting out to find Mr Durdles. Armed with this, he made his way along the High Street, judging that to be the shortest route to the stonemason's home.

Mr Sapsea had certainly been correct in saying *'No man is better known in Cloisterham than Durdles'*: having missed the hole in the city wall twice, Samuel felt obliged to enquire the way and was guided securely to a yard freely littered with *gravestones, monuments and stony lumber*. At the yard-gate, he saw a mound of quicklime, and he stepped nimbly to one side of it. Two of Durdles's *journeymen had left two great saws sticking in their blocks of stone,* and these cast ghastly shadows across the entrance to Durdles's home, the day now fading into night and the moon usurping the place of the sun.

"Mr Durdles?" called Samuel, injecting a questioning note into his voice.

A man appeared at the door holding a lantern. He was dressed in *a suit of coarse flannel with horn buttons, a yellow handkerchief with draggled ends* about his neck, *an old hat, russet-coloured and laced boots*. From hat to boots he was covered in the dust of his trade, and even had not colours been dying with the light Durdles would have assumed only one: stony.

"Does Durdles know you?"

"I am a friend of Mr Jasper, and Mr Sapsea recommended me to your company," replied Samuel, bending the truth rather than indulging in a direct lie.

"And why would that be?"

"Why, Mr Jasper and I share a common interest."

"You'll be a man of the tombs, vaults, towers and ruins, would you?" asked the stonemason, eyeing the bottle of brandy Samuel held in his hand.

"I have come up from London," said Samuel, hoping that Durdles might take his trip to relate to the objects he had mentioned.

"Durdles is your man, then."

"A quick snifter before we set out, I think, would put us in the right mood," said Samuel, stepping past the stonemason and entering his home for no other reason than he liked to place a man.

It was a *bare room: brick with rafters overhead and no plastered ceiling*. On a block of stone stood *a bottle, a jug and a tumbler*. Samuel poured a generous measure of the brandy into the tumbler and handed it to the stonemason, taking a swig directly from the bottle himself. It was always good to share a drink: the action encouraged a feeling of sociability and engendered trust.

"*This is good stuff*, Mr ...?"

"Warden."

"Good stuff, Mr Warden."

"And when we've finished for the night, we'll find more measures at The Golden Lion, no doubt."

Samuel was not sure what he meant by 'finished for the night', except that Durdles had jumped to the conclusion he wished to view the cathedral in the same way as John Jasper had done. The expedition might lead to nothing, but it would help build a picture of those few crucial days last Christmas.

"Durdles will be with you in a moment," said the stonemason, as he proceeded to unhook a lantern from the wall and place some items of food into a small bundle, looking up at

Samuel as he did so, "Never go without my dinner-bundle.
Never!"

They set out, passing the Travellers' Twopenny as Samuel
had done earlier, but this time bearing up through the Monks'
Vineyard, through the gap in the wall, along Minor Cannon
Corner and so to the precincts of the cathedral.

"It was on a winter's night Durdles brought Mr Jasper
here," said the man, as if suddenly remembering the occasion,
"It were bitter cold, as always *among them tombs afore it's
well light*. It's bitterer still *down in the crypt among the earthy
damps there, and the dead breath of the old 'uns.*"

They stood in the graveyard of the cathedral. Durdles ran
his tongue over his lips and made a choking sound as though
his throat was dry, and Samuel handed him the bottle from
which the stonemason took a lengthy swig. The detective was
familiar with the commonly held belief that 'if I lose my keys
when I am drunk, I must be drunk again before I can remember
where' but agreed only up to a point. Drunkenness always
reached a stage where nothing could be remembered with any
clarity. If this expedition was to reveal anything at all, and a
night spent among the dead be more than a waste of a good
brandy, Durdles needed to be sober enough to retrace his steps
with the choirmaster.

"This is Mrs Sapsea's monument is it not?" asked the
detective.

"That's when your friend showed his interest – the day
Durdles measured up the inscription. That's when he said he'd
like *to go about with me and see some of the old nooks* in
which Durdles passes his days. It was here – no, not here,
nearby – when Durdles showed him what he could discover
with a tap of his hammer."

Durdles proceeded to tap the walls of Mrs Sapsea's
monument with his hammer: tap, tap, tap.

"Hollow, see! But she's there – *six foot inside the wall*.
Now, let's go on."

He moved to another monument and tapped again, clearly knowing what he would find; tap, tap, tap.

"You hear the different sound, Mr Warden? Solid – there's one in there – stone coffin. Now listen here."

He moved to the other side of the tomb and tapped again with his hammer: tap, tap, tap.

"Do you hear? *Solid in hollow – some rubbish left by Durdles's men.*"

"*Astonishing!*"

"That's what Mr Jasper said. Listen again."

Durdles moved on to another tomb and tapped; this time the sound echoed.

"Solid, see, but hollow inside – empty coffin – *an old 'un's crumbled away*! Mr Jasper said it was a gift, but Durdles worked it out for himself."

"Nevertheless, it is a gift you have. It's not just anyone could have worked it out as you have," replied the detective, wondering and wanting to compliment the mason.

It was dark, now, the warm darkness of a summer's night. Listening carefully, Samuel heard the sounds of the city street, but no sounds emanated from the precincts of the cathedral, even on such a night, when lovers might have sought a quiet place. The quiet of the precincts was eerie: an unnatural silence that groped its way into the imagination.

Durdles paused by a side door and from a coat lined with keys selected one, giving Samuel a sideway glance and a secretive smile as he did so.

"You've never seen so many pockets of keys have you, Mr Warden? Nor so Mr Jasper. He were fascinated. These are the keys to Durdles's work. *They all belong to the monuments.*"

They entered the cathedral – Durdles taking a special delight in locking the small door behind them – and descended well-worn steps into the crypt. It was Samuel's first experience of such a place, and he was taken aback by its size. Heavy pillars supported the roof, which formed the floor of the cathedral, and these cast black shadows before the two men.

Across these they trod from the darkness into the light thrown by the moon through the *groined windows*.

This, then, was a passageway for the dead: coffins, sar-cophagi, a burial vault to store the deceased. The same, almost crafty, smile crossed Durdles's face as he looked up at Samuel in the light of the lantern; he, obviously, enjoyed his work and savoured the lack of composure in those he brought to this place. He was at home here; Samuel could see that was so. Occasionally, the stonemason would tap a wall with his hammer and comment on those interred.

"*Stoned and earthed up*, Mr Warden," he said, with a chuckle.

He seemed on familiar terms with all who ended their days in this chamber and was in no hurry to be gone. Samuel kept hold of the brandy, passing it across to Durdles when he coughed or licked his lips but otherwise keeping it close. They must have spent the best part of half-an-hour wandering back and forth before Durdles mentioned the tower.

"You took my friend, Mr Jasper, up the tower?" asked Samuel.

"Oh yes. He insisted. You can view the whole of Cloisterham from up there."

And so, they left the crypt and began their ascent of the tower, rising first to the cathedral and by a small *passage at the side of the chancel* arriving at the twisting staircase. It was a breathless walk for the mason who paused frequently on the steep climb. The winding steps were narrow, and they brushed often against the walls and, as often, Durdles sat to rest, while Samuel stood watching him and waiting.

"Do you believe the dead come back, Mr Warden?"

"I wouldn't care to speculate, Mr Durdles," replied the detective, "but it would make for an uncomfortable world if they did."

The stonemason-cum-sexton-cum-gravedigger smiled a grim smile.

"I was here on Christmas Eve two years ago, welcoming the season as was the right thing to do. I must have fell asleep because I was woken *by the ghost of a cry, the ghost of one terrific shriek, which shriek was followed by the howl of a dog: a long dismal woeful howl, such as a dog gives when a person's dead.*"

"This would be the Christmas Eve before last, before the one when Mr Drood disappeared?"

"That'd be the one," replied Durdles, "Come, let's be moving on."

It seemed an age – an age dominated by the waving lantern, angels' heads, narrower and steeper staircases, the cries of startled birds and falling dust – before they emerged on the ramparts of the tower and the warm wind of the summer's night blew fresh upon their faces. From here, as Durdles had promised, they were able to look down upon the town of Cloisterham, upon *the sanctuaries of the dead ... the red-tiled roofs ... the red-brick houses ... the river winding ... its way towards the sea.*

"Is this where your expedition with Mr Jasper concluded?" asked the detective.

"For an age we stood here. You'd wonder what there was to keep someone looking so long. It was a winter's night, then – dark as pitch. You couldn't see as much as tonight ... There's my house – down there. See that long stretch of trees and grass just off the High Street, just behind the Dean's house? That's mine."

Samuel looked to where the stonemason pointed. Even on a summer's night, the area around the cathedral, behind which stood the Deanery, was shrouded in shadow.

"We finished in the crypt," said Durdles, suddenly, as though keen to be gone, "He wanted to go back there. It was a long night before we made our way home."

Samuel passed the bottle of brandy to Durdles, intending to leave it in his safe keeping while he contemplated the scene. It was dark below, especially in those parts of the town overshadowed by the cathedral. He was not troubled by heights, but the top of the tower was no place for a drunken man, and he retrieved the brandy from Durdles before the mason became too drowsy to keep his balance. Durdles cast him a vicious glance.

"Come," said Samuel, kindly, "I'll buy you the drink I promised and then see you home."

"Durdles don't need no seeing home. Durdles will make his own way," snapped Durdles, pausing before continuing, as though a befuddled memory was nudging its way into his mind, "Deputy was there ..." he said, grabbing suddenly at the elusive recollection, "He sees Durdles home."

"Who is Deputy?"

"The boy from the Travellers' Twopenny. He didn't ...,"

Durdles stopped himself, as though about to break a confidence. Samuel waited but the drunken man said no more, and the detective did not press him. There would another moment – possibly that very evening at The Golden Lion – when drink would loosen the man's tongue. It had been an expedition that raised more questions than answers, but it was always so at this stage of an investigation.

And so, they descended the tower and left the cathedral, locking doors and gates behind them, before emerging from under the arch of Jasper's Gate House into the lights of the town and the companionship of The Golden Lion.

Chapter 9

Mr Datchery is Unsettled

The following morning, the arch of Mr Jasper's Gate House led Samuel to Mrs Tope. It was another bright morning, heralding an even brighter day. He had expected little from his expedition with Durdles but, truth to tell, the expedition had left him wondering; it was hard to account for such an enterprise at such an hour.

Mrs Tope, however, promised a fuller version of what had passed on December 27th when the solicitor, Grewgious, visited Jasper at his Gate House to impart the news of the broken betrothal between Edwin and Rosa.

Samuel consulted his notebook: Crisparkle arrived to find Jasper 'collapsed in his easy chair – the remains of a meal provided by Mrs Tope were on the table'. Hiram Grewgious had been deliberately less than helpful regarding John Jasper's reaction to the news of the broken engagement; indeed, had the detective not known about it from Rosa Bud he thought it unlikely that the solicitor would have mentioned the matter at all. Again, the thought came to him. Why?

Samuel consulted his notebook: 'he (Jasper) was very upset, he collapsed – What did he have to say? – At that moment, nothing. – And later? – I am a lawyer, not a man given to speculation'. Grewgious was not being cautious, Samuel thought, but evasive.

He made his way along the High Street to the residence of Mr and Mrs Tope, whose house adjoined Mr Jasper's and who provided for him. Mr Tope was absent.

"He is about his business, sir, as Chief Verger and Showman to the Cathedral," said Mrs Tope upon Samuel's enquiry, expressing her husband's importance by the use of capitals, which she managed to emphasize by holding her breath on their enunciation.

"Showman?"

"He is *high with excursion parties*, sir."

"I am sure, ma'am, being married to a woman such as yourself, he could be nothing less. But ...," replied Samuel, holding her eyes as he paused, "it is you I have come to see, ma'am – you who might bring a little sunshine into a detective's life."

Mrs Tope's face blanched slightly at the word 'detective', but she held herself beautifully, her rosy face and plump figure bearing up against the forces of law and order. She lifted her ample chest high, supporting herself by folding her arms beneath it.

"Samuel Warden, ma'am, Detective Sergeant of the Detective Police, London, and here at Mr Jasper's request to shine some light on the disappearance of his nephew, Edwin. I believe it was you, ma'am – according to the Rev Crisparkle – who looked after him when he collapsed with fatigue after three days of searching for the young man?"

Once he had his informer onside, Samuel never wasted time. The mention of two names who Mrs Tope held in high esteem was enough to mollify any doubts she might have about the policeman, and this was clear to him from the expression in her eyes.

"That is so, sir," she replied, dropping her face to one side and then lifting it again to look him straight in the eyes; this being her way of suggesting she would be offended if he supposed otherwise.

"Mr Grewgious asked for your assistance?"

"He called, sir. Who else could he ask?"

"Quite, ma'am. My word," he continued, not wishing to appear to pry by bombarding the lady with too many questions, "those crumpets smell delicious."

"Freshly baked for breakfast, sir. Mr Tope is partial to a crumpet or two with the butter thickly spread and the tea scalding hot before he goes about his cathedral duties."

"Lucky to have a wife such as yourself, Mrs Tope."

"You are not married, Mr Warden?"

"Not yet, ma'am. I have yet to find a woman who will have me."

"In a city the size of London, sergeant, you must be spoilt for choice."

"I always think, ma'am, that it should be the lady who does the choosing ... even if it appears to be otherwise."

Mrs Tope laughed, loud and heartily, at this compliment to her sex and immediately invited the detective to sit and enjoy a crumpet or two. Though already more than replete with the enormous breakfast he had enjoyed at his lodgings, Samuel sat at the Tope's kitchen table while Mrs Tope warmed the crumpets on the grate and brewed a fresh pot of tea. 'Let's be comfortable,' his mother would say, sitting across their kitchen table, looking at her son; and Samuel had always found it was at those times a woman enjoyed talking, it was at those times she would 'open up'. Mrs Tope was no exception to his golden rule.

"I'm pleased Mr Jasper has called you in," she began, "He has never given up, you know, never given up on his nephew. He was devoted to that dear boy and is determined to find him or ... or what happened to him. I found Mr Jasper collapsed on the floor. He looked nothing like himself. He looked just like *a heap of torn ... clothes*. Oh, it was dreadful to see him brought so low – he was singing so beautifully only a few days before.

Mr Grewgious helped me get him into his easy chair, and then I went and fetched him some food. I told him *he ought to take some wine ... and the jelly that I had ready for him, and that he wouldn't put his lips to at noon, though I warned him what would come of it ... and him not breakfasted*, and I said *he must have a wing of roast fowl that has been put back twenty times if it's been put back once.* I told him *it shall all be on table in five minutes* and that Mr Grewgious *will stop and see him take it."*

"Did the gentleman eat with him?" asked Samuel, reluctant to interrupt the lady's flow but pursuing a thought of his own.

"Why no, sir, but Mr Jasper ate voraciously. He mustn't have eaten for days."

The picture Samuel had of that encounter was incomplete, but the lines of the drawing had been shaded and the whole sketch was filling out into a shape more three-dimensional than previously.

He sat with Mrs Tope awhile as she expounded on the citizens of Cloisterham, his eyes remaining attentive on her face while his mind roved elsewhere, his ears pricking up when the name of Durdles was mentioned. "A sot is Durdles, a libertine. Some say as he's *a wonderful workman – which, for aught that anybody knows, he may be, as he never works.* He's better acquainted with the cathedral crypt than anyone else – even the dead. They say it's where he sleeps off his drunkenness."

That was at it may be, thought Samuel, but the man knew his monuments and his inscriptions, his empty tombs from his full ones and his way about the cathedral after dark. The crumpets consumed, and the tea gone cold, Samuel made his excuses, thanked Mrs Tope profusely for the 'abundance of her wisdom' and strolled out into the High Street to find himself, once more, standing under the arch of Mr Jasper's Gate House.

He needed to speak with John Jasper again and wondered whether the choirmaster was at home. He was standing by the postern door, considering his course when a cheery voice called out:

"Who are you looking for?"

Samuel turned and saw, for the second time since his arrival in Cloisterham, beyond the arch, an open door through which he glimpsed a man with a shock of white hair. The memory jarred him, but for the moment he was unsure as to why this was so.

"Mr Jasper, Choirmaster," he said.

"You're the second person to stand on that spot asking after Mr Jasper in as many days," was the reply, and the man emerged into the sunlight.

The man was *a white-haired personage with black eyebrows. Being buttoned up in a tightish blue surcoat, with a buff waistcoat and grey trousers, he had something of a military air.* He gave the impression of being elderly, but the lack of lines on his face suggested otherwise; the skin was pale and the complexion on the puffy side, but it was the face of a man no older than Samuel's own thirty years.

"And who was the first?"

"An elderly lady, sir," was the short answer. "Allow me to introduce myself – Dick Datchery at your service," he continued, and extended his hand, which Samuel took.

"Samuel Warden. You are a local in this place, are you, Mr Datchery?"

"*An idle buffer living upon his means. I have taken lodgings in this picturesque old city for a month or two, with a view to settling down here altogether.* And you, sir?"

"A visitor, Mr Datchery, lodging, for the moment, at the Royal Victoria and Bull."

"I looked for something odd and out of the way; something venerable, architectural, inconvenient … Cathedral!" replied Mr Datchery, with a touch of the stage in his delivery.

"You are an artist, are you, Mr Datchery?"

"And what makes you think that, Mr Warden?"

"Why – your manner of dress, your fascination with the inconvenient and the pile of paper upon your breakfast table. I glimpsed you as I passed the other morning. Only an artist – a writer, in particular – would be working at that hour and over his breakfast."

Mr Datchery was clearly flattered; had he been a bird, he would now be preening himself ready for flight. Instead, he *shook his shock of hair.*

"You are a magician, Mr Warden!"

"An observer of human nature, Mr Datchery – nothing more. May I?"

Without waiting for an answer, the detective strode past the idle buffer and stepped into his room. It was *a chamber of no describable shape, with a groined roof, which in its turn opened on another chamber of no describable shape, with another groined roof: their windows small and in the thickness of the walls … close as to their atmosphere and swarthy as to their illumination by natural light.* In one corner there was cupboard, empty and with its door open. On the inside of this door were a few chalked strokes.

"*I like the old tavern way of keeping scores,*" said Mr Datchery, who had followed Samuel, hurriedly, into his own room.

"Very clever, Mr Datchery – if I may say so: *illegible except to the scorer – the scorer not committed, the scored debited with what is against him.* I said you were an artist, sir, and everything about your room speaks of that truth. I see you had a successful day, sir, not many days since – this *one thick line extending from the top of the cupboard-door to the bottom* tells all. But only to you, Mr Datchery: an artist has his secrets! Are you a playwright, sir, or a novelist?"

"A playwright," replied Mr Datchery, with something of a gasp, as though confiding the information was an intrusion, and with a swift movement to the papers on his table.

"Fear not, Mr Datchery. Fascinated by your persona as I am, my discourtesy would not extend as far as casting a philistine eye upon your writings. What I would crave, sir, are your impressions of this city, Cloisterham. You say you are a stranger here, hoping to become a settler – if I may use the term. What of its people, Mr Datchery, Playwright? What does an artist make of its people – the very bread and butter, sir, of your craft!"

Mr Datchery opened his mouth, about to speak but with a disconsolate – not to say, gloomy – expression in his eyes, an expression that obliged the detective to prevent him speaking lest he might border on a refusal.

"I have, myself, spoken with the bountiful Mrs Tope, the worshipful Mr Sapsea, the devoted Mr Jasper, the muscular Rev Crisparkle and Mr Durdles, who you, sir, as a writer, would – I humbly suggest – describe as a character! And you, Mr Datchery?"

The idle buffer's eyes had widened several times and seemed about to invade his forehead, as the detective reeled off the list of names, and had veritably sparkled at the name of Jasper. Samuel did not miss this reaction and leaned towards the man, expectantly.

"You've certainly been busy, Mr Warden," replied the playwright, a touch of pique in his voice, "I have yet to meet the clergyman but met Durdles briefly."

"Durdles the stonemason and I spent an informative evening only yesterday in the depths and heights of the cathedral, Mr Datchery, in the footsteps of Mr Jasper. We were, you might say, travelling between Heaven and Earth. And you, sir? You spoke of Mr Jasper."

"It was he who spoke for the respectability of Mr and Mrs Tope – or, at least, referred me to the mayor as being a person whose recommendation was more important than his own when testifying on behalf of others."

"Ever the humble choirmaster,"

"As you say, Mr Warden, ever the humble choirmaster."

"You found him so?"

"I met him only the once."

"But you are an artist, Mr Datchery! You formed an opinion above the gossip of the common herd. Did he not strike you as a man hemmed in by his circumstances? A man, perhaps, like yourself, though in another field, whose light was dimmed by Cloisterham, whose light yearned to shine in the great metropolis."

"He did."

"And his visitor, Mr Datchery – the elderly lady who stood at his postern door – did she not stir your imagination? Did you not wonder, Mr Datchery, Playwright, what she sought with the Choirmaster and Lay Precentor of the cathedral in whose precincts you live and write?"

Mr Datchery seemed puffed up by the praise heaped upon him, puffed up to bursting point. Here was another stranger in Cloisterham, a man who seemed to acknowledge he lacked the talents required for the artistic life but stood in admiration of those who did, a man hungry to feed upon the imagination and insights of himself. And this stranger had persuaded Durdles the stonemason to show him the secrets of the cathedral.

These thoughts, at least, Samuel hoped were passing through the mind of Mr Datchery; put a man on his mettle, set him back upon his heels, and who knows what might come of it. It was often the odd word, the odd insight, that led a man on to greater things; and what better than the insights of a stranger to the town, one who could step back and view its happenings without prejudice.

"She asked after his calling" began Mr Datchery, adding, gloomily, "but when I explained seemed unsure what a cathedral was. Nevertheless, I pointed it out to her – it being hard to miss: a substantial enough object against the sky, would you not say, Mr Warden?"

Samuel said nothing but continued to focus his full attention upon the playwright.

"She didn't want to speak with him, something I found it difficult to understand and so I suggested she *might admire him at a distance three times a day if* she cared to go to the cathedral," continued Mr Datchery, looking quizzically at the detective, as though waiting for the obvious question. When it failed to come, he continued, "She then begged money for her lodgings from me and went on her way."

Mr Datchery clammed up, granted Samuel a look that suggested enough had been said and, at the same time, gave *that shock of white hair of his another shake.*

"And did she go to the cathedral the next day?" persisted Samuel.

"You are certainly of an inquisitive disposition, Mr Warden. You have asked mine, and so may I enquire what might be your business in the town?"

The old buffer's eyes betokened no further thoughts unless Samuel shared his, and so the detective, set slightly back on the proverbial heels himself, replied:

"A mere visitor."

"A mere visitor who persuaded Mr Durdles to take him in Mr Jasper's footsteps."

"The purest of accidents, Mr Datchery. Mr Sapsea told me of the stonemason's expedition with the choirmaster. I simply could not resist the temptation to do likewise," replied Samuel, eager to climb from the hole into which Mr Datchery seemed to be dropping him, and suggesting, "It would be an adventure for an artist, sir – an experience to set the creative juices flowing. Let me show you our stonemason's home."

The playwright seemed mollified by this offer and continued:

"She went to the cathedral next morning and stood watching the service from behind a pillar ..."

"And that is all?"

"What more were you expecting, Mr Warden?"

"She was a stranger to the town and, therefore, must have travelled here, perhaps by train and certainly by Joe's omnibus. It seems she made a determined effort to find Mr Jasper, only to watch him from a distance."

"Human nature is curious, Mr Warden. As a student of its finer points, you must be aware of the fact."

It was obvious to the detective that the playwright was holding back. Under normal circumstances, he would have badgered the man; if his on-the-spot persistence bore no fruit, a march to Cloisterham police station and a night in the cells would have found Mr Datchery to be more obliging. But Samuel desisted from applying pressure. He wasn't sure why: call it intuition or his feelings about time and chance. Certainly, the race was not to the swift ... nor yet riches to men of understanding, but the riches, in the form of justice, would come to him, he felt sure.

"Where did the lady spend the night?" he asked, suddenly: despite his intuition, seeing no other way forward but a direct question.

"At the Travellers' Twopenny."

"How do you know that?"

"Deputy told me," replied Mr Datchery.

"Deputy?"

"A boy who works at the Travellers. I met him on my first day here. He was stoning a sheep grazing in the burial ground. I told him to let it be, and he directed me to Mrs Tope's lodging."

"And so, this boy met your old lady, Mr Datchery? I am sure there will be a place for both in one of your plays, and I should be fascinated to meet them."

"You will find that somewhat of a difficulty at the moment, Mr Warden," replied Mr Datchery, with a dry laugh.

"Why so?"

"Because three days ago they set off to London."

"Together?"

"Perhaps they formed a friendship overnight at their lodgings."

Samuel detected the change of tone in Mr Datchery's reply: an almost off-hand flippancy had entered his voice, which indicated at the best an evasion, at the worst a lie; and the detective did not approve.

"Did he or she tell you this?"

"You sound like a policeman, Mr Warden."

"Detective Sergeant Samuel Warden of the Detective Police, Mr Datchery, at your service. Now, I am pleased to leave you at your writing – the artist must have his solitude as the policeman must have his witness. You are not being too forthcoming, are you, Mr Datchery, Playwright? You are jollying me along. The lady's name is ...?"

"Why do you suppose ...?"

"Never mind why I suppose, Mr Datchery, Playwright! You have sent the boy into the heart of the criminal cesspit known as London, where he will meet – along with other detritus of humanity – prostitutes and their procurers, sneak-thieves, house-breakers and burglars, swindlers and card-sharps, beggars, cheats and – if he is unfortunate enough to end up near the Thames – smugglers and river pirates, and – possibly worst of all from a young lad's point of view – pickpockets, who will welcome him into their sordid lives. Now – let us hope that young Deputy told you the lady's name."

"Her Royal Highness the Princess Puffer," blurted Mr Datchery.

"I shall return, Mr Datchery, and expect to find you settled here. In the meantime, if I hurry, I might catch the midday omnibus to the rail station at Maidstone."

Watching the detective making haste away, Mr Datchery felt anything but settled.

Chapter 10

Helena Landless Displays Her Unusual Powers

Helena Landless would brook no denial in her desire to search for her brother that very night, despite Lt Tartar's warnings of the difficulties and dangers inherent in such an undertaking.

"I have said, Mr Tartar, that *there is a complete understanding between my brother and me, though no spoken word may have passed between us*, and he is gone from me. I must find him."

The solicitor, Hiram Grewgious had called for Lt Tartar's assistance as soon as the young woman had coming rushing to his chambers well past the midnight hour, and the three of them now stood in Neville Landless's rooms: the solicitor with a coat thrown hurriedly over his night attire, Helena and Tartar now dressed to walk the streets of London for as long as it may take to find the missing young man.

Helena was calm and resolute despite harbouring the possibility that her brother was no longer among the living. She seemed enervated rather than subdued by the thought: her dark eyes blazed with a determination that Lt Tartar had previously seen in men under fire but never in a woman.

She led the way into the dark streets and the sailor followed. They pursued the trail along Oxford Street before turning towards the great slum of St Giles. Ahead lay Covent Garden, to their right St Martin-in-the-Fields and to their left Drury Lane and London's theatreland. It was in the latter direction that Helena Landless turned first.

The young Ceylonese girl reminded Lt Tartar of a beagle on the scent of a fox, but the knowledge that guided their path came from within rather than on the warm air of the summer's night. To the sailor it seemed as though she was in some mysterious way connected to her brother, as though a field of energy – perhaps of understanding – linked them throughout the tumultuous streets of the city.

It was after one o'clock. *Parties returning from the different theatres footed it through muddy streets; cabs, hackney coaches, carriages and theatre-omnibuses, rolled swiftly by. The frequenters of the theatres thronged to the different houses of refreshment; and chops, kidneys, rabbits, oysters, stout and cigars were served up amidst a noise and confusion of smoking, running, knife-clattering and waiter-chattering.* Nothing drew Helena Landless from her quest, or even distracted her, for one moment.

They turned from the gaslit streets into those with the dark corners, where prostitutes plied their trade and both they and their customers welcomed the lack of light. The streets in such places were dirty as were the dwellings on either side, dwellings that crowded in upon the thoroughfares, overlooking the walkers and nudging them from the pavement. The refreshment houses were replaced by the baked potato and kidney pie merchants. Oyster and fruit venders hung about on corners offering sustenance to the those who lounged or idled their time away, reluctant to return home – if, indeed, they had a home.

After so many years abroad, Tartar had yet to come to terms with the state of his homeland. His initial wanderings in the city had been confined to daylight hours, but now he saw his own countrymen homeless, *lying coiled up in nooks.* He brushed aside *the drunkards and the slinking men, who whistled and signed to one another at corners and then darted off at full speed.* He caught the eye of a woman, her infant upon her arm and wrapped loosely in a shawl, *attempting to sing some popular ballad, in the hope of wringing a few pence from a compassionate passer-by*; she looked no older than

Helena. Tartar grabbed two pies from a nearby vendor, dropping two pennies into his tray, and handed them to the woman, who smiled weakly. He kept close to Helena, guiding and protecting her without actually placing a hand upon her, so keen was he not to impede her mission.

The night wore on, but it was not yet time for those first streaks of day to begin, shyly, invading those far reaches of the horizon far beyond the city and start their steady trickle through the alleyways and across the terraces. There came a time when the crowds dispersed, slowly, inevitably, to their beds, when the venders and the merchants walked away with their ovens on their arms and the shopkeepers drew down their shutters.

The city grew silent and the intensity of their pursuit became more apparent, their isolation from the rest of mankind goading them on. They passed the time of night with a policeman on a street corner, his brief conversation more concerned with a supposed spell of prevailing sunshine than their business abroad at such an hour.

As they neared the river, Helena's pace quickened and the sailor, used as he was to be navigating the seven oceans of the world, felt himself losing track of where they were placed. He had noted Covent Garden, *its flagstones stained green with the leaves trodden underfoot* and the smell of fruit and vegetables – apples, broccoli, potatoes, cabbages and rhubarb among them – still redolent in the warm air, accompanied by the muskiness of the sacking in which they were carried. From here they veered towards the Strand through a labyrinth of passageways to the Adelphi Terrace and the north bank of the Thames.

On the bank, Helena paused for the first time and looked down into the river. The heat of the previous day and the warmth of the night drew a faint miasma from the waters. It hovered for a moment and then dispersed as quickly as it had appeared. They heard the tide beating against the supports of the Hungerford Bridge, and Tartar noted that it was on the turn. On the other side of the river and stretching also along the north shore were dozens of warehouses served by docks and basins from where the masts of ships pointed towards Heaven. The going underfoot became treacherous, covered as the walkways were with the slime of the cargoes landed here and the treading of watermen's feet.

At the bridge, Helena hesitated, making her way, first, down three flights of steps until she came to the space beneath the arch of the bridge. This was the first time Tartar had seen her puzzled. It was a dismal place under the dark bridge. The young woman shuddered and looked at Tartar, her eyes suggesting for the first time since they set out that she was grateful for his company.

A church clock somewhere struck four. As its final peal faded, Helena turned and made her way to the terrace. She looked both ways along the shoreline and up at the steeple of St Clement Danes, which loomed above the surrounding buildings of the waterfront.

"He is gone this way," she said, speaking for the first time in three hours.

Tartar followed her until they came to the very central arch of Waterloo Bridge, the 'Bridge of Sighs' from where it was said many prostitutes had flung themselves into the dark waters below. They both looked down into the turgid flow of the river; the gas lights that spanned the bridge were reflected on the surface but illuminated nothing beneath, and they stared for a long time into the murky, hidden depths.

"Neville has brought me here," said Helena, "and now we must follow him along the river."

"Miss Landless – Helena – we must wait until dawn. It is summer, and the daylight hour is not far off. There is no chance of finding your brother … in the dark."

The sailor paused, only briefly but it was enough to alert this young woman who seemed able to read other minds than her brothers.

"What are you keeping from me, Mr Tartar? What is it I need to know? I am not a child and will not be treated as such."

"The Thames is a tidal river, Miss Landless. We are now approaching the ebb – perhaps in an hour, the water will begin to flow once more towards the sea."

"You mean that if my brother found himself in the water earlier, the tide would have taken him inland?"

"Yes."

"And may now bring him back to us?"

"Let us repair to a hostelry I know of along the shore," replied Lt Tartar, avoiding the question, "We will find a comforting drink there while we wait, and I will send a message to my man, Lobley. I have a boat moored at Greenhithe. He can be here in a short time and his assistance will be invaluable."

There was a considerable hesitation before Helena Landless agreed to the sailor's proposal. She was a young woman used to deciding matters for herself; after all, it was she who led when her brother and herself ran away as children. She looked down at the watermen along the shore and wondered; she looked up at the young man with the old figure, robust and broad of shoulder, at the sparkling eyes and the laughing teeth – the sailor with whom, she was sure, her friend Rosa was already in love – and decided to trust his judgement.

The snug, little room at the Three Jolly Sailors, into which they were shown by a plump young woman, warm and rosy of complexion, enveloped Helena in its comfort as soon as they were seated. The gaslight cast its glow around them, and Lt Tartar ordered, without consultation, a steaming jug of glogg.

The potboy was called and instructed to hire a cab and get himself down to Greenhithe, post haste, where he would find Mr Lobley, who he was to bring back to the Sailors. At this request, the plump young woman demurred, on the grounds that the boy was far too valuable to the house, and called, instead, on the services of another boy who was prone to hang about the hostelry waiting for odd jobs, such as polishing the brasses and cleaning the cutlery. The lad, who could not have been more than six or seven years of age, took Lt Tartar's money with a ready smile and was off like a shot from a gun.

All they had to do now was wait. It seemed to Helena that the glogg provided sustenance as well as refreshment following their travails of the night, after she was provided with a spoon to extract the almonds and raisins. The plump, young woman, Pleasant by name and pleasant by nature, was a novelty as far as Helena was concerned: where the Ceylonese girl came from, women knew their place, and that place was not conducting the business of a public house, however respectable and hospitable the hostelry may be.

While the two women chatted, Lt Tartar excused himself and sought out some watermen he knew along the shore and who he had seen in the bar. Among these men – most of whom were employed, quite legitimately, in such pursuits as ferrying fish to the market at Billingsgate – were those who pulled corpses from the river.

It was profitable enough line of business and those involved in the trade were well versed in the requirements of the law – as those working on the edge of it are prone to be. A body once found would almost certainly be relieved of any encumbrances, such as money and jewellery, before being brought before the appropriate authorities. Once the police had taken possession of the deceased, a notice alerting the public to the fact that someone had been found in the river would be printed and handbills circulated *offering rewards for drowned men.* Those involved in such a trade took pride in conducting their business in what they considered to be a *regular* manner. It was such a man that the sailor now sought.

His guide, a waterman who had provided Lt Tartar with advice and assistance ever since the sailor arrived in London, led him along the *shelving bank of the river, among the slimy stones of a causeway* to where a number of boats were moored. Here, he was told to wait and did so, leaning back on the gunwale of a rowboat that stank of fish. Lt Tartar had sought out Billingsgate soon after his arrival and knew well the variety of catches marketed there: turbot (brought alive in tanks on the decks), roach, plaice, dabs, flounder, salmon, sole, haddock, skate, cod and eel were all to be had from the market. Perhaps with such a beneficence of choice, thought Lt Tartar, one should not complain of the smell.

He had, anyway, not long to wait. His guide returned accompanied by a stocky figure with a shock of grizzled, raven-black hair and a rough beard that equalled it in colour. Lt Tartar, used to summing-up men in an instant, disliked and distrusted him on sight, but realised that this man would know his business, know where Neville Landless, if he was drowned as the sailor expected, was most likely to have washed up.

The trader-in-corpses listened intently as Lt Tartar explained the circumstances, tide and time and place, where the young man was supposed to have been last seen. When the sailor finished speaking, the man, whose name the lieutenant had not been given and not requested, spoke quietly and thoughtfully.

"If, as you say, he went on the flood tonight, he's like as not to be up river past the Westminster and could have gone as far as Millbank," he said, uttering the last name, renowned and dreaded for the prison sited there, as though he had just sucked on a lemon, "but there's many a place he could have dropped off on his journey, many a nook and cranny in the shore that way as could harbour him in safety, as there is when he makes his return journey – if he makes his return journey – this morning. If I was you, I'd cast my eyes on the southern shore below Vauxhall and on the northern shore above Westminster. If he gets past Hungerford, you're likely to have lost him. The tide pulls quickly there and many a good man has left us for foreign shores, as they say."

The man watched Lt Tartar as he spoke, and the sailor knew that he, also, intended to search for Neville Landless: there was money in corpses. But the ex-Royal Navy man had no regrets about asking: the more who searched, the more likely were they to find the young man. Whatever Helena Landless's thoughts were on the matter, Lt Tartar had no doubt that her brother had gone from the bridge into the river, and there was no hope in those waters.

Many a comrade had been recovered, having fallen into the sea, but these were men who knew the art of survival: not a callow youth unused to combating such elements. One sailor who had to all intents and purpose drowned while in the lieutenant's command had actually been recovered, declaring that a man cannot be drowned twice; it was an old idea common among sailors and the man concerned had borne out it's truth, having been washed ashore, after three days at sea, on a foreign coast.

After Lt Tartar returned to the snug of the Three Jolly Sailors, he had not long to wait for the coming of his man. Lobley *was a jolly-favoured man, with tawny hair and whiskers, and a big red face. He was the dead image of the sun in old woodcuts, his hair and whiskers answering for rays all around him.* He sat without saying a word while Lt Tartar explained the circumstances that brought them to the public house, his face deepening into a frown that ran from between his eyes to his pursed lips.

"We'd best be off to Temple Stairs," was all he said by way of acknowledgment, and soon they were in the cab the lieutenant had retained, having paid off the odd-job, orphan boy who had brought Lobley to them.

"We have a rowing boat at Temple Stairs," explained Lt Tartar, "and we shall make our way upriver. It will be against the tide going, of course, but if you take up your position in the stern, Miss Landless, I am sure we shall have the best lookout on the Thames."

It was as he planned. The two men *pulled the oars*, Lobley *resplendent in the bow of the boat ... with a man-of-war's shirt on ... and his arms and chest tattoo'd all sorts of patterns. Lobley seemed to take it easily, and so did Mr Tartar; yet their oars bent as they pulled, and the boat bounded under them.* Both men had an instinctive understanding of the other and the rowboat made steady progress, its passage dependent on their ability to steer with their oars, since Helena was otherwise occupied.

She leaned forward in the stern, her eyes scanning the banks. The natural width of the Thames was narrowed by the amount of shipping moored on either bank alongside the quays. The early morning sun, heralding another fine day, shone upon the water so that the little ridges of water in the wake of the boat caught its light and sparkled. It was a busy sight that met the young woman's eyes: barges floated on the tide, men hauled at sails either raising or lowering them as they approached or passed one of the bridges, a raft of timber towed by a small boat passed close on their port side. Along the banks, rank upon rank of warehouses, lifeblood of the city, rose black and ugly. Dark figures – costermongers and watermen – scurried back and forth on the wharves, carrying cargo from the boats to the barrows to the markets. Steamers, hurrying past, flung white spray into the air and shook the water into such a frenzy that the smaller craft and even the barges, laden low as they were with barrels of beer, sacks of flour or coal, were threatened.

The wharves, seen none too clearly through the mast and rigging of the sailboats, were decked out with ungainly cranes, so cumbersome a sight that they seemed likely, at any moment, to topple forward into the river.

Helena gaze never faltered; her intensity never diminished. Whatever concerns might be running through her mind, they remained camouflaged within a deep, abiding concentration. She appeared to be listening for a voice as much as watching the sights that scurried before her eyes: a glimpse of boats through the arch of a bridge, the feet of men making their way from causeway to stairs, the black sides of steamers towering from the water, the early morning mists rising from the waters.

With foresight as to what their day might involve, Lobley had brought with him a small luncheon consisting of ham sandwiches, cheese-cakes that he had by, some cherries and a bottle of sherry he offered with water, but Helena would eat nothing, although she urged the men to do so, insisting that their physical effort required them to eat, while her mental one was served better by fasting.

The two men said not a word that might hearten or discourage the young woman in this search for her brother, loath to encroach upon her thoughts and her hopes. All morning and far into the afternoon they pulled, searching as closely as possible both banks of the river for where a young man might have been washed ashore; but the nooks and crannies mentioned by the trader-in-corpses were many: hidden between the hundreds of ships and the shore, concealed against the rotten woodwork of a staithe, lying unseen at the foot of a vacant causeway, masked by a tangle of rope, veiled among the detritus washed up against a quay.

The question as to whether or not the young woman wondered if her brother had been dragged down by a medley of rope or heavy chain uncoiling in the dark as a boat came to its moorings in the night was never raised, even as a thought, by either man; but on their return journey, drawn back to Temple Stairs on the afternoon ebb tide, both men noticed that Helena Landless's lips were drawn, her cheeks hollow, her eyes glistening with a semblance of madness.

She said nothing, except to thank Lobley for his help, when they reached the boat's mooring, and she took Lt Tartar's arm as he walked her back to Staple Inn. She felt lighter than when they had left, when her hopes and anger raised her to the search, as though something had gone from her; her concentration had been such that she was now drained not only of energy but of the spirit that kept her going, much as a doctor might be drawn having worked with a deeply troubled patient. The full power of her mental resources had been focussed on her brother, and now the circuit that linked them was broken, the field of their energies spilled into the streets and waters of the city.

These, at least, were Lt Tartar's thoughts as they progressed slowly back to their rooms. He was surprised, therefore, when Helena turned to him as he bid her good evening.

"My brother is gone from me, but I have not given up, not abandoned hope, Mr Tartar. Under no circumstances will I believe that my brother has left me forever. I shall rest tonight and such powers as I have will be refreshed by sleep. I will find my brother or join him in the attempt."

*

On the flood tide that very night, a rowboat pulled out from a causeway close to the Three Jolly Sailors. In the boat was a stocky figure with a shock of grizzled, raven-black hair and a rough beard that equalled it in colour, dark enough to be visible above the shadows of that late hour. His *eyes watched every little race and eddy* in the river, one hand on the rudder, moving with the tide. He gazed at *every mooring-chain and rope, at every stationary boat or barge ... at the paddles of the river steamboats as they beat the filthy water, at the floating logs of timber lashed together lying off certain wharves.* The river was *meat and drink* to him, and he was familiar with the comings and goings of corpses on the many tides.

Chapter 11

Princess Puffer Smokes a Pipe

Samuel regretted losing his temper with Dick Datchery. He was sure the man was a fountain of knowledge, if not wisdom, and leaving him calm in Cloisterham, rather than unsettled, the detective would have a man on the spot: a fountain from which he felt sure he could eventually tap what he needed to know; but the knowledge that the boy, Deputy, was in London – sent there, Samuel's intuition told him, by the playwright to follow the woman – had forced his hand.

Besides, he knew Her Royal Highness the Princess Puffer: not by that name, but by the more accessible, Eliza, purveyor and smoker of opium. Eliza kept an opium den in Shadwell Court. He had some idea as to where she may have originated although her nationality was difficult to determine, but the area in which she thrived was a mish-mash of races: Lascars brought over by the East India Company and Chinese and Greeks – all seaman or militiamen who cohabited, and sometimes married, local women. Shadwell was a place where outbursts of random violence were common; a few years into his work as a beat constable, Samuel had been called to the East End to help quell a street brawl that resulted in more than a dozen men being arrested. For the young policeman it had been a baptism of blood, cuts, bruises and broken bones. It was a miserable place, the dark and ghastly side of London.

He arrived in the metropolis in the early evening and made his way immediately to Shadwell's High Street. He knew the landlords of both pubs – The Three Crowns and The Grapes

– and he needed their help to find the boy, Deputy. The former pub was licensed for dancing and was a magnet for sailors and their women. A knot of prostitutes was standing outside but made no attempt to proposition Samuel, whose manner advised them of his occupation.

The bar cleared when he entered, and the landlord gave Samuel his full attention. Neither he nor his fellow officers had ever experienced any problem with entering any premises in the area or in seeking help when needed; eager to get rid of them, the occupants were always found to be cooperative. A corner table was vacated, brandy and water provided, and a conversation held discreetly. The description he had of Deputy, gathered from Dick Datchery when that idle buffer had been sufficiently unnerved, covered a multitude of such children: dressed in rags, malnourished, with a jagged gap in what remained of his front teeth and a propensity to throw stones at anything or anyone. The only distinctive mark was his habit of contradiction, his use of the term 'Yer Lie!' when challenged.

"Mark it well, James Brooks, Landlord, pass on the word, make it known that Detective Sergeant Warden wants that boy, needs that boy, and that no one here in the city need fear the consequences once he is apprehended. You know me as a man of my word. It shall go well with you if you are obliging."

Samuel had learned the technique of assertive persuasion from his superior officer, Detective Inspector Charles Field, a man who might enter a den of thieves and quell those there with his composure. 'Be bold, Samuel! Let all present be aware that you know who they are and what they are about. Be polite. Wish them all the good tidings of the day. They will know that in your time you have, or will, collar half the people there and will have *motioned their brothers, sisters, fathers, mothers, male and female friends … to New South Wales.* They will keep their eagle eye on you, *answer when addressed,* laugh at your jokes. They could, if they wished, murder you on the spot – but they will not do so. Be business-like and nab your man or woman!'

James Brook, Landlord and Brothel-keeper, knew his place and knew Mr Warden's business; and the policeman left with a smile all round. The boy had been in London three days according to Mr Datchery, but he would be found. Thus comforted, Samuel went on his way.

The alleyways veered off in all directions from the High Street, leading into dark and dank corners amidst houses held together more by hope than plaster or brickwork. The few, unbroken windows were stained with the wet and dirt of years and those less fortunate were stuffed with rags or paper to waylay the draught. The quarrels and drunkenness with which he was familiar from his days in E Division permeated every turn and corner.

It was fortunate for Samuel that it was a summer's evening, the days long and the night's short, for *the solitary oil lamp in the centre of the court had been blown out, either by the violence of* a winter *wind or the act of some inhabitant who had excellent reasons for objecting to his residence being rendered too conspicuous.* As it was, he made his way easily along the *broken and uneven* pavements and avoided the *gutter that ran down the centre* of the court and from which *all the sluggish odours of the place were called forth.*

He turned from the court down a grubby passageway and entered a house that had no street-door and found himself in a kitchen where a woman was crouched over a coke fire, whose fumes filled the place and made his eyes water. She paid no attention to Samuel, used as she was to the customers of the prostitutes, who paid her four shillings a week for the use of the hovel, barging past. He went upstairs and found the room he sought.

A Lascar lay prone across the bed covered by a couple of tattered blankets. By the side of the bed sat the woman Samuel wanted to question. Both reeked of the opium they had been smoking; the seaman slept, and the woman gaggled to herself. Her face was grimy and unwashed, wrinkled and careworn; she was desperate for another pipe and clutched an empty one in her bony fingers. Samuel wondered how she had found enough stamina to make the journey to Cloisterham in search of John Jasper, so broken in body and spirit did she seem.

He walked across the mean room and pulled the newspaper from the window, both to allow the light an entrance and the stale smell of the room an exit. The movement stirred the woman and she looked up at him, unrecognisable in the darkness of her lodging.

"Come in, come in, deary," she cried, "*I can't see you till I light a match*, yet I seem to know you. *I am acquainted with you, ain't I?*"

"We have met, Eliza," replied Samuel, keeping his voice low so as not to wake the Lascar.

"I knew you'd be coming. I say to myself, 'he'll be coming, have a pipe ready. *He'll bear in mind the market price of opium and pay accordingly*'. No one mixes it like me – not Jack Chinaman across the court – *he doesn't have the true secret of mixing it.*"

As she spoke, the woman turned to a small table at her side on which stood a candle, a pair of scissors, a saucer, a tray, a horn spoon, a thimble and a number of penny inkbottles.

Watching her eager movements and the lack of attention she paid to him, Samuel realised he had been mistaken for a customer, and an idea suggested itself as the woman prepared the pipe.

He had seen the process before on several occasions when visiting the dives of London with Inspector Field and it never failed to fascinate the detective. There was something of the artist in those who specialised in the craft. He had watched while a Chinese called Chi Ki had taken the raw opium and shredded it into slices. These were held on a piece of canvas suspended in a small, iron pot filled with water. The pot had been heated over a small oil lamp and the essence of the opium drained through the canvas to form a sediment at the bottom of the pot.

It was this sediment that the Princess Puffer now held in her thimble. She dipped the tip of her needle into the treacly substance, which smelt like burnt sugar, and withdrew a little drop of it. This she held in the flame of her candle, having first trimmed the wick, until the opium was toasted. Over and over again she repeated the process until a lump of the drug the size of a large pea was ready to be placed in one of her inkbottles and a bamboo mouthpiece attached.

"*I've got a pretty many smokes ready for you ... haven't I,* deary?"

"*A good many*," replied Samuel, moving to the one chair in the room, which he placed back to the wretched window, "You enjoy the first pipe, mother. You've been good to me. No one knows the secret of mixing like you. Business slack, is it?"

"*Worse luck for me*," replied the woman.

"I've all night. I'm in no hurry. We can smoke a few together and enjoy a laugh or two."

Princess Puffer drew on the pipe: three whiffs and she relaxed, her eyes glazed over, her breathe shortened.

"Are you home from a voyage, deary?"

"Home, mother, and money to spend," replied Samuel with a hearty laugh.

"I'm a mother to you all – land customers and sea customers," she replied, laughing with him: a laugh that turned into a coughing fit, "*Oh my lungs is awful bad, my lungs is wore away to cabbage nets!* Let me mix another for you, deary."

"And one for yourself, mother, and one for yourself. Whilst we have the money we might as well spend it."

She looked up at him, but the detective's face was in shadow. The Lascar on the bed stirred, and the opium woman, leaving her preparations, went over to the man and turned him on his side.

"He sleeps better like that," she said, "and we don't want him disturbing us."

The mixing complete, Samuel took his pipe and waited while she mixed another for herself from the treacly essence of opium.

"Me matches," the women cried, "I coughs so much, I coughs them out."

Samuel reached over, struck the match and held it steady. When she was ready, he handed her the second pipe, which she seized, gratefully. Samuel waited until the opium had taken hold.

"I've had some dreams with you," he said, knowing of the stories smokers told, "Dreams of far-away places, strange lands and even stranger people ... the smoking opens up another world, such things as dreams are made of ...I've travelled far while in this room. I imagine you have tales to tell ... customers beyond the far seas."

Tap, tap! Samuel tapped away at her unconscious mind, leaving his pipe to cool and fade.

"*Do it in your fancy, over and over again,*" replied the Princess Puffer with a contented groan.

Samuel waited. He needed to strike a chord. He was here to discover how much this woman knew of John Jasper and why she had sought him out with such persistence. Was it to blackmail him, or was there more to her determination? How often did he visit? A chord! He must strike a chord.

"I was a child chorister," he said, "and my singing, like my smoking, brought dreams and relief. It is a hard world this, and a man must escape."

"*This is the place where the all-overs is smoked off,*" she said."

"So true, mother, so true."

"A sweet singer ...," she said.

"Sweet enough, mother – the sweet voice of a child."

"He was *a sweet singer when he first come.* Used to sing himself off to sleep."

"And dream away."

"And dream away. His dreams were journeys ... *the journey he was away upon ...*"

Samuel did not so much as make a sound with his breathing: *perfect quietude* freed the memories.

"He made the journey in many ways, when he made it so often ... but no, only the one way, in the way it was made at last ... and always with the same pleasure ... never tired he was ... he came o'purpose to take the journey. I might have known it ... there was a fellow traveller ... great landscapes and glittering processions ... couldn't begin till it was off his mind ..."

"Fellow traveller ...," crooned Samuel as softly as he was able.

"How could the time be at hand unless the fellow-traveller was ... The journey's made. It's over."

The woman slumped forward in the chair, the pipe slipping from her hands. Samuel was tempted to help her back onto the seat but disinclined to intrude on her memories, memories that had dwelt within her and festered. Memories that had sustained her on her journey to Cloisterham?

"The journey's over," he said, hopefully.

"So soon? So soon it seemed not worth the doing, it was done so soon."

The detective sat dead still; not so much as a whisper came from him, not so much as a faint breath, but she was gone from him, asleep in a drugged-filled world of her own.

How much of that particular memory had she shared with John Jasper? She had just returned from her pursuit of the man and business had been slack: she had time on her hands. The woman dropped further into sleep, and Samuel walked over to the window. He took his notebook from his pocket and wrote down her words, words he would dwell on time and again as the case wore on.

There was nothing more to be culled from her now. In the morning he could return or have a constable haul her off to the local station, where she may be frightened into telling more of what he hoped she knew; but for the moment there was nothing more to be gained from staying in the woebegone room that was her home. Samuel looked down at the creature in the chair. She was huddled up and looked more like a bundle of animated rags than a human being. He felt no pity for her kind but could not suppress a feeling of sorrow for the woman she must once have been.

He *groped his way down the stairs* with their broken banister and so out into the street where the odours from the gully and drains still corrupted the air.

Chapter 12

Samuel Warden Ponders *the Gritty State of Things* Past

Samuel woke late the following morning. This annoyed him, given his habit of rising and being off for work early. He put it down to the heavy meal his landlady, the widow, Mrs Sarah Rowse, had provided the previous evening when he arrived in Camberwell and she realized he had not eaten all day; a fact he, too, had been unaware of until the pangs of hunger struck on his walk home.

He went downstairs to find a *very neat, clean breakfast* waiting for him, and *he fell to with an appetite*, often the case following a heavy supper. It was quiet in the little cottage. Mrs Rowse had left before dawn, carting her baskets of fruit and vegetables to Covent Garden market. He helped on his days off but was glad to be spared the trouble this particular morning: he had much on his mind, and the absence of the sounds of the market – men shouting, carts backing, horses neighing, boys fighting, basket-women talking, piemen expiating … and donkeys braying – was welcome.

He cleared the dishes, leaving them stacked neatly in the corner cupboard, and made his way back upstairs. The cottage was, essentially, a two up and two down with the kitchen as an extension into the back garden, and Mrs Rowse, early on in their acquaintance, had organized one of the upstairs rooms so that it served Samuel as a study and, initially, a bedroom. Here, he would sit and write his reports to his superior, Detective Inspector Charles Field, who would then pass them on to his superior, Sir Richard Mayne, Joint-Commissioner of the Metropolitan Police and the man who had created the detective branch.

Standing at the back-bedroom window, looking out over the market garden that provided Sarah with her main income, he changed his mind about starting work on the report immediately and decided, instead, to take a walk to Peckham High Street where the police station for the Camberwell Division was situated.

It was a neat and orderly place with its whitewashed walls and scrubbed wooden floor. The Duty-Inspector, who knew Samuel well, sat at his high desk writing up his books and ruling them off, while a drunk called from one of the cells along the corridor that led from the rear yard. He exuded the type of calm one found in libraries, where silence ruled the roost and even a cough might raise an eyebrow. He glanced up as Samuel entered and then looked down again, quietly intending to complete one task before attending to another. When his last line was ruled, he graced Samuel with a smile.

"Detective Sergeant Warden, to what do we owe the privilege of your presence in our humble station at such an hour? How may we be of service, sir?"

The words were uttered with an overwhelming politeness, so overwhelming that they would have bordered on the discourteous had not Samuel earned the admiration of the Inspector when as a constable he had, single-handedly, brought in a roaring drunk who had been within an inch of beating his wife to death.

"If you could arrange for one of your officers to convey a message to H Division, I should be most grateful, Inspector Rees."

"And the nature of the message would be?"

"That I would appreciate them bringing in a certain Princes Puffer for questioning. She runs an opium den in Shadwell, and I think she may be able to help us with our enquiries concerning a Mr Edwin Drood."

"I thought I hadn't seen your around this week, Samuel. You've been on a quiet, country retreat, have you?"

Given that Camberwell, itself, was a village – a place of market gardens with merchants' villas at one end and terraced cottages for the poorer inhabitants at the other – the Inspector, himself, could hardly claim to be troubled by an excess of crime. Admittedly, there were always going to be the shifty types and a few outright villains, but the Inspector's daily round was untroubled by the criminal cesspit of the metropolis, and Samuel excused himself a smile.

"You could say that, John. Thanks for your help."

"We shall convey your message, or have it conveyed, in one way or another. When will you be interviewing the lady in question?"

"This afternoon, once I have delivered my report."

The chat and the walk had cleared his head. It was nice to know that business was being conducted as usual and in a methodical manner. He could rely on the fact that by the time they spoke Her Royal Highness the Princess Puffer would be clear of opium and desperate for another smoke. It was also nice to have his own head clear regarding the Drood case. It was too early to draw conclusions – behaviour that began by pointing one way often turned out to be pointing another – but he had the whole case so far in his head and so, aided by his notebook, Samuel sat down to write. He outlined what he had discovered so far that supplemented the original reports by the local constabulary his superiors had in their possession.

He opened his report by stating that as far as he could ascertain only two people had a motive for killing Mr Drood – Mr Jasper and Mr Landless – and their motives were almost the same: a professed admiration for Mr Drood's fiancé, Miss Rosa Bud. In Mr Landless's case, there was also the factor of his ungovernable temper, witnessed on several occasions by people well-disposed towards him and denied by none. There was, however, no evidence that Mr Drood had been murdered; it was equally possible that he had simply decided to disappear.

It was also conceivable that others had been involved, either before or after the fact, in Mr Drood's murder or disappearance.

He then went on to summarise the key points of evidence gained in his interviews with those involved:

'Neville Landless stated that he had not only desired to cut Mr Drood down but also confessed he might have been drawn to kill his stepfather, had not the man died when he did. Mr Drood goaded him beyond endurance: speaking almost dismissively of Miss Bud and telling Mr Landless that he was 'no judge of white men'. He was 'unsettled and unhappy and unsettling and interfering with other people'. During our interview, he repeatedly clenched and unclenched his fists. He was the last person, as far as we know, who saw Mr Drood alive and, at that time, knew nothing of the broken engagement between Mr Drood and Miss Bud. He obtained an unnecessarily heavy walking stick only the day before – an ironwood stick – and left very early for his planned walk the morning after. Joe, the omnibus driver, confirmed others' impressions of Mr Landless's temper, stating that he 'fought like the devil' when they attempted to arrest him.

Rosa Bud, by reports a demur young lady, struck me as anything but: her flight from Cloisterham following Mr Jasper's accosting of her in the garden of the Nun's House and her decision to end the betrothal to Mr Drood shows her to be both determined and resourceful. If Miss Bud knows more than she is telling and has exaggerated the fervour of Mr Jasper during their encounter, it seems to me that she does so from a sense of her own guilt.

Helena Landless's loyalty to her brother would provide sufficient justification, in her own mind, for offering him unequivocal support. I do not suspect her of anything save this fearless affection.

Mr Grewgious was less than helpful and is, clearly, withholding information that might prove vital in resolving the case. He would say nothing more than that he had 'conducted a small piece of business' when Mr Drood visited him on December 16th and was reluctant to disclose his presence in Cloisterham over the Christmas period until pressed. Even then he would only repeat what I already knew and would offer no comment on Mr Jasper's reaction to the news that Miss Bud and Mr Drood had broken off their engagement.

Mr Jasper spoke of his affection for his nephew, Mr Drood, and this has been confirmed by others to whom I have spoken. The uncle took a very active part in the search for his nephew following the young man's disappearance; this search lasted several days. He stated that the two young men left his home amicably after their reconciliation meal on Christmas Eve. This had been brought about as the result of a conversation between Mr Jasper and Revd Crisparkle after the violent arguments between the two young men to which I have already alluded. He clarified the purpose of Mr Grewgious's visit to him on December 27th: it being to relay the news of the broken engagement. This appears to have given Mr Jasper momentary hope that his nephew had simply disappeared. He confirmed Miss Bud's statement that his nephew was 'in fear' of him but clarified the nature of this fear as a desire not to disappoint. He became very agitated when I questioned him on Mr Landless's possible affection for Miss Bud, terming it 'an expiable offence'. I discovered that he made regular trips to London and questioned him on this; Mr Jasper stated that his business there was of a 'personal nature'.

The Revd Crisparkle confirmed his 'absolute faith' in Mr Landless, while acknowledging his ill temper. He had seen Mr Jasper's diary and stated that he was shown the entry we have already seen and another speaking of the uncle's fear for his nephew; an entry that spoke of him having to 'assure himself that he (Mr Drood) was sleeping safely, and not lying dead in his blood'.

He refrained from mentioning many aspects of the enquiry, including his reasons for visiting the Princess Puffer, his meeting with Dick Datchery and his tour of the cathedral with Mr Durdles. These matters might, or might not, fall into place as time and tide moved his investigation forward; at present, his thoughts on these angles were dangerously speculative and Samuel did not want to be drawn.

He also avoided mentioning any thoughts he might have on the Rev Crisparkle's finding Edwin Drood's jewellery. This had always troubled him. On the surface it suggested that the young man had been murdered, since he would hardly have thrown possessions away if he planned to disappear; but impressions on the surface were best avoided. A calculating young man, one cold and indifferent to the feelings of others, wishing to disappear, might deliberately create a false impression rather than take the risk of others seeking him among the living. His uncle had spoken of the 'crumbs of comfort' he had felt on learning of the broken betrothal, hoping that Edwin 'finding himself in his new position' had taken flight. He had gone on to say that prior to this news it had been 'impossible to entertain the idea of his nephew voluntarily leaving Cloisterham in a manner that would have been so unaccountable, capricious and cruel'. Samuel did not share John Jasper's belief in the character of his nephew. Besides, other unanswered questions suggested that Edwin Drood may have found it advisable to disappear when he did, possibly with the knowledge and even assistance of others.

It was less than a week since his investigation began, and he was pleased with his progress so far. Samuel signed off his report and dated it. He was not to know, as he stood and gazed from the back-bedroom window at Mrs Sarah Rowse's fruit and vegetables, how far matters had moved on since he was last in London.

*

The Rev Crisparkle sat on the long, wood and iron bench that offered a resting place on the banks of the Thames not far short of Putney Bridge in one of the *everlastingly green gardens* that bordered the river; with him was Helena Landless.

Rev Crisparkle had come down immediately he was informed of Neville's disappearance, and following the cessation of the search by boat he had accompanied the young woman on her walks along the banks north and south of the river.

Her calm acceptance of what she supposed to be Neville's fate amazed the clergyman. Helena was infused – or so it seemed to him – with an angry righteousness, so quiet, so subdued that it was far more terrifying than an outburst of temper.

For three days, she and Lt Tartar with his man, Lobley, had scoured the river during daylight hours, working sometimes with and sometimes against the tidal flow. In all that time she had spoken barely a word. It was only on the evening of the third day that she turned to her two companions and said:

"I knew my brother was gone from me that first night before we came even to the bridge, but I had to search for him. He will come now. I know that to be true. I only wish it was given to my hand to draw him from the waters."

She said nothing else other than to thank the two men, and neither felt able to ask whether she supposed her brother to have committed suicide or to have been murdered. Lt Tartar later commented to the Rev Crisparkle that there seemed no reason for either eventuality on the young man's nightly walk but harboured, silently, his fears over the detective's interrogation of one so fragile as Neville Landless.

On his nightly, and then daily, walks with Helena Landless, the clergyman's thoughts returned frequently to Neville's savage outbursts of temper but he, too, remained silent, hoping that the young woman would eventually say something. She did not. She seemed grateful for his company and content in his soundless presence.

Only once did she speak, and her words sorely grieved the priest.

"I do not wish to be cleared of my anger, Mr Crisparkle, but I wish you to help me forge it to righteous ends. I make no apologies for the rights and wrongs of the feelings I carry in my mind. *My nature must be changed before I can do so, and it is not changed*, and never will be changed. *I am sensible of inexpressible affront*, and my anger is the anger of the abused and it is directed at the abuser. I will have justice for my brother. I will avenge his death."

"I am sorry to hear such words coming from one so young and of such a good nature," replied the clergyman.

"You cannot soften my resolve, Mr Crisparkle. I am as determined as my brother made clear to you. The time will come when I shall do what I must, and I hope, then, to have you by my side as my adviser and the saviour of my soul."

"I will go with you and be your guide ..."

"... in my most need to be by my side?"

"Yes," he replied, simply.

Helena Landless took his arm and they walked on, an understanding, one not to be broken, firm between them, as binding as any oath.

*

It was when he left his report with Inspector Field's office that Samuel Warden heard of Neville Landless's disappearance. Unlike Helena Landless, he jumped to no conclusions but kept his options open: an accident seemed unlikely, suicide in such an unstable young man more so, and murder needed motive, opportunity and means. All three of these might have been in place but were open to investigation.

He made his way to Staple Inn and found Lt Tartar enjoying a pipe in the small garden and on the same seat Samuel had shared with Helena Landless. The sailor immediately and succinctly brought Samuel up to speed on the progress of events, his reserve about the detective's probable part in a possible suicide left ashore.

The detective asked whether a lookout had been kept for handbills proclaiming 'BODY FOUND' in the river and emanating from the local police station, whether that establishment had been paid a visit and whether the trader-in-corpses Lt Tartar mentioned had been questioned a second time. To each of these queries, the sailor was able to reply in the affirmative.

"You have done well, Mr Tartar, Lieutenant Retired. Admirable! We can now wait."

"Waiting isn't a natural activity for a man used to action Sergeant Warden, Detective," replied the sailor with a smile.

"No doubt, sir, but when one is unsure what to do it is often better to do nothing at all, and it seems to me. sir, that you have, for the moment, done all possible. Where might Miss Landless be now?"

"Ever since we came ashore, she has walked the banks daily with Mr Crisparkle."

"Ah – the Muscular Christian. An admirable man, and no doubt a comfort to the young lady."

"One of the best is Septimus Crisparkle, Sergeant Warden. We were at school together, you know. I was his fag. It was my good fortune to save him from drowning."

"And no doubt his good fortune, too, sir," replied the detective with a jovial chuckle, adding, without quite knowing why, "One good turn deserves another, as they say."

He stood, suddenly, and turned to the sailor.

"Do you know, sir, I think my time might be well-spent having another talk with Miss Rosa. An astute young lady and still waters run deep … as they say."

He paused deliberately, watching the sailor's expression, an action not missed by Lt Tartar, who was unable, however, to hide the blush, part-embarrassment, part-annoyance, that crossed behind his eyes.

"You do not miss much, do you, Sergeant Warden?"

"Nothing at all, if I can help it, sir. Perhaps you would care to take an afternoon stroll with me in the direction of Southampton Street?"

The sailor smiled, knocked out the remains of his pipe beneath the seat and the two men set off together to find Miss Twinkleton's summer retreat.

A maid opened the door, followed – unnecessarily abruptly, Samuel thought – by a stout woman with a loud mouth.

"I'll deal with these gentlemen, Maisie," she said and swiftly positioned herself between them and the hallway.

"And to what may I ask do we owe the pleasure?" she enquired, her tone suggesting the pleasure, if it existed at all, would be fleeting.

"You are Mrs Billikin are you not?" said Samuel, glancing at the brass doorplate on the wall, which spelt out her name in *uncompromising capitals of considerable size.*

"I ham, sir. I do have that consideration. May I ask to whom I have the courtesy of addressing?"

"I am Detective Sergeant Warden, and this is …"

"The gentleman and I are acquainted, if you please. He is a frequent visitor to my residence."

"In that case perhaps you would let Miss Twinkleton and Miss Rosa know that we are making a courtesy call," replied Samuel.

"If only I could, sir, but *I will not deceive you; far from it.* I regret to say that neither person of whom you speak are at present abiding here."

"Do you mean they have left?" asked Lt Tartar, hurriedly.

"Left – oh, good gracious no, sir," replied Mrs Billikin as though such an idea would be nothing short of an insult to her establishment, "They are but promenading."

Images of the seaside must have occurred to both men at the same time because they looked at each other and it was all they could do not to burst out laughing.

"I cannot apprise you of when they will return, for of that fact I am unacquainted, but I might say, since you asked me, *my open and honest answer* must be that they are seldom, if ever, gone for long. An afternoon perambulation is seldom extended, for who might wish *to take advantage of your sex, if you was not brought to it by inconsiderate example ...*"

The conversation, or extended monologue, might have gone on for ever had not, at that moment, Miss Twinkleton and Miss Rosa appeared at the corner of the street. The young woman's eyes lit up at the sight of Lt Tartar and her look was returned by his own. Neither was missed by the three other people who watched them: Miss Twinkleton with a faint air of disapproval, Mrs Billikin with the expectation of her experience and Samuel with interest. It suddenly occurred to him that an alliance of sorts was building itself in the metropolis.

"You may safely leave our guests in my hands, if you please, Mrs Billikin," said Miss Twinkleton, with a proprietorial air and adding through pursed lips, somewhat waspishly, Samuel thought, "I am sure your *flow of words* has been enlightening, but now we might favour them with a little conversation."

"I am sure that neither gentleman felt subjected to any such flow, Miss Twinkleton. There are those of us whose flow of words is not of a stipendiary flavour but more inclined to the homely and the comforting," replied Mrs Billikin, marching off with her head held unnecessarily high.

Miss Twinkleton acknowledged the two men she felt she had rescued and led the way, sedately, upstairs to where she and Rosa lodged on the first and second floors. Tea was served and the four of them conversed amicably for half-an-hour or so before Samuel wondered whether he might speak with Miss Rosa "confidentially" (he avoided the more exact 'privately'), trusting that Miss Twinkleton might entertain Lt Tartar for a few moments. The lady's eyebrows rose, marginally, suggesting that she would not be incommoded by what might be considered an impropriety by one of a less sophisticated disposition, and she indicated by a slight move of her head that the detective and Rosa might retire to the back parlour.

Once seated with the young woman, Samuel got down to business.

"Miss Rosa, I am struggling with this case. As soon as I think a road might be leading somewhere, it turns in to a dead end. I need your help if – and only if – you are willing to share what, for you, are painful thoughts with me."

"If it will help to find Eddy, of course you must ask me what you need to know."

"It is not so much 'know' as 'thought', Miss Rosa. When you spoke to me of Mr Jasper's intrusion into your life in the garden of the Nuns' House, you spoke of a 'dreadful suspicion'. What did you mean by that remark?"

"Is it so important, Mr Warden? It was only a giddy girl's trifling thought."

"There's no such thing as a trifle, Miss Rosa, whether it's a man leaving his room only occasionally to purchase half-pints of coffee and penny loaves or a young woman's thoughts."

"It was after he had gone that it came to me, so desperate was I to escape; but it was a thought that had crept in and out of my mind ever since Eddy disappeared – I still say 'disappeared', Mr Warden, because I do so hope that he is alive and well somewhere safe."

"There is always hope, Miss Rosa," said Samuel, softly.

"Since Eddy disappeared – so long ago now, it seems – I have been confused. It's only a half-formed suspicion, too wicked to be considered true … Mr Jasper was so devoted to his nephew and, since his disappearance, so devoted to his search for him that to even think … even consider *the possibility of foul play at his hands* is unconscionable."

The young woman turned to the detective, her eyes pleading for an answer.

"*Am I so wicked in my thoughts as to conceive a wickedness that others cannot imagine?*"

Samuel reached out and took her hands in his own.

"*What motive could he have? The motive of gaining me!* Surely, no one could consider *founding murder on such an idle vanity?*"

She looked at the detective for an answer, perhaps an assurance that her thoughts bore no truth. Samuel said nothing but squeezed her hands gently.

"Besides," she continued, "Mr Jasper has encouraged the idea of a murder. If he were involved in something so vile, *would he not rather encourage the idea of a voluntary disappearance?*"

"Miss Rosa, have you ever wondered whether you might have encouraged Mr Jasper in his attentions?"

"Oh, I do not think so. I do hope not," she cried, her eyes filling with tears.

"If it were so, you must not blame yourself. You are a young woman on the verge of adulthood – seventeen are you not?"

"Yes."

"And what young woman would not be flattered by the attentions of an older man – a man young himself. Mr Jasper is but twenty-six, I believe?"

"Yes."

Samuel took a handkerchief from his pocket and handed it to the young woman so that she might dab her eyes clear of the tears.

"You must no longer trouble yourself with such thoughts, Miss Rosa. Sharing them relieves you of their burden and helps me in my search. Let us sit quietly for a while until you are quite recovered and then, I think, I will suggest that you, Lt Tartar and I take a little stroll. Miss Twinkleton can have no serious objections to you being accompanied by a policeman, especially one in plain clothes, and I think you may have no serious objection to Lt Tartar being allowed to see you safely back alone," said Samuel with a wink and a smile.

Rosa Bud's face blushed a deep scarlet, but her eyes lit up and the tears fled from her face.

Miss Twinkleton had no objections; indeed, Miss Twinkleton seemed quite flushed herself with the attentions of Lt Tartar. What tales he had regaled her with Samuel had no idea but the dry spinster on the doorstep had blossomed in the parlour: her hair appeared curlier, her eyes brighter and the pursed lips fuller. She might almost have been described as sprightly. Perhaps the *tenderer scandals* of the world had come to her in the sailor's tales and enlivened her afternoon. Samuel wondered whether memories of times past had been stirred in her mind: perhaps a gentleman caller, perhaps a certain season in her life?

*

He left the young couple in Holborn Square and made his way rapidly to Bow Street police station, where he expected Her Royal Highness the Princess Puffer to be have been residing since the morning. He was not disappointed. The Duty-Inspector gave him a smile and a wink and ordered a constable to open the cells for him. As Samuel entered, she looked up from the bench on which she was crouched, bent forward, her hands clutching at her mouth.

"I know you," she said, "I've seen you somewhere before."

"You know me, Eliza, and I know you. I am Detective Sergeant Samuel Warden of the Detective Police. You are going to help me and when you have, I shall see you safely home with a little something to keep you going. But first you are going to tell me what I need to know because it's the right thing to do."

"Eliza," she croaked through dry lips, "No one's called me Eliza for as long as I can remember. Who are you?"

"Always Eliza, wasn't it, until you took up with that Bengalee chap and he showed you the way of mixing the opium? Am I right? Of course, I am! No father and no mother to speak of ..."

"She was took with the pox. I wasn't for that life."

"You might say your Bengalee friend saved you from a life of sin and disease, Eliza – you might ... but, then again, you might not."

"He was good to me while he lived."

She drifted off into memories ancient and dark: 'the light of a dying fire flickered in a dirty grate; a few coins passed hands; the room was so low it was impossible to stand upright; lying on a foul mattress placed on the ground were Chinese, Lascars and a few English; lit by a dim lamp a Bengalee with dishevelled, white hair, a thin face and dull-looking eyes was blowing a cloud of smoke into the stagnant air and coughing so much, now and then, that this frame shook; he looked up at the young woman dipping the tip of her needle into the treacly substance and withdrawing little drops of it, which she toasted in the flame of the small lamp.'

"How do you know all this?" she asked, trembling from head to toe.

"It's our business to know, Eliza. We keep our ears to the ground."

The image seemed to amuse the old woman who cackled with laughter, laughter subdued as quickly as it had begun. She threw torrent of abuse at Samuel and reached for him with long, bony fingers. He moved to sit on the bench next to her and took a few shillings from his waistcoat pocket.

"Three and sixpence is all it takes to put me right," she cried, "There are those who think kindly of an old woman."

"A few days ago, Eliza, you were in the town of Cloisterham. Why were you there?"

She gave him a shifty look, a sideways glance through eyes almost closed, a glance that meant she wanted to keep her secrets but was desperate for the drug that kept her going.

"In less than no time, Eliza, you shall be back home puff, puff, puffing but first ..."

"He weren't like that! He were kind!"

"Who Eliza? Who was kind?"

"The young man."

"The young man?"

"'*Are you ill?*' he says. No, deary, I say. '*Are you blind?*' No, deary, I say. '*Are you lost, homeless, faint? What's the matter*', he says, '*that you stay here … so long without moving?*'"

She looked up at Samuel sitting beside her and whimpered.

"*My lungs is weakly; my lungs is dreffle bad. Poor me, poor me, my cough is rattling dry!*"

She coughed uncontrollably. Samuel did not move except to rattle the coins in his hand. Her memory was returning, and it was best not to interrupt. But what young man was she talking about? What young man had she met in Cloisterham only a few days ago?

"*Give me three and sixpence, I says, and don't you be afeard for me. Give me three and sixpence, and I'll lay it out well, and get back … if you do give me three and sixpence, deary, I'll tell you something.*"

Samuel dropped a few coins into her hand. She clutched it tightly.

"'*What's your name?*' I say. '*Edwin*', he says. '*You be thankful that your name ain't Ned*', I say, '*it's a bad name to have just now, a threatened name, a dangerous name.*' He laughs and says, '*The proverb says that threatened men live long.*' '*Then Ned should live to all eternity,*' I say.

She leaned forward, placing her face beneath Samuel's, and looked up into his eyes. She was shaking uncontrollably again. Her chin rested on her hands. She could barely see Samuel: her eyes shut and then blinked open. A haze passed over them and she rocked back and forth. Thick drops stood out on her forehead and she caught her breath. The memory had gone as suddenly and unexpectedly as it came. She was back in her cell, speechless, leaving Samuel bewildered.

Chapter 13

Samuel Warden Takes on a Deputy

A brandy-and-water was what Samuel needed: about that there was no doubt. He had called for the constable, given him money for the old woman and instructions to see her safely back to the den in Shadwell. He now made his way to the Three Crowns and its landlord, James Brooks, who, hopefully, would have something to accompany the brandy-and-water: a boy called Deputy.

"You've got yourself a handful there, Sergeant. It took a clout or two to quieten him down and if there's damage to the room I've locked him in, I'll expect some compensation."

"Lively, is he, James Brooks, Landlord?"

"Lively! I had to tie him to the chair in the end, while a couple of the girls held him down. They're black and blue."

The 'girls' in question glanced up from their drinks and their customers as the landlord spoke and gave the detective a knowing look, as though he might keep in mind that they were respectable citizens, not averse to a little inconvenience when carrying out their public duties. Samuel smiled his thanks and nodded towards the stairs that led to the upper rooms.

"Should any of your ladies need to avail themselves of the use of a room here in the next hour or so," he said, "I will have no objection."

James Brooks, in his role as brothel-keeper, viewed the policeman up and down for a moment or two, scepticism in his eyes, amazement on his face, his hands fidgeting with his apron.

"We don't want the boy lured by the attractions of the city, do we? I'm expecting to take him back to his hometown tonight and it will be in his interests – and mine, at this present juncture – to remain there. Where was he found?"

"Haunting the railway station with a group of other tearaways, offering to carry bags or push carts."

It was an honest occupation, at least, thought Samuel. Many homeless boys earned their living that way: helping travellers or the porters. Others would follow overladen cabs into the city, eager to help with the luggage once it arrived at the home or hotel of the traveller. The more experienced would stand outside offices, clubs or inns waiting to hold a horse while the rider conducted his business or his pleasure within the establishment. They would earn a penny for standing with a horse up to half an hour. It was a law-abiding livelihood and told Samuel that the boy, Deputy, had bags of initiative and not a little courage: it took both to intrude on the territory of the regulars.

It was the attractions of those other occupations – the ones he had mentioned to Dick Datchery – that troubled the detective; and he hoped that Deputy would be calm enough for a walk on the dark side once their little chat was completed.

The boy's scowl, the resumption of his foot stamping and struggling with his bonds when Samuel entered the room did not bode well. The detective looked him over, pulled across a chair and lit a cigar, eyeing the boy without speaking. It was early evening, yet, and a long night ahead would trouble him less than the boy; best that he should work out his anger before the policeman started to squeeze him for information.

Deputy struggled and writhed for fifteen minutes or so, and this was accompanied by several long and tortured howls, which reminded Samuel of the wolves he had seen in the zoo when he first came to London. When the howling subsided, it was replaced by more boy-like yells and screams, anger and desperation apparent in every syllable. Throughout this performance, the boy favoured the detective with looks of such anger and hatred that he seemed more beast than human; although, on reflection, Samuel decided that such emotions were rarely seen in animals.

All the while, he sat smoking calmly, a look of dreamy innocence pervading his face. At first, this seemed to rouse the boy on to greater efforts; but when he saw that nothing was to be gained by such an exhibition, he collapsed against the ropes that bound him and watched while the policeman's cigar burned out.

"I've been talking to a friend of yours," said Samuel, eventually, when the boy's anger had once again reverted to a sullen grimace, "Nice lady by the name of Her Royal Highness the Princess Puffer."

"What's she to me?"

"I understand from Mr Datchery that you followed her to London."

"Yer Lie!"

"I don't think so. What did you make of her home?"

"You'll ketch nothin' from me. I'll stone yer first."

"We smoked a pipe or two. She was good company."

"Yer Lie!"

"Of course, I've known Eliza a long time – knew her mother, knew her father."

He looked at the boy, guessing that he had known neither of his own. He had seen it before: the very mention of parents raised both hope and disappointment in the same expression. The detective continued to gaze straight in front of him, through the haze of his cigar smoke. From the bar below, the sounds of revelry rose: a piano was played, there was laughter and song. Footsteps mounted the stairs; the sounds from the adjacent rooms more muted than usual, no doubt in acknowledgement of his presence.

"Stoning sheep in the burial ground. That's no way to earn your keep."

"Yer Lie!"

"You can keep saying that over and over again, all night long, if it pleases you, or ... I can cut you loose and we can have a little chat. Only I need to know that if I do right by you, you'll do right by me. Are you thirsty?"

"He gave me a drink."

"Are you hungry?"

"I'm always hungry."

"What's your fancy – eel stew?"

Deputy looked at the detective. Eel stew was not a dish with which he was familiar, despite Cloisterham being on the river. Samuel raised his eyebrows, placed his spent cigar in an ashtray and left the room.

On the street he found what he was looking for; it was not difficult: streets stalls sold food from dawn to dusk – before work began and after the theatres closed. The eels were bought at Billingsgate and the street traders' wives would slice them up, boil them, thicken the pot with flour and add parsley and spices. Samuel bought two cups for a penny, had a word with the landlord and returned to the room, where he untied the boy and handed him one of the cups, leaving his own untouched.

By the time the landlord arrived with another brandy-and-water for Samuel and a half-pot of ale for the boy, Deputy had accepted Samuel's cup of stew and was well into his unexpected supper.

"You followed her home, did you – Eliza, the Princess Puffer? Mr Datchery needed to know where she lived? He told me. I could have saved you the trouble, had I known. I've just been speaking with her, as I said."

"You don't need me then!"

"Oh, but I do. She told me she'd been to Cloisterham, but I never saw her there. You did ... at the Travellers' Twopenny. Where else was she?"

"Shaking her fists in the *Kinfreederal*."

"Shaking her fists at Mr Datchery?"

The boy laughed, the idea struck him as so amusing. It was an unusual sound to come from his mouth and he looked surprised at his own audacity.

"No – at him!"

"Him?"

"Him as lifted me off me legs and all but burst me braces and choked me. *Wait till I set a jolly good flint a flyin' at the back o' 'is jolly old 'ed some day!*"

"Whose Him?"

"*Jarsper!*"

"Mr John Jasper, the Choirmaster?"

"That's him!"

"Now why would he do that. Do you suppose?"

"I don't go supposin' nothing. He did it, I tell you."

"When?"

"When they came out of the *Kinfreederal*."

"Mr Jasper and the Princess Puffer?"

The boy laughed again, and once again seemed surprised at the act.

"Stony Durdles and him!"

"Let us take this slowly, my son …"

"I ain't no son to you!"

"… because I am older than you and nowhere near as sharp. You are telling me that you saw Mr Durdles and Mr Jasper come out of the *Kinfreederal*. Would that be at night?"

"That's what I'm a-tellin' you, aren't it!"

"And what did you see?"

"Nothin', I didn't see nothing. Yer lie. *I'd only just come out for my 'elth when* I saw them a-coming out of the *Kinfreederal*."

"Well, that's very helpful, my boy. Now, who was Mr Jasper shaking his fists at?" asked Samuel, deliberately twisting the facts, knowing it would tickle the boy's sense of the ridiculous.

"It weren't him. It were her – in the *Kinfreederal*. I saw her shaking her fists at him. I was watching through the grating and there she was behind the pillar a-shakin' her fists at him and grinning like the devil."

Whether the opium woman knew more about Mr Jasper than she was letting on, Samuel couldn't be sure; that she must have followed him to Cloisterham there was no doubt and with some purpose in mind. Blackmail? Did she hope to squeeze more out of the man than he paid for his opium smoking? Probably. It seemed clear, now, to the detective, that John Jasper indulged in the habit – an unseemly habit, in the public and ecclesiastical mind, for a Lay Precentor and Choirmaster. It was unlikely his bishop would admire the sight of John Jasper collapsed, sodden with the drug, on that dirty, old bedstead in the Shadwell den. But every man to his pleasure, Samuel thought, so long as it did no harm to others.

So long as it didn't – that was the question. Samuel had seen many men under the influence of the drug, and it seemed to take each of them differently. He had seen Lascars, Chinese and English mad with excitement after a smoke or two – some fighting mad, some delirious with imaginings. He had hauled some into a cell for the night to sleep off the effects of the habit for their own safety and the safety of others; he had watched them rage and bang at the bars until they could no longer muster the energy. Then, they had collapsed, often in convulsions, and lay twisting and shaking on the cold floor until sleep overcame them.

An old Duty-Inspector had once put forward the view that a violent man became more so, while another became torpid, as with drink. 'It exaggerates a man's preoccupations,' he had said. He had gone on to speculate that the drug 'unleashed tendencies that would end up destroying the user'.

What were John Jasper's preoccupations? 'It is then I go to the city, to find those pleasures denied me here by the very *vocation to which I must subdue myself*,' were the Choirmaster's words. No doubt he was obliged to subdue many emotions within the cramped monotony of his existence that ground him away by the grain. The words of John Jasper's confession came back to Samuel.

And did this matter, given that the opium woman claimed to have spoken with Edwin Drood less than a week since when she had been to Cloisterham and shaken her fists at John Jasper within the cathedral?

'… proceed systematically and quietly, in a workmanlike manner … moving from clue to clue, steadily pursuing your man through the deductive process …'. Detective Inspector Field's words came back to Samuel, haunting him like the warnings, even forebodings, of some Christmas ghost. He turned to the boy.

"Now, there needs to be trust between you and me if we are to get on as we should. Have I been fair by you?"

"I don't know no more."

"And I'm not asking you for more – not even your name. Deputy you are, and Deputy you shall be, however many of you there may be looking out for the lodging houses. Tomorrow, I'd like to take you back with me to Cloisterham and the Travellers' Twopenny, where you'll feel comfortable. Tonight, I'd like you to accompany me on a little walk around the town. How does that sound?"

"I don't mind."

"Good! But I mind that you don't run off, 'cause if you do, I'll have to have you found again. Do I make myself clear?"

The wary look came back into the boy's eyes, the look of some fierce animal cornered and ready to fight for its life. 'Yer lie', didn't seem an appropriate response, but it was the only form of denial left to Deputy and so he remained silent.

They left the Three Crowns after Samuel had spoken a few words of thanks and warning to the landlord. Summer was upon the city and it was still light, darkness a mere suggestion on the horizon. The detective was taking a risk; he knew that to be true. The boy might do a bunk and then the tiresome business of searching for him would start all over again, but the chance he was taking would be worth it.

He made his way to the police station at St Giles and introduced Deputy to the Duty Inspector.

"If ever you're lost in the city, son, make your way here and the boys will find you a bed for the night. But it's best you don't get lost," said Samuel with a wink to his fellow policeman. "That's right, isn't it, Mr Inspector?"

"We'll find you a bed, my boy, and a nice cup of char and a bit of bread and dripping for your breakfast," replied the other, with a smile and a wink.

Deputy watched them both, unsure whether to believe either. 'Yer lie' didn't seem appropriate, somehow, and so he satisfied himself with a scowl. He heard a *raving drunk woman in the cells, screeching her voice away* and as they left saw another woman, *a quiet woman, with a child at her breast,* brought in for begging. How many people, he wondered, were there in London who ended up here.

Samuel took him on down streets strewn with filth of every kind, filth that overflowed into the black road and sent upwards a *compound of sickening smells.* People were crouched against *the tumbling houses,* people with *lowered foreheads, sallow cheeks and brutal eyes.* They seemed like *infected vermin-haunted heaps of rags* to the boy. Samuel said nothing but moved on at an accelerated rate.

Deputy heard the clock of St Giles strike an hour – he wasn't sure what hour – as the detective turn from the main thoroughfare into a dark square and so to yet another dilapidated house from which issued a breath so pestilent that Deputy gagged. On the floor of the house lay twenty or thirty people – *men, women, children, for the most part naked, heaped upon the floor like maggots in a cheese.* The children woke as they entered, sat up and stared. In their eyes, Deputy saw just one craving – the need for food.

"Who's in charge here?" asked Samuel.

"I am, sir, to be sure," called a voice from a dark corner, a voice shrouded in a rough sack.

"Are you to be trusted?" asked the detective, "*Will you spend this money fairly, in the morning, to buy coffee and food for 'em all?*"

"*Yes, sir, I will!*"

"*O he'll do it, sir, he'll do it fair,*" cried a chorus of voices.

And Deputy saw the detective hand over a sum of money to a blackened hand.

They pressed on down a narrow street, full of low lodging-houses. It was quieter here, more orderly. A bunch of men were playing cards in the doorway of one of the houses. They looked up when they saw Samuel.

"Why, Mr Warden!" cried the one with bleary eyes, "I hope I see you well, sir."

"Well enough, Deputy," replied Samuel, without looking at the boy by his side.

"It's steady here, now, sir," said the bleary-eyed Deputy, "Steady as they come."

"*Who have you got upstairs?*" asked Samuel.

The Deputy placed his cards on the floor and led the way up *a wooden staircase outside the house,* lighting their path with *a flaring candle in a blacking-bottle.* The upstairs room contained *crowds of sleepers, each on his own truckle-bed coiled up beneath a rug. They turned their slumbering heads towards* Samuel and the boy, and as they did the *intolerable smell* aroused by their movements pervaded the confined space of the dormitory.

Outside, once again, assailed only by the smells from the gutters, Samuel turned to the boy.

"Wherever we go, son, you'll find a Deputy in charge of the beds and the lodgings. Why Deputy, I can't say. I only know that it's always so."

"*All us man-servants at Travellers' Lodgings is named Deputy,*" replied the boy.

"Yes, just one of many," said Samuel, knowing his point had been made, "Now, I'll show you where the sailors dance. I've a little bit of business there."

And so, they made their way to the river and the snug, little room at the Three Jolly Sailors, where the plump, young woman, Pleasant by name, sent for the potboy who ran off to find a stocky figure with a shock of grizzled, raven-black hair and a rough beard that equalled it in colour: the trader-in-corpses.

"Nothing," said the man, "It can take many tides."

"Keep looking. I don't want you giving up on this one, and when you find the young man send word to Mr Field at this address," replied Samuel, writing the necessary instructions on a slip of paper he tore from his notebook. "I'll leave word with him and he'll see you right."

They left the riverside, *the creeping river, black and silent, rushing through sluice-gates, lapping at piles and posts and iron rings, hiding strange things in its mud, running away with suicides and accidentally drowned bodies*, the river that was the *very food and drink* to those who lived by its waters, from their cradles to their graves.

"Where are we going, now?" asked Deputy, tiredness in his voice.

"Home," replied Samuel, "to a warm bed and a comfortable night's rest. It's a tidy walk but worth every step and, in the morning, Mrs Rowse will waken you with a hearty breakfast. Perhaps a cutlet or two – unless you prefer sausages or a savoury omelette – and some buttered cake or toast and marmalade to round things off."

Deputy looked up at the detective but didn't feel in the mood to contradict him or even ask who Mrs Rowse might be. By the time they reached Camberwell, Samuel Warden, Detective, was carrying a sleeping burden in his arms.

Chapter 14
Mr Durdles Shakes Off Some Stony Dust

Joe's omnibus brought them into Cloisterham just after noon. The sun was in the sky and the day promised much. *A brilliant* afternoon shone *on the old city. Its antiquities and ruins are surpassingly beautiful, with the lusty ivy gleaming in the sun, and the rich trees waving in the balmy air. Changes of glorious light from moving boughs, songs of birds, scents from gardens, woods, and fields … penetrate into the Cathedral, subdue its earthy odour and preach the Resurrection and the Life. The cold stone tombs of centuries ago grow warm, and flecks of brightness dart into the sternest marble corners of the building, fluttering there like wings.*

Back on his old stomping ground, the only place he had ever known with any clarity, Deputy regained some of his edge. Despite the detective's kindness, despite Mrs Rowse providing a breakfast such as he had never seen before, Deputy trusted neither of them; experience had taught the boy that nothing was for nothing.

"I'll walk back with you to the Travellers'," said Samuel, "we don't want them thinking you've run off and neglected your duties."

"Yer lie!" cried the boy, "I don't need no one to see me home. I sees meself home. I sees Durdles home."

"You see Mr Durdles home?"

"*I make a cock-shy of him. He gives me a 'apenny to pelt him home if I ketches him out too late.*"

As he spoke, the boy began to dance. It was an ugly sight, half-dance, half-savage ritual, the sight exacerbated by the rags in which he was clothed and *the laces of his dilapidated boots.*

"It's Mr Durdles I desire to see, "said Samuel, "If you could take me to his home, I'd be grateful, but I can do without the stoning."

"Yer lie!" replied the boy, laughing and bringing his dance to an end.

He set off along the High Street, glancing back occasionally, with an assumed nonchalance, to see if the detective was following him; but Samuel was pleased to note that when he crossed the road to purchase a bottle of brandy at Gordon House Hotel the boy waited for him, lounging idly against a shopfront while he did so. Their route took them past Mr Jasper's house and a view of the cathedral and so to Mr Durdles hole-in-the-city-wall.

There were certain matters the detective needed to clarify in his mind, one being the unaccountable expedition undertaken by John Jasper with the stonemason. On their previous reconstruction of the journey, the detective felt that Durdles had left much unsaid.

The yard was still freely littered with *gravestones, monuments and stony lumber*, the mound of quicklime held its place at the gate; only the two great saws had come to life in the hands of Durdles's journeymen who now moved them back and forth *in their blocks of stone.* They looked up at Samuel as he entered, the sun on their backs, the sweat of an honest day's toil on their brows. Durdles appeared at the door, dressed as before, covered in the stony dust of his trade.

"Durdles knows you," he said, adjusting the dinner bundle under his arm and making for the gate as though he might leave Samuel in the yard without enquiring as to why he was there.

"Might I have a word, Mr Durdles?"

"You might. It depends who with," replied the stonemason.

"Since I'm in your yard, one might suppose it's you."

Durdles strolled on past his men without looking back, speaking to the air in his face rather than the detective at his back.

"Durdles is on his way to see the Dean. If you care to go with him ..."

He left the sentence unfinished, implying that Samuel might please himself whether he did or not but that Durdles cared neither way; and so, the detective fell in step alongside the man.

This time, however, they did not go via the Travellers' Twopenny, as they had done previously, bearing up through the Monks' Vineyard, through the gap in the wall, along Minor Cannon Corner and so to the precincts of the cathedral; this time, they took a route that went directly by the Deanery, passing the incumbent's entrance drive and so to the precincts of the cathedral, where they met not only the man himself but also the mayor, Mr Sapsea.

When they drew nigh to these two, Samuel smiled to himself. It was one scene that would never leave his mind's eye. He had the whole cathedral: its self-proclaimed proprietor in the shape of Mr Sapsea, its spiritual heart in the shape of the Dean and its rough repairer in the shape of Mr Durdles. If only Mr Jasper, the voice of its song, were to appear, it seemed to Samuel that the picture would be complete.

It was Mr Sapsea who took it upon himself to speak first, which was unfortunate because in introducing Samuel to the Dean he quite forgot he had not troubled to acquaint himself with the detective's name on their first meeting. Pulling himself up to his full height and expanding the folds of his waistcoat with a breath deep enough to emphasise his corpulence and turning to the Dean, the Mayor of Cloisterham began:

"Ah – my Very Reverend Sir, may I introduce ..."

At this point he could only remember what he had said to the stranger rather what the stranger may have said to him. He caught sight of Durdles smiling and images of tombs, vaults, towers and ruins appeared in his mind.

"… may I … It was I who brought Mr Jasper and Durdles together …"

"This is Mr Warden, your Reverence," said Durdles, with a smirk, "He's a friend of Mr Jasper and he asked for a tour of the cathedral."

"Mr Warden, I am most gratified to meet you," said the Dean, extending his hand, which Samuel took, "Are you, too, working on a book, like our Mr Jasper?"

"I am here at Mr Jasper's request, Reverend Sir."

"Our good Choirmaster has suffered much in the past few months, Mr Warden. Perhaps you may bring him some comfort?"

"That is my intention, sir, and Mr Durdles has very kindly been assisting me in my search."

"I took it upon myself to introduce Mr Warden and Mr Durdles. The Very Reverend Dean will please to bear in mind that I have seen the world."

Quite what this attribute might have to do with anybody at that moment was uncertain but from the mayor's point of view it enabled him to gain a foothold in the conversation.

"Why, Very Reverend Sir," he continued before any of the others could intervene, "it was but last Christmas that I, in my capacity as Mayor of Cloisterham, was consulted on this very matter of concern to our Choirmaster. It had a *dark look* then, and it has a dark look now. The vagabond brought before me in my parlour had an *Un-English complexion*. I said then and I'll say now – *to take the life of a fellow-creature is to take something that doesn't belong to you*. We hounded him from the city, sir. We can do without his sort in Cloisterham."

"Mr Landless was not convicted of any crime, sir," said Samuel, quietly, "and is now missing. It is feared he may have ended up in the Thames."

The Mayor opened and closed his mouth and the Dean looked uncomfortable. Dressed as they were in black and almost identically, for Mr Sapsea dressed in the style of the Dean – indeed, much to his pleasure had *been bowed to for* the Dean, in mistake, and had *even been spoken to in the street as My Lord, under the impression that he was the Bishop* – the two men looked like two old rooks in a parliament passing judgement on another less fortunate than themselves.

Durdles, standing with the cap he had pulled from his head on spying the Dean in hand, muttered something under his breath and shuffled his feet.

"Mind you take care of Mr Jasper's friend," said Mr Sapsea, attracted by the movement.

"I might have more time for that if I were to settle my business here," replied Durdles.

"Your tone, sir, is inappropriate in the presence of the Dean."

"*With submission to* the presence *of his Reverence the Dean, if you'll mind what concerns you, Mr Sapsea, Durdles he'll mind what concerns him.*"

"*You're out of temper,*" replied Mr Sapsea, with a nod and a wink to the Dean and Samuel, indicating he knew that Durdles understood who was master, "*My friend concerns me, and* Mr Warden, as a friend of *Mr Jasper, is my friend* also ... *And you are my friend.*"

The last phrase, uttered majestically following a slight pause, sounded as the final injunction from the pulpit might sound when the incumbent rounded off his sermon. Watching him, Samuel was aware that Mr Sapsea thought so, too.

"*I own it,*" replied Durdles, sharply.

"Mr Durdles," said the Dean, having recovered from the uncomfortable recollection of having refused Neville Landless sanctuary and keen that Durdles should not lose countenance at that moment, "I think we have the small matter of an inscription to discuss and then I will be able to release you to assist Mr Warden with his enquiries."

Durdles gave Samuel a look suggestive of his recollection that he had offered the detective no particular assistance and then slouched off after the Dean. Alone with the Mr Sapsea, Samuel turned his attention to a small dog that had remained quietly looking up at the mayor's feet throughout the parleying. He knelt and stroked the animal gently behind the ears, wondering what such a tiny creature could be doing in the company of so large and important a person.

"My late wife's companion, sir," said Mr Sapsea, in answer to Samuel's question, "She admires me, sir, as once did Mrs Sapsea. *When I made my proposal, she did me the honour to be ... overshadowed with a species of Awe ...*"

For a moment, Samuel wondered whether the mayor referred to the little dog that was, indeed, gazing up at him with wonder in its eyes or to his late wife, but the remainder of the mayor's eulogy to himself clarified the point.

"I have since asked myself the question: *What if her husband had been nearer on a level with her? If she had not had to look up quite so high, what might the stimulating action have been upon the liver?*"

Samuel felt as sorry for the little dog, forever looking upwards, as he might have once felt sorry for Mrs Sapsea, and refrained from commenting. Affronted perhaps by the detective's lack of awe, the mayor bad him Good Afternoon and strode off with the little dog at his heels, leaving Samuel pleased to be relieved of his company, pleased and wondering as he recollected Durdle's words at their last meeting: '*the ghost of a cry ... followed by the howl of a dog: a long dismal woeful howl, such as a dog gives when a person's dead*'. This would have been the Christmas before Edwin disappeared, at about the time Mrs Sapsea was called to pastures new. He pictured Durdles sitting on the steps that led up the tower telling him the story.

'Time and chance happeneth to them all'. The phrase came to his mind again and Samuel saw himself sitting in the pew at the little church in the village of Wherstead, snug between his mother and father, listening to their local vicar. He remembered the words from Ecclesiastes had suggested patience. Had he returned and chanced upon an understanding? Had his patience had been rewarded?

It was in this frame of mind that he saw Durdles approaching from the north door of the cathedral and Samuel hurried to meet him.

"Mr Durdles, Stonemason, I need to spend some time with you in your crypt."

"I'm a busy this morning ..."

"Not too busy to help me, Mr Durdles, I hope. We need to stir a memory or two."

"Durdles don't remember nothing."

"I'm sure that's true, sir, but a little moistening of the lips often refreshes the memory – or so I've heard. A few minutes of your time, sir, is all I ask."

There was no sense in which Samuel's tone suggested he was making a request: 'ask' did not come into the question. Durdles guessed this and when the detective took him by the elbow, he was sure of it.

"By the side door," he said, "we'll go by the side door."

"Just what I had in mind, Mr Durdles, just what I had in mind."

And so, they entered the crypt once again by the route taken by John Jasper the Christmas his nephew disappeared and then by Samuel not so many days since.

Once again, Samuel was taken by the sheer size of the place, by its size and its unkempt and worn appearance: the heavy pillars cast dark shadows throughout. Such light as there was from the groined windows only seemed to intensify the blackness elsewhere. The floor was paved in places by stone slabs; in others, the earth seemed to suffice. Heaps of dust and mounds of earth were scattered here and there, as were the tools of the stonemason's trade. A few baskets, used for what Samuel could only surmise, were propped against the pillars or left lying on their sides.

He handed Durdles the brandy he had bought on his way, taking a swig for himself first as he had no intention of relieving the stonemason of it once he began drinking.

"Where did you sit with Mr Jasper?" he asked.

"Durdles ain't …"

"Think! You entered this crypt for a second time that night – or so you said …"

"Twas true! Durdles don't lie. There! There it was!"

They settled by the pillar he indicated: Durdles with the bottle to his mouth, Samuel pacing back and forth.

"Did you sleep?"

"Forty winks. No more!"

"And Mr Jasper?

"He walked up and down, like you."

"Like this?" asked the detective, walking to and fro, "Drink up, man."

"It's good stuff."

"It's very good stuff."

"That's what he said – Mr Jasper – *very good stuff, I hope. I bought it on purpose.*' There!"

"And you slept – as you want to sleep now?"

"It was restless," said Durdles, dreamily, as the brandy took effect, "I was asleep. I could hear him walking back and forth, and then he'd die away – his footsteps. I was *alone for a long time*, and then *something touches me, and something falls from my hand.* I slept while …"

"While?"

"I don't remember."

"Take a swig and cast your memory back."

Durdles did. He had cleared half the bottle by now and was fuddled by drink and tiredness.

"The tower bells struck two."

"At what time did you set out?"

"Nine, perhaps ten …"

"So, you were here four or five hours?"

"It must have been. I slept like the dead," replied Durdles.

"And Mr Jasper?"

"He waited. Tried to wake me, he said," continued Durdles, taking another swig, "I dreamed … there were footsteps coming and going, and the clinking of keys. I must have dropped them 'caus when I woke – when Durdles finally woke – there was his crypt key lying on the pavement."

"You're sure it was the crypt key?"

"Durdles knows his keys!"

"It's very dark in here."

"They weigh different. They clink different. Mr Jasper, I thought he was going to play us a tune on 'em. Held 'em in his hands he did. Held 'em and weighed them."

"Us?" questioned the detective.

"Mr Sapsea and me. It was when Durdles measured up the inscription for his widow."

"Mr Jasper was there?"

"Approving the inscription, while I measured up. Like you, he'd never seen so many pockets of keys," said the stonemason, glowing with pride and brandy.

"Come, Mr Durdles, let me see you home."

"Durdles don't need no seeing home, not by day."

"Nevertheless, I'd like to see your yard once more and I'd like to return by the way we came today."

Once more outside in the sunshine of the summer's day, Durdles, still gripped by the elbow, found himself being steered back to his yard.

"I brought your Deputy back from London, today, Mr Durdles," said Samuel, as they passed the entrance to the Deanery, "He's a wild one."

"*Own brother to Peter the Wild Boy,*" replied Durdles, "*But I gave him an object in life. I gives him a 'apenny to pelt me home if he ketches me out too late ... What was he before? A destroyer. What work did he do? Nothing but destruction. What did he earn by it? Short terms in Cloisterham Jail. Not a person, not a piece of property, not a winder, not a horse, nor a dog, nor a cat, nor a bird, nor a fowl, nor a pig, but what he stoned, for want of an enlightened object. I put that enlightened object before him, and now he can turn his honest halfpenny by the three penn'orth a week.*"

"He has no time for our Mr Jasper."

"I told Mr Jasper to *recollect* himself. The boy enraged him with the stone throwing. Called him a *baby-devil*, he did. Said he'd *shed his blood. He rushes at Deputy, collars him*, took him by the throat. I thought he was going to strangle him, but the boy twists himself free and hides behind Durdles, he does, swearing at Mr Jasper. *'I'll stone yer eyes out, s'elp me!'* he says. But Durdles says to Mr Jasper *'Don't hurt the boy'*."

The recollection left Durdles shaken. Beads of perspiration sprang from his forehead, sweating out both the memory and the brandy.

"He was there the night you left the cathedral with Mr Jasper, was he not?" asked Samuel.

"That's what riled Mr Jasper – that and the stone throwing, but the boy swore he'd only just come by, and I believe him, Mr Warden."

"So, do I," replied the detective, as they made their way back to Durdles's yard along the short route that on a summer's day enjoyed the cool shadow of the cathedral.

Chapter 15
Helen Landless Under Many Circumstances

Helena had spent that evening – the evening she was to remember forever – with Rosa and Lt Tartar at the theatre in the Haymarket, known since Queen Victoria's accession to the throne as Her Majesty's, engaged in watching the comic drama, *The Knight of Arva*. Her friend thought it would help "to take you out of yourself" and she and the lieutenant would have a chaperone, one not in the shape of Miss Twinkleton.

Truth to tell, the young people had enjoyed their evening. The sailor knew London and its ways, and he steered them to a restaurant he hoped would prove a novelty for a pre-theatre supper. The surprise meal arrived scalding hot and in a covered dish, and Lt Tartar teased the young ladies as to what they were about to enjoy. Moving aside the cover slightly he said:

"I'll give you three guesses."

Both young women leaned over, their noses to the dish, and inhaled the aroma.

"It's very nice," said Rosa, "Is it polonies?"

"No, not polonies," replied the sailor, grinning, "although it is well-spiced, it is mellower than the sausage."

"Liver?" asked Rosa.

"No, *there's a mildness about it that don't answer to liver*."

"Chitterlings!" guessed Rosa, moving closer to the sailor in her excitement.

In answer, the sailor threw back his head and laughed.

"You guess, Helena," said Rosa, turning to her friend, who had remained silent, not wishing to interrupt the joy shared by her friends.

"I've no idea," replied Helena, "I have found English food so strange. But it smells like a soup we had in Ceylon, a soup made from the stomach of a cow."

"You nearly have it," said Lt Tartar, "but this is a stew."

"Tripe!" cried Rosa.

And *it was the best tripe ever stewed* with vegetables and spices, and the young people had set to with a hearty appetite, their loss forgotten for the moment.

The play, too, had enlivened Helena's mood – not only the play but the theatre crowd who enveloped the young people in the foyer with an excitement and a warmth the Ceylonese girl had not experienced for a long time. It seemed to her that they had entered another world. There was something heroic in the very act of performance. It lifted the actors and audience alike above their everyday lives. Somehow, it brushed reality aside, making the very act of living more manageable. In the theatre, it was the actors and the experience they shared with the audience that controlled events, that brought about the resolution she so desperately sought.

Standing outside the theatre as the audience crowded past her, Helena still carried the mystery of the drama with her – the mystery and the denouement.

"We can summon a carriage, ladies, or we can walk," said Lt Tartar, "Staple Inn and Southampton Street are a pleasant stroll from here and the night is still warm."

Sensing the sailor's keenness to remain for as long as possible in their company, the young women elected to walk. The summer had settled the dust on the streets and the crossing sweepers had only the dung to brush aside. Dry now, the thoroughfares of the city were a joy to walk. The baked-potato stalls and the kidney-pie stands were doing brisk business. Their appetites, rather than their hunger, roused by the smell, the young threesome made their purchases and walked on, moving the hot pies from hand to hand as they ate.

They amused themselves discussing the play they had seen: the young knight, out of funds and out of luck in Spain, urged by the duchess's minister (who mistakes him for an ambassador) to woo her on behalf of the Prince of Wales – the knight's astonishment, his subsequent vigorous wooing of the duchess on his own behalf and his banter with the Austrian and French ambassadors, particularly the Frenchmen, who insisted his ancestors were granted a place on Noah's Ark. The very ludicrous nature of the plot, all happily resolved and greeted by uproarious laughter by the audience, kept their conversation animated as they made their way home.

The streets were also lively: the eager patter of feet on the pavements, the cries of the vendors, the rushing back and forth of the potboys, family laughter coming from household windows opened to the air, the smell of coffee brewing, the tinkling of shop bells, the singing of a popular song emerging from the upstairs room of a public house, the policeman standing on the corner grateful for a quiet night.

As the evening darkened the gas-lamps were lit, and the lights of shops seemed to be bright for their benefit. Arm in arm they walked, the sailor supporting both women, one on each arm, Rosa content to be with the man she found herself loving more as the days passed, Helena pleased for her friend and her companionship.

It was Rosa who the lieutenant saw safely home first: not by choice – he would have lingered awhile with her alone – but of necessity because Miss Twinkleton saw herself as forming *the future wives and mothers of England* and considered that *rakish habits* were best avoided by such.

And so it was that Helena arrived alone with him to her brother's former rooms at Staple Inn to find Mr Grewgious waiting, his forlorn face telling all. The news had been conveyed to him earlier in the evening by a constable from the Limehouse station and the old, angular solicitor had waited for the young woman's return. He broke the news as gently as a man lacking all the social graces was able to do. When he had completed his task – and a task it was – his eyes glistened as did those of the sailor who had remained standing by the window, his face in shadow. The only dry eyes in the room were those of the dead man's sister.

"There is no need for you, my dear, to … to venture to the police station … to … I am quite able to undertake such a mission."

"If you would be kind enough to accompany me, I should be grateful," Helena responded, "but it is I, and I alone, who must identify my brother. Lt Tartar, if you would also come with us, I should be grateful."

The sailor inclined his head in agreement but did not speak lest he should choke on his words.

A carriage duly summoned, they made their way along various winding thoroughfares until they came to *the wicket-gate and bright lamp of the police station, where they found the Night-Inspector, with pen and ink, posting up his books.* He looked up quickly as they entered, casting a careful eye at the lieutenant, a stranger to him and therefore to be scrutinized. He greeted the solicitor with a grim inclination of his head, stepped down from his high desk and approached Helena with the tenderest of expressions on his face.

"Are you sure, my dear?"

Helena answered with a nod, her face set, the decisiveness of her intention very clear; and so, he ushered her before him, leaving the two men to follow if they so desired. They passed out from the station into the yard, where he used a large key from his bunch to unlock the door of a small shelter at the far end. The air inside was fetid. The body had been placed on a sort of bench and covered by a tarpaulin. The policeman looked at Helena, once again a question hovering in his expression. When hers did not change, he drew back the covering.

Both Tartar and Grewgious moved forward to support her, to catch her should she fall, but there was no need. Helena stood like a rock beside the corpse of her brother and closed her eyes but once, having expressed recognition (if only by the clothes he wore) with them to the policeman.

"I should like to be left alone with Neville, now," she said, "If I might have a chair?"

The chair provided and the men dispersed, she sat quietly with her own thoughts.

"I thought I heard you call me, Neville," she said to herself and to the body of the brother before her, "I heard your voice on the air. I read your thoughts as we sought for you in the water. I cannot touch you, now, but I still feel your presence within me. You are not without a voice while I live. If you can still speak to me, if you can still reach me from beyond the grave, I am listening. You would not have left me willingly, Neville. I know you too well to harbour any such thought. Once, I could share your feelings and your understanding though we might be apart."

She was silent for a time, her mind roving over her brother's fate. She heard the boisterous rushing of the water and saw Neville struggling against the pull of the tide. He never cried out: of that she felt sure. The waters filled his mouth and bore him on, while the currents tore at his legs. All this she knew, sitting quietly by his side. He looked up as his back brushed roughly against the side of a boat – or was it one of the piles that supported the jetties? And then he was washed away, and there was the Thames mud and the coarse grass of the banks where, for a while, at the whim of the waters, he was dumped. Somewhere, out there on the dirty, slimy waters, he had been alone and friendless. And his handsome face, once lovely to her stroke, became as it was now, here on this lonely bench in this hut, made close and muggy by the warmth of a summer's night, a warmth he would never feel again.

"May the Resurrection and the Life be with you at this time and bring you to me. Amen."

Helena left the hut knowing that forever, from that moment on, she would, in some way, always be alone.

*

It was only two days later when she announced her decision. The Rev Crisparkle had arrived to bring her comfort and the four young people had walked together but alone, each pleased to be in the company of the others, each pleased to be silent.

In truth, Helena had reached her decision while she sat with her brother's corpse in the small hut in the yard of the police station. The funeral arrangements seemed but a formality, awaiting the release of Neville from the authorities, and she knew, with the quiet determination she had always possessed when running away as a child, that she now had to make her own way in the world. It was while the four of them sat on the small bench on the footpath reached from the steps that led down from Waterloo Bridge that she spoke her thoughts.

They had returned each day to that bridge, the Bridge of Sighs, from where so many, desperate to leave this world, had thrown themselves into the waters of the Thames: drunkards, a baker whose business had collapsed, a servant girl who had 'fallen', a boy who had lost his job and many women of the streets. It was the last place on this earth where she had felt Neville's presence, where *a complete understanding* had existed between her brother and herself, *though no spoken word* had *passed between* them.

"I must make my own way in this world," said Helena, "and to do so I must leave London. Apart from you, my dears, and Mr Grewgious" she continued, turning to Rosa and Lt Tartar and resting her hands on them both, "I have no one who cares for me here. Besides, I am called elsewhere. I have spoken with Septimus and he is sure I may find both work and lodging in Cloisterham."

"Cloisterham?" cried Rosa, her voice almost a squeal, "How can you ever return there?"

"I will have justice for my brother," replied Helena, "and it is there I shall find it. Do not ask me how or why, Rosa, my dear friend. I only know that it is so. In Cloisterham, I shall have Septimus by my side, my guide and the saviour of my soul."

Neither the lieutenant nor Rosa felt like questioning the distraught young woman further; neither could conceive what she might have in mind, what work she might consider finding in Cloisterham, but both knew her determination was such that it could not be breached. When they spoke of their friend later that evening, it seemed to each of them that she now inhabited another world, a world where she might find the resolution she so desperately sought.

Chapter 16

The Fall of Mr Datchery

The news that Neville's body had been drawn from the river came to Samuel Warden several days later. This was not due to any slackness on the part of the postal service – deliveries were frequent in those days – but because Detective Inspector Field had waited for the results of the post-mortem; they were succinct in their detail and the essentials contained in a one sentence:

> The state of the body was such that no firm conclusions could be drawn but it was the pathologist's view that when he entered the water Mr Landless was alive.

Samuel placed the paper gently on the table in front of him with the remains of his breakfast. He was disappointed. The opinion took him back to when he first heard Neville Landless had disappeared only a few days before: they were still left with the three possibilities of accident, suicide or murder. Signs of a blow to the back of the head or of a struggle would have settled the detective's deliberations. Now, he was left with the unlikelihood of an accident and the strong possibility of a suicide; murder needed a motive and who could have reason to kill the young man?

Samuel finished his repast with a strong coffee and some hot, buttered rolls. It was going to be a long day and a trying one. He was obliged to see John Jasper with the latest news, had much to ask Dick Datchery and wanted to catch hold of

Deputy long enough to caution him against visiting London again.

It was still early, and the choirmaster had only just put paid to one of Mrs Tope's breakfasts of pickled salmon followed by pigeon pie when Samuel arrived, unannounced as was his wont, by way of the postern stair. The coffee pot was still hot and the choirmaster, though taken aback, promptly offered the detective a cup, which he accepted.

Samuel gazed round the room as he had done on his first visit. Nothing had changed: *the grand piano was in the recess, the folio music-books on the stand,* the books upright on their shelves, the unfinished painting of Rosa Bud hung over the chimneypiece. Everything precisely in its place, neat and ordered. Samuel admired neatness and order: it showed a tidy mind.

"And how are our investigations proceeding, Mr Warden?"

"To be honest with you, Mr Jasper, they are not. I have acquired a great deal of information. I have a clear picture of who was where and when on that fateful evening and who has done what, when and where since. At one point, only yesterday, I felt I may even have traced Mr Drood's progress after he left your house last Christmas Eve and parted company with Mr Landless," replied Samuel, his eyes fixed, if only languidly, on John Jasper's face, "but there are too many unanswered questions and too many unexpected occurrences."

"You leave me mystified," said the choirmaster.

"Perhaps, sir, we might begin with a piece of news that will, I anticipate, shock you, but which you may welcome ... or, there again, may regret. Has it come to your attention that, only eight days ago, Mr Landless also disappeared?"

"The news has not reached us here in Cloisterham, Mr Warden. Why do you suppose I might regret hearing this?"

"I was of the opinion, sir, that you considered Mr Landless responsible for the murder of your nephew."

"That is so – ah, I see, you would expect me to regret that he could no longer be brought to account, no longer face the justice of the courts?"

"I believe your exact words, sir, were," continued Samuel, taking a notebook from an inner pocket of his jacket and referring to the first interview with John Jasper, "'*I will fasten the crime of the murder of my dear dead boy upon the murderer ... I devote myself to his destruction.*' I believe, at that time, sir, you had Mr Landless in mind?"

"I did. I have no doubt that he is responsible for Edwin's death."

"Mr Landless's body was pulled from the river three days ago, Mr Jasper."

"He is dead! Excuse me – the shock. I see what you mean. He can no longer be brought to justice, no longer face the hangman ... The river, you say?"

"Yes, sir."

Samuel waited. John Jasper stood, unsteadily, and walked to his piano, where he paused for several minutes in the sombre shadows of the recess, his face masked from the detective. His concentration suggested he might be running a tune through his head. When he turned to the detective, his face was drawn.

"I am, of course, disappointed to hear this news, but ... where might we go from here, Mr Warden? My dear boy is still not found and the only person able to lead us to him is dead, you say."

The revelations – particularly the one revelation – Samuel had gleaned from the Princess Puffer was on the tip of his tongue, but he refrained from mentioning them. Call it instinct, call it a feeling for a sense of the dramatic: whatever it was, held him back.

"I have interviewed several people over the past few days, Mr Jasper, and they have raised questions I think you may be able to resolve for me."

"Of course, but I don't see, now, how any questions will lead us to find Ned."

"I understand, sir, that you paid a visit to Miss Bud at the Nuns' House after Miss Landless left for London – indeed, after Miss Twinkleton's establishment closed for the summer? May I enquire the purpose of your visit?"

"I don't see ..." began John Jasper, throwing the detective a look that might have been suggestive of either anger or fear.

"Let me do the seeing, sir. Why did you visit Miss Bud?"

"I wished to speak with her about my nephew. We both loved him in our different ways. It was over half-a-year since his disappearance, we were both still in mourning and I supposed we might be of some comfort to each other."

"And what was Miss Bud's reaction to your visit?"

"She was distressed, naturally."

"And you were unable to comfort her?"

"To my everlasting regret, that is so."

"So distressed, sir, that the next day she fled from Cloisterham?"

"Yes."

"Have you any idea, sir, where she went?"

"No – not immediately ..."

"But since?"

"Yes."

"And so, you know that she is now safe – and being comforted?"

"I do know that, Mr Warden."

"It must be a great relief to you, sir."

"I do not understand where your questions are leading, Mr Warden ..."

"They are not *leading* anywhere, Mr Jasper," replied Samuel, placing stress on the verb, and adding, "as yet."

The choirmaster's confidence in him was still critical and Samuel decide to proceed with caution as he had on their first and only meeting.

"Miss Bud is of a nervous disposition, is she not, Mr Jasper. One might say, highly strung?"

"I don't see why you ask this, Mr Warden."

"There was an incident, was there not, sir, at the Rev Crisparkle's house on the occasion of Mr and Miss Landless's arrival? Miss Bud was singing, I believe, and she stopped abruptly in a state of some agitation?" Samuel once again consulted his notebook before continuing, "She cried out '*I can't bear this! I'm frightened! Take me away!*' and Miss Landless caught her and placed her on the sofa. You were accompanying her, were you not, sir? Can you account for Miss Bud's behaviour?"

"You're not suggesting Miss Bud has anything to do with Ned's disappearance, Mr Warden?"

"I'm not suggesting anything, sir. Can you account for her behaviour?"

"I cannot."

"Mr Drood suggested that you were, I quote, '*such a conscientious master*' you had frightened her."

"How can you know that, Mr Warden. You cannot have spoken with Ned – of course, of course, Miss Landless."

"Indeed, sir."

"I am a stern teacher, no doubt, Mr Warden, but I was Miss Bud's Music Master. She was used to my ways. I cannot think I frightened her."

"Of course, of course. You've not visited Miss Bud since her flight to London?"

A look of relief passed across the choirmaster's face, as though Samuel's question assured him that the detective did not know everything.

"No, no, I felt … I felt she had comfort enough and have no wish to … to distress her further."

"Of course not, sir. I take it that your visits to London, which we spoke of when we last met, do not bring you within the vicinity of Miss Bud?"

"No, no, they do not."

"And Mr Landless?"

"Mr Landless?"

"You are aware of where he lodged?"

"I believe the Rev Crisparkle has mentioned something of the kind."

"But you have never been tempted to visit Mr Landless, despite your conviction that he was responsible for your nephew's disappearance?"

"My own investigations brought me nought, Mr Warden, which is why I asked for the assistance of the Detective Police."

"Of course."

Samuel left the agreement hanging in the shadows of John Jasper's room and walked to the door as though he was about to leave. He paused for a moment, as Jasper had done by the piano, and then turned to the choirmaster.

"I am interested, sir, in the solicitor Grewgious's role in your nephew's disappearance. He came to you, did he not, soon after the mystery began and found you exhausted and slumped in your chair?"

"I had been assisting in the search for Ned for many days."

"What did Mr Grewgious have to say?"

"He came to tell me that ... that Ned and Miss Rosa had ... had called off their betrothal."

"It must have been a shock, Mr Jasper."

"Yes. It was."

"I understand Mrs Tope attended to you."

"I was famished."

"She found you collapsed on the floor, I believe."

"I am ... I am unsure ... of how I might have been found, Mr Warden."

"I see ... I believe Mr Grewgious's words were '*After some innocent and generous talk, they agreed ... to dissolve their existing, and ... their intended, relations, for ever ... and ever.*' Would that be so, sir?"

"Yes, I believe that is what was said."

"It would seem as though the young couple had come to a mutually agreeable decision?"

"Yes, I suppose that to be so."

"In some respects, at least, you must have been relieved that they had resolved a situation that proved to be a burden to them both."

"On reflection, possibly ..."

"But not immediately?"

"No."

"Immediately, you were bitterly disappointed," said Samuel, twisting round the words of their last interview.

"For Ned. Ned feared I would be bitterly disappointed."

A glazed, faraway look had come over John Jasper's face: his eyes blanked and beads of sweat sprang from his forehead and upper lip. The pallor of his face was ghastly to behold in one so young. Samuel had to remind himself that the man before him was only twenty-six years old, little older than his nephew and a few years younger than Samuel.

He wanted to keep the choirmaster's confidence and yet he had to pressure him for answers. He was torn between breaking the man and holding the pieces together.

"The last time we spoke, sir, you mentioned your need to go to the city, to find those pleasures denied you here. I think your very words, sir, were 'denied me by the very *vocation to which I must subdue myself*'. Would one of those pleasures be opium smoking, Mr Jasper?"

"My words were in confidence!"

John Jasper looked up at the Samuel, who had not moved from his position on the door, as though the detective was a disciple of the Devil. On his lips was the question he seemed unable to ask - 'How did you know?' – as his mind tussled with wondering what else the man from the Detective Police had dug up.

"Always, sir, always. Take a pipe, now, sir. It will calm you down and do you good. As I said, I am also from a small town – indeed, a village in my case – and I know how suffocating such a life can be."

"Not now, Sergeant! I have my cathedral duties to attend to later this morning. Despite *the cramped monotony of my existence,* I am devoted to my art."

John Jasper stood as he spoke, once more a dark young man, deep and good of voice, his manner a little sombre as befits one of his calling, a man used to being seen about the cathedral, a folder of manuscripts tucked under his arm, on his way to see the Dean or another of the important clergy, a man respected throughout Cloisterham, a man of God, his intention to pass Samuel in the doorway clear.

"That, sir, if I might say so, is very transparent – and admirable," replied the detective, who did not move but stood wondering whether he might pursue the question of the unaccountable expedition with Durdles and deciding against it, deciding that it was, perhaps, unnecessary.

But there was one thing he must mention, the very thing that had troubled him from the lips of the Princess Puffer, casting aside all those unacknowledged conclusions he had drawn: unacknowledged because a man of the Detective Police did not jump in that direction.

"Before you leave on your daily round, Mr Jasper Choirmaster, there is one more matter with which I must acquaint you."

When John Jasper did not budge, Samuel indicated the easy chair, but still the choirmaster stood his ground.

"I was speaking to a witness only a few days ago, sir, who informed me that she had been to Cloisterham this summer. She was here about some business connected with the cathedral, when a young man approached her, asking after her welfare. She was a wretched-looking person, and he offered her money for lodgings and food as an act of kindness. He gave his name as Edwin."

John Jasper still did not move but, instead, *burst into a fit of laughter*, a merriment so all-consuming he had to bury his face in his sleeve *to have his laughter out. The sense of destructive power ... expressed in his face* was so frenzied that even the detective was taken aback.

"Stand aside, Sergeant. I asked for your help to find my darling boy and all you can do is come here with a pack of impertinent questions and a cock-and-bull story that would have difficulty finding its place in even a pantomime.

I *pledged never to relax in my search*, never to relax until I fastened *the crime of the murder of my dear dead boy on the murderer*. That pledge was fulfilled when the body of Neville Landless was drawn from the waters of the Thames.

When we first met, you said I might stake my life on you finding my nephew. Empty words, sir – as empty as your investigation. I have no more time for your badinage. My work for the cathedral calls to me.

Later, today, I will be in touch with your superior, Detective Inspector Field, who will doubtless have you removed."

With a final, contemptuous glance at the detective, John Jasper strode past him on his way to the cathedral.

Having come down the postern stair, Samuel waited under the archway of John Jasper's Gate House watching the choirmaster disappear into the north transept and the safety of the cathedral. He had known it would be a trying morning and he was now exhausted; exhausted and, apparently, running out of time.

Samuel was wondering whether a quick brandy-and-water might perk him up, when he heard a familiar, cheery voice:

"Detective Sergeant Samuel Warden of the Detective Police, we meet again!"

The *idle buffer living upon his means,* still *buttoned up in a tightish blue surcoat,* despite the warmth of the day, stood smiling in his doorway.

"Mr Datchery, Playwright, we do indeed, sir, and with an apology from me. I was a trifle sharp with you when we parted and for that lack of civility on my part I apologise most humbly."

"No offence taken, Mr Detective, I assure you. You were quite right. I should not have sent the boy off alone on such a mission. But he tells me you saw him safe and brought him back."

"You have spoken with him this morning?"

"And apologised, Mr Detective. The boy and I get on well. I call him Winks, and he seems to like the familiarity."

"If I might trouble you for some of your time, Mr Datchery?"

"Enter and welcome!"

The room was as before: close, groined, the small windows allowing just enough northern light and no more. Samuel noted the corner cupboard and the realignment of the chalk marks; he noted the scattered papers on the table, once again hurriedly scooped into a pile as he entered.

"I see your investigation progresses, Mr Datchery, Playwright and Detective."

"Detective, sir?"

"Detective, Mr Datchery – amateur, perhaps but assiduous, judging by the proliferations of strokes upon your tavern board. May I trouble you for a brandy-and-water? I find it lubricates the social wheels to a fine extent. You do have some of the lubricating spirit on the premises, do you, Mr Datchery? If not, I can pop out ..."

"There is no need, sir. We are able to provide for a guest."

And so, the two men sat, one on either side of the small table, smiling at each other, sipping their pick-me-up and waiting for the other to open the conversation. It was Samuel who spoke first.

"You were less than frank with me during our one, previous conversation, Mr Datchery, regarding what you saw of the Princess Puffer's activities here. You omitted to mention her shaking her fists at Mr Jasper in the cathedral, for example, but your little helper, Deputy, has completed the picture, and it proves an informative one, does it not? You also omitted to mention why you had such an interest in the lady that you felt obliged to send a child to London to discover where she lived."

Mr Datchery said nothing. His cheery face, the face of *an idle buffer,* had become, suddenly, pale and puffy, one might even say *doughy*, as an actor's face might look with the make-up removed. The white hair, too, seemed out of place, crowning as it did the face of a man no older than Samuel's own thirty years.

"We will forgive you that, Mr Datchery, Playwright and Detective, as long as you are open with me now."

"And what might I be open about, Mr Samuel Warden of the Detective Police?"

"You might start by being honest about your business in Cloisterham. I feel, sir, that you are just a trifle more than a*n idle buffer, living upon his means,* who has *taken lodgings in this picturesque old city for a month or two, with a view to settling down here altogether.* Indeed, I would go so far as to say that you have no intention of settling down here at all once your business is concluded."

"And what would that be, sir – my business in *this picturesque old city?*"

"I was hoping you might tell me that, Mr Datchery. I feel I am pumping at a very dry old well. Have you, as yet, spoken with those people I mentioned before – the bountiful Mrs Tope, the worshipful Mr Sapsea, the devoted Mr Jasper, the muscular Rev Crisparkle – and have you taken a journey with Mr Durdles, following in the footsteps of our Mr Jasper?"

"And why would I do any of those things, Mr Warden, Detective?"

"Because that is what you were sent here to do, Mr Datchery, Solicitor's Clerk."

Mr Datchery's face fell, the doughy complexion became even more so, as though, having been kneaded thoroughly, it was waiting *to be sent to the bakers*, and an air of dissatisfaction overcame the man. He seemed but a shadow of his former self, a walking shadow, a poor player who having strutted and fretted his hour upon the stage was to be seen and heard no more.

"Come, come, Mr Bazzard, cheer up," said the detective, feeling sorry for the man, "You may yet have a part to play. Your employer, Mr Grewgious, had faith in you or else you would not be here, and your two month's leave is but little spent."

"I thought I recognised you," said the clerk, mournfully.

"It was the Marylebone Lady's Maid case, sir. I came for a list of valuables owned by the gentleman who placed the advertisement in 'The Times'."

"I remember. Mr Grewgious was reluctant to hand it over. You were very persistent."

"The quality comes with the work, sir. I like to be amiable, like to do things nicely," said Samuel, taking a reflective sip of his brandy-and-water, "and that is how I wish it to be with you. We can spend the morning comfortably enough together sharing what we know – that's the way I would like it to be – or we can continue our conversation down at the station. But you wouldn't want that, sir, would you?"

Mr Bazzard looked across the table at the detective much as a runaway dog might look when cornered, but then seemed to recover himself. He walked to the open corner cupboard, retrieved the bottle of brandy, topped up their glasses and pushed the water jug towards Samuel.

After a brandy or two, Mr Bazzard loosened-up somewhat, and even cheered up. He corroborated what Deputy had already passed on to the detective, confirmed that he had established an "amiable enough" friendship with John Jasper and the mayor and had followed in the choirmaster's footsteps on the unaccountable expedition.

"And what did you account for?" asked Samuel.

"Very little, I must say. Mr Grewgious asked me to find out what I could and keep an eye on …"

"… Mr Jasper," continued the detective, when the clerk hesitated, "to whom it seems he took an unaccountable dislike at their meeting last Christmas. You made nothing of the journey through the cathedral precincts, Mr Bazzard?"

"I can't say as I did. Did you?"

"Not at first, but Mr Durdles was kind enough to afford me a second tour. Did he mention the keys to you?"

"I never thought to ask. The keys?"

"No matter. Have you spoken with the Rev Crisparkle?"

"We have passed the time of day. Nothing more."

"Always the difficulty of the amateur detective, Mr Bazzard: he cannot be seen to be asking questions. It's your eyes that are valuable, Mr Bazzard – your eyes and your imagination. Do not give up, sir."

The detective replenished both their glasses, toasted the clerk and tossed off his drink, obliging the other man to do likewise. He leaned forward.

"I have a respect for you, Mr Bazzard. I know of your loyalty to your employer, and I would not ask what I am about to ask of you if it were not to save me another return journey to London, where I might put the same questions to Mr Grewgious, Solicitor, who has yet to take me into his full confidence – and will, when I account for the unaccountable at our next meeting ... Mr Edwin Drood paid a visit to Mr Grewgious on December 16th of last year. Is that not so?"

"If you say so."

"No! Mr Grewgious said so! What I need to know is the nature of your involvement at that meeting."

"I did nothing more than I was asked."

"And that was?"

"Ask Mr Grewgious."

"I am asking you, Mr Bazzard."

What he was asking, Samuel was very unsure; all he knew was that the solicitor had been less than helpful, an *angular* man who had unbent only slightly. He was not hopeful a second visit would prove any more profitable unless Bazzard was able to open some door, however narrow the chink, and let in some light; if, of course, there was any light to let in.

"I was asked to witness a ... transaction," replied Mr Bazzard, raising himself in his chair, if not to the height of a playwright, then at least to the height of a solicitor's clerk.

"And the nature of the transaction was ...?"

"Mr Grewgious handed Mr Edwin a ring. He required me to witness the said transaction."

"Go on."

"That's all I know, unless you wish for an account of how we dined," replied Mr Bazzard, enjoying the note of disgruntled sarcasm in his voice.

"What sort of ring?"

"A ring of diamonds and rubies."

"Where had this ring come from?"

"From one of many of Mr Grewgious's safety boxes, I imagine."

"You imagine! You were there!"

"I dozed off," replied Mr Bazzard, unable to hide his smile, "Mr Grewgious was obliged to wake me."

"And you have not seen the ring since?"

"Mr Edwin took it away with him."

"And you had never seen the ring before? You have no idea of its significance?"

"Unlike you, Mr Warden, I am not a detective."

"Wait here! Do not leave your room, while I am gone."

The detective, unable to fit the significance of the ring into any pattern of events he had constructed, walked out onto pathway that led up to the cathedral. He walked briskly, not wishing to meet anyone, not wishing to be engaged in conversation. The cathedral precincts behind him, he made for the river, following the end of the route he had taken on his first day in Cloisterham. He passed the cream house, and thence downhill to the Medway. On the Esplanade, he gazed, once again, down into the waters, and stood there a long time. As on that first day, the sun was rising towards its noontime place in the sky and causing the waters to sparkle and flicker.

He turned, looked at the town and made his way along the High Street, where workmen were again cooling themselves at the public pumps, walked past his hotel and so to John Jasper's Gate House. Beyond the arch he saw Mr Bazzard's door still open and, entering, found the clerk still sitting at the table. He had not moved even so much as a muscle and was surrounded by gloom.

"Mr Bazzard, thank you, sir, for your patience. The matter you have confided in me will remain so. If I seem bewildered, sir, it is because I am. Now, may I suggest we repair to the Royal Victoria and Bull where my hosts will shortly be providing lunch. It will be my pleasure to treat you, and where, I hope we may continue our conversation. Always enlightening, sir, always enlightening."

Samuel's mood was pensive when he returned from the river and alongside Mr Bazzard's, whose own demeanour verged on the lugubrious, a rather doleful lunch seemed in store, but the meal itself lifted both their spirits.

The coffee-room of the Royal Victoria and Bull, where lunch was served, smelt of cigar smoke. It was furnished with an old sofa and flag-bottomed chairs and had the general air of being worn but comfortable. An immense round of beef was placed on the table, along with a flagon of ale, and some smoking-hot potatoes. Accompanied by some pickled cabbage and fresh, home-baked bread to go with the local cheese, the fare brought nothing but praise from both men and soon – replenished and relatively jovial – they were laughing together.

Over a fresh cigar and a neat brandy to settle their stomachs, Samuel broached those other matters he had on his mind.

"I have the feeling, Mr Bazzard, that I might soon be recalled to London, and yet I know – and have always thought – that the search for Mr Drood would end here in Cloisterham, where it began.

Your disguise seems to have worked well, sir. I take it that anyone associated with Mr Grewgious – and many here, including Mr Jasper, will have had dealings with him, however transitory they might have been – would recognize you as his clerk but, as yet, have not.

On my return to London – not my wish, I assure you, sir – I shall be in touch with Mr Grewgious to clear up a few matters for what will, I'm afraid, be my final report. I shall express the view that sending you here was an excellent idea, and I shall suggest most strongly that you remain in post. Your mission is to keep your eye on Mr Jasper and nose around in a general way …"

"If you say so," interrupted Mr Bazzard, curtly, leaning forward on his chair.

"Let's not find areas of disagreement, sir. There is still much to be done, and no way clear to see to the doing of it. We need to be in league, sir – in league. You are clearly an actor of some consideration, Mr Bazzard, and there lies one of our strengths."

Relaxing into the flattery, Mr Bazzard eased himself back again and drew firmly on his cigar. Samuel continued.

"I want you to keep an eye on the boy, Deputy. Once these lads have clapped their eyes on London, it acts like a magnet on their imaginations – and there's nothing good waiting for him in the city, I can tell you. I showed him the sights – so to speak – but doubt whether they will put him off venturing there again."

"I think you can rely on me," replied Mr Bazzard, adding a slight sniff to the comment, as though to suggest that doubting him was not an option.

"Lastly, we come to something that turned my view of Mr Drood's disappearance on its head. He hasn't. He's been seen here in Cloisterham this very summer by The Princess Puffer – and seen only a few days ago."

"When she was here watching Mr Jasper in the cathedral?"

"So, she told me. According to Eliza, she met a 'kind young man' who asked if she was ill. She then went on to wheedle some money from him, making no pretence but that it was for opium."

Mr Bazzard sat up in his chair and leaned forward once again; this time, the curtness was gone, replaced with a sly smile on his face.

"'*Give me three and sixpence,* she says," continued Samuel, "'*and don't you be afeard for me. Give me three and sixpence, and I'll lay it out well, and … if you do … I'll tell you something …*'"

"'*What's your name?*'" she said, continued Mr Bazzard, his voice streaked through with laughter, almost to the point where he was choking, "'*Edwin*', she says. '*You be thankful that your name ain't Ned*', she says, '*it's a bad name to have just now, a threatened name, a dangerous name ...*'"

Mr Bazzard found it impossible to continue, such was his laughter. It had begun on his lips, moved to his mouth and now seemed to consume his whole body. Merriment was not a word one would have normally associated with Mr Bazzard: a titter tarnished with cynicism, perhaps, but not a chortle, and certainly not one that shook him from head to foot in paroxysms of mirth.

Samuel sat and watched; there was nothing else he could do. The only explanation for the clerk's behaviour was that he, Samuel Warden of the Detective Police, had broken a golden rule and drawn a false conclusion. 'Never believe anything or anyone until you have checked their story': Inspector Field's words rang through his ears and but for his natural composure would have shown as humiliation on his face.

"The old woman ... did speak with Mr Drood," said Mr Bazzard, almost in control of himself, but not quite, and so his explanation was broken up by coughs and giggles that rattled in his throat, "She told me the same story when we reached the Monks' Vineyard ... but that was last Christmas, '*last Christmas Eve, just arter dark, the once that I was here afore*' ... I can hear her saying it now ..."

Samuel Warden stood, stubbed out the remains of his cigar in the ash tray, apologised to Mr Bazzard for his behaviour and left. He was not, naturally, a rude man but he needed – needed desperately – to be alone, and for the second time that day. If only he had not lost his temper with Mr Bazzard on their first meeting, he might have spared himself two reconstructions, on the same day, of what might have happened to Edwin Drood. A walk was needed, a long walk around Cloisterham, back and forth, up and down, round and about.

As he left the hotel, Mr Bazzard's laughter was still ringing fretfully in his ears. He rather hoped the man might choke to death.

Chapter 17
John Jasper Takes the Train

Summer had come and gone, and the first mists of autumn were in the air when John Jasper took the train, once again, to London.

Cloisterham was beautiful in the autumn, even to the choirmaster whose yearnings drew him elsewhere. It was the mellow season and the city in which he felt enslaved over his work in the church seemed to mellow with it. The sun was calmer and less likely to rouse the spirits to disenchantment with its scorching. The fruit hung plump on the vines and branches; in the Dean's orchard, the boughs were borne low with the weight of their apples. Passing beneath them, while strolling in harmony with his superior, John Jasper felt their swelling sweetness with his hands and was almost tempted to pluck one from its twig. But he could wait: another month and they would drop into his hands.

The fruits of the woodlands were also in abundance: hazel nuts and blackberries ready for the early picking. Mrs Tope had already introduced the berries into her dishes; sitting over his breakfast that morning, the choirmaster had enjoyed their sweetness. The honey had already been harvested and a jar of that, too, had its place on the neatly laid table.

The previous evening, she had placed a bowl of nuts by the side of his sherry decanter, and he had recalled the time, getting on for a year ago, when he sat cracking walnuts with Ned, while his nephew talked of Rosa.

The season tempted him to walk often, to walk fiercely and with energy, and he had ventured into the countryside around the little city that seemed destined to be his home forever. He passed farms and the smell of apples being pressed reached his nostrils. A farmer's wife, seeing him pause to wipe his brow, offered him a drink of the sharp, biting juice. In the hedgerows, the bees buzzed around the ivy and the finches pecked at the elderberries. The farmer's men had begun work on the hedges and the stubble was being ploughed ready for the winter sowings. The world seemed at peace with itself.

Overhead, swallows gathered in readiness for their migration south; and John Jasper returned to his cathedral and his sombre room above the Gate House, once again unsettled.

He had been taking the opium in his own way, a pipe or so when the rages called him; but he needed it in what she called the *'artful form'*. He hated it there in that grubby den in Shadwell: *stale streets, a miserable court, a broken staircase, a stifling room.* But go he must.

He sat silently in the omnibus, ignoring the other passengers. He preferred the box seat by the driver, but Joe tended to want to talk and the choirmaster preferred to be close when he was bent on a mission; his purpose was all-consuming. It was a tiresome journey from Cloisterham over the loosely gravelled roads and John Jasper was only too pleased when he was nestled comfortably in the railway carriage at Maidstone.

He always travelled first-class, expensive though it was, as he considered it best befitted his station in life; besides, even the second-class carriages were uncomfortable. There the passengers sat, five a side, facing each other on wooden benches; ventilation, by means of small wooden louvres in the doors, was poor and the smell of tobacco, being smoked or chewed, and snuff nauseated the choirmaster. He liked his own pleasures in life, but he preferred to take them in comfort and privately.

Eastward and still eastward he went, when he arrived in the city, making his way through thoroughfares as mean as the lives of those who lived there. The clientele of the public-houses spilled on to the streets: thieves, pickpockets, burglars, prostitutes and all manner of ruffians. Jasper wondered whether any of them did an honest day's work or whether they preferred to scrape together a living as best they could and by any means that came to hand, however criminal or disgraceful it might be.

He witnessed a fight in one of the drinking dens: a pugnacious man, drunk and urged on by one of the whores, picked a quarrel with a workman who had dropped by for a drink on his way home. Soon all the regulars were involved, taking one side or the other for no better reason than it gave them something to occupy their time. When the workman was knocked to the ground, one of the regulars helped him to his feet, rifling the man's pockets as he did so.

At the corner of one lane he came across a group of women talking. They were dressed raffishly, their wares on display, their dresses and bonnets and shawls garishly bright. They looked up as Jasper passed them but made no attempt to accost him. As they were women used to taking any man back to their grimy room for a shilling a time, this was unusual, but something about Jasper's manner told them he was not to be molested.

One of them did catch his eye. He recognised her for a moment as a girl he had seen years before, sent out by her gin-sodden mother to pick up a few pence as a flower-seller. The choirmaster, feeling sorry for the child, had overpaid her for a small bouquet; but he had been younger then and less versed in the ways of the world. She must have been five or six at the time; now, she might be in her late teens or early twenties but looked nearer sixty with her painted face and unwashed skin.

He had come to distrust beggars, although he knew well the plight of many. Too often, as a young man, he had been touched by a child slumped in a doorway, half-frozen by the cold in winter, half-starved all year, apparently asleep from exhaustion, their pale face summoning his pity. But it was a pretence, all a pretence: on receiving his alms, the child would cease rubbing her eyes and groaning piteously, as she resumed her pose for the next gentleman passer. Somewhere by, her mother – or owner – would be waiting to relieve the child of her money.

He came at last to the grubby passageway, entered the house that had no street-door, *groped his way* up *the stairs* with their broken banister and so out into the sordid room with its sweet odours that corrupted the air.

*

Samuel Warden, thrown out of countenance as he had been by Mr Bazzard's revelations, was not a man to waste time with regrets or let the grass grow under his feet.

On that July day, now two months or so gone, he had wandered the highways and byways of Cloisterham for the last time, accepting that John Jasper's threat to remove him from the case would bring about his return to London.

He was focussed on a fervent desire to solve the mystery of Edwin Drood's disappearance once and for all: the news of the ring opened an avenue of hope, his mistake in supposing Edwin to have been in Cloisterham that summer returned him to the path of thought he had been pursuing since his meeting with Durdles the previous day.

The letter from Detective Inspector Charles Field requesting his return to 'metropolitan duties' had arrived the next day and by then Samuel had laid his plans. To be sure, they could not be finalised until he had spoken with several people, not least of all his superior and the solicitor, Grewgious, but Mr Crisparkle might be persuaded to play a useful hand and Mr Bazzard a critical one.

He was not, then, to know of Helena's decision or of the outcome of her move to Cloisterham and the effect these might have on his scheme; but time and chance happeneth to them all.

He had walked Cloisterham on the two days left to him, covering, yet again, the tracks of the missing man as far as he could determine what they might have been. The Nuns' House, the Monks' Vineyard, Minor Cannon Corner, the Esplanade, the precincts of the Cathedral, the Gate House, the High Street and Durdles' Yard all witnessed the wearing of his shoe leather on that day.

It was in the High Street that the idea came to him, while he stood outside the Lyceum Theatre, remembering when, on his first visit, he had met the young actor cross-gartered to his calves and bemoaning the lack of enthusiasm among audiences. It was also where he had met, for the second time, the choirmaster. Samuel was conscious, again, of having been drawn here, as though by some strange influence.

*

John Jasper woke the morning after his visit to Princess Puffer's opium den at his usual place of residence when in London, The Falcon Hotel, which was situated in Falcon Square, near the General Post Office. It was a discreet establishment, one that asked no questions of its guests but provided, for two-and-ninepence a day, bed, breakfast with meat, room service and an all-night porter.

He felt heavy in all his limbs and could not prevent an ugly twitch jerking him from side to side. When he sat up, he felt chilled and shook from head to foot despite the gentle warmth of the season and the closeness of the room. It was some while before he felt able to call for water so that he might wash, and even later when he felt the desire to order breakfast. It was a dismal meal, not so much because of the food itself but rather that he had no appetite.

He wanted to be alert that day: he had much to reconnoitre before his plans could be laid so that he might pursue his object without interruption. He had watched before, the last time he was in the city, but he still needed to be sure, needed to know that when he accosted Rosa Bud, she would be alone.

John Jasper dressed carefully once he had come to his senses - his shoes shone, his cravat neatly tied, his coat brushed – and when he left the hotel sometime after the hour when he would normally have taken coffee he was looking as sharp as any man-about-town.

He knew she had walked with Miss Twinkleton over the summer, but that good lady was now otherwise engaged at her Seminary for Young Ladies in the Nuns' House, and little Rosebud, his one-time music student, would now be walking alone, unless the sailor, Tartar, arrived to escort her. Mr Jasper had not made up his mind about the sailor: he wondered whether the man might simply be an agent of the solicitor, Grewgious, or had interests of his own in Miss Rosa. He always seemed attentive without ever encroaching on the young woman's dignity.

Mr Jasper knew that Rosa's favourite walks usually led her to one of the parks: Regent's to the north or Hyde to the west, but that sometimes she had strolled further and sat, discreetly and quietly, with Miss Twinkleton in the gardens off Russell Square, before visiting a small teashop nearby. He favoured these gardens as a place where he might, once again, press his suit. Pausing only for a moment on the edge of Smithfield Market to buy flowers from one of the girls there, he sped away from the *crowding, pushing, driving, beating, whooping and yelling; the hideous and discordant din that resounded from every corner of the* cattle *market* towards the relative quiet, if not bustle, of Holborn. The solicitor, Grewgious lived in the vicinity and John Jasper had no desire to bump into him. He hurried on and arrived in less than half-an-hour at a spot where he might find and pursue his quarry.

The house in Southampton Street – where she still resided, having had no wish, he learned, to return with Miss Twinkleton to Cloisterham – was visible from the Bloomsbury Square Gardens and John Jasper positioned himself where he could watch without being observed. Anxious as he was like any ardent lover, the morning seemed to drag remorselessly, but eventually, alone and unaccompanied, Rosa emerged from her lodgings and headed west through Mayfair and hence to Hyde Park.

He followed her at a distance, perturbed lest he lost sight of her, while she crossed the park, pausing only once to pass the time of day with one of the nannies who walked her charges there, and so beyond. Was it possible his prayers were to be answered? Was she making for the quiet spot enjoyed with Miss Twinkleton over the summer months?

He had but two days at his disposal, and then his work at the cathedral would summon him back. If needs must, he would speak with her in Hyde Park, but the gardens were less open, less conspicuously public. If only, if only his luck was in, he would be careful. The extremeness of his passion had driven him, before, to express desires best left unspoken. He had urged his case in a storm, bombarding the young woman with the lightning bolts of his ardour. He had been too vehement, and burnt out his proposal in threats and cravings. He would remain calmer this time, drawing her to him with affection and the necessity of their mutual circumstances. She was, after all, alone in the world, at the mercy of Fate; he would be her saviour and possess her future.

While his strategy raged in his head, John Jasper never lost sight of the young woman he pursued. Now and then, he would offer up a prayer, trusting that God was on his side and would lead her where he, John Jasper, most wished to see her; and when she skirted Holland Park and continued onward, he knew his prayers had been answered.

Rosa Bud sat on one of the benches, quite away from the general view, her hands in her lap, looking about her in an expectation of some kind. It was considered not quite respectable for ladies to sit on the benches, unless accompanied. For a moment, John Jasper wondered but drove the thought from his mind and walked quietly up to her, raising his hat in greeting.

The start she gave almost panicked him. There was fear in her eyes; he knew he must not rise against it but draw back and give her space.

"Miss Rosa, I am here for a few days only, and happy circumstance seems to have brought us together," he began, and added, "if only briefly," as she seemed about to rise and leave. "It gives me a chance to apologise for my behaviour at the beginning of the summer. I was overcome. I spoke in haste and with an unforgiveable vehemence. I …"

"Mr Jasper, you spoke with an unforgiveable violence, a violence so frightening that I was forced to flee to the protection of my guardian, Mr Grewgious."

"I know, and I can only beg your forgiveness."

The young woman did not speak but merely looked at him. She was aware of her position – alone on a bench in a public garden with a man who terrified her and had threatened her and her friends – and she wished to end the conversation and for him to be gone, gone without a scene because she did not doubt that he would pursue her; and she did not doubt that he had pursued her to this very place. Where could she fly now? Where else might she find sanctuary?

"Miss Rosa, if I might have a few minutes of your time?"

He did not wait for an answer but sat with her on the seat, making sure he was as far from her as possible so as not to drive her away. Rosa shifted her position. The idea of flight and the thought of this man hunting her down across the city was more than she could bear. He must leave her and not the other way around; she must drive him away, now and forever.

To a passer-by they might have looked like a young couple discussing their future, which in some respects they were.

"Miss Rosa, when we met in the garden of the Nuns' House, I offered you protestations of love. I spoke of how I felt, without regard for your sensitivities and circumstances at the time. I had no right to speak so, but I am a man untutored in these matters. My life has been spent in the church and in the service of the church. I have very little experience with women."

He paused at that point, his eyes upon Rosa, his mind wondering what effect his confession might engender. Her face remained composed and she looked straight ahead, not meeting his eyes, not daring to meet those eyes.

"I am calmer now, and if my speech is still awkward, if I am still unable to express my thoughts and feelings as eloquently as I should then I must ask your forgiveness for my shortfall. I will not speak of love, but of admiration. I have always admired you, Miss Rosa, from the very day we met, from the very first time you sang for me while I played. I dreamed then – though I had no right to do so – of a time that might be. But it was a time that was never to be, for I knew you were betrothed to my dear boy who is now gone from us."

She shuddered at the mention of Edwin, remembering her harboured fear that she had in some way been responsible for encouraging those feelings in the choirmaster, feelings that may – only may, please God – have driven him to murder his nephew.

"I cannot bring my dear boy back and even were this possible I now know that you and he had decided to go your separate ways, and so ... and so I want to address myself to the thoughts of your future ..."

"Mr Jasper, I am but eighteen years of age ..."

"I know – hence my shame at my awkwardness," cut in the choirmaster, not wishing her to dismiss him until he had played his coup de grace: a stroke he hoped would be both merciful and fatal. "Please hear me out. I may not gain another chance. A man cannot go through life alone, but until I met you, I had never come across anyone who I might wish to share my life. There is not so much of a gap between us. I am, this year, but twenty-seven, and a man well-established in his field of work. I have much to offer should you ever feel – and I do not press you for an answer at this time – should you ever feel there might be a chance that we could, perhaps, come to know each other better."

Rosa sat without moving; her fear keeping her rigid, not daring to show any response lest he should seize upon it. Had it been another declaring his love, she would have found his plea enchanting, but she loathed this man, remembering his strange hold over her when they were together, remembering the piano and the sundial.

"You invade my thoughts, Miss Rosa. No day passes but that I think of you in some way or another," he continued, adding as though not to alarm her, "at my music, on my walks, in the quiet hours of my life ... There are people who think well of me, people who have not seen me as you have – at my worst – people who, indeed, hold me in some esteem."

Still, Rosa sat as if unmoved, though her heart was churning in her breast: a churning so desperate it made her feel nauseous. Her hands gripped the bag she carried and held on her lap, twisting the strap around itself. John Jasper noticed this agitation and was both alarmed and pacified. He dared not threaten her, not again; he must plead.

"My feelings for you are such that they confuse my days. I have even feared they may be the ruin of me ..."

"Mr Jasper, I cannot be held responsible ..."

"Hear me out, please. I only wish you to know how I feel so that you might consider ... might consider my plight and my offer. I have no claim on your affections. I know that to be so, but in time ... in time, we might come to know each other better. You might come to see the better side of my nature ... even to love me!"

There! He'd spoken the very word he had sworn not to use under any provocation.

"Mr Jasper, I can never love you."

"Is there another?"

"I have listened to you, Mr Jasper, though I did not ask you to impose yourself upon me in this way, and I have been considerate towards you, but I ask you now to leave me in peace. If you wish the truth to be said, you frighten me. Even when you speak quietly and with reflection, as you have done today, I am fearful of you, for there is a passion in you, Mr Jasper, that knows no bounds ..."

"I am respected in my work and among the people of Cloisterham. The clergy hold me in high regard. Other opportunities have come my way, as I have said, but never have I felt attracted to anyone as I am attracted to you. Never have I felt so sure of the certainty of happiness. I must be seen to be as I am ..."

He hesitated as he made this demand, as though even he who thought he knew himself was unsure of what he meant. For the first time since they had begun speaking, he seemed to lose himself in his thoughts, and he struggled for the words to express what he felt and what she might fear in him.

"I am not a man who is unable to control his passions ..."

"But you are, Mr Jasper, even in those moments when you are calm, as just now when you spoke your innermost thoughts to me in a manner you deemed to be quiet, there was a rage in you that I fear would prove to be ungovernable."

He stood up and backed away from the bench on which they had conversed. The words she spoke were true, although he could not acknowledge that to be so. Whenever he thought of her – and it was often during the course of his days – his thoughts were fierce and animated. He knew himself to be a zealot of Love.

"There, you see," said the young woman, "You know what I say to be so. I see it in your eyes and your demeanour."

Whatever there was in his demeanour that was obvious to the young woman, to a casual stroller they might still have seemed to be a young couple in earnest debate; despite the intensity of their argument, nether had raised their voice. Facing each other, the man standing, the young woman sitting, both held their ground, their eyes fixed upon the other.

Rosa Bud had changed since fright drove her from Cloisterham, and it was at this moment, perhaps, that she realised this to be so; fearful of him as she was, the young woman was no longer frightened as once she had been. But they were at an impasse: neither moved, neither seemed able to do so.

It was as each held their position that the sailor appeared. He rounded one of the bushes that shielded the spot Rosa had chosen to sit, and it was obvious he expected to find her in just that place.

John Jasper saw him first and it was the turn of the choirmaster's head that alerted the young woman who stood at once and went to her friend. Unspoken understanding of the situation in which they found themselves was apparent in all three faces. It was a silent comprehension, bewildering – not to say staggering; a telepathic grasp of the circumstances. It was Lt Tartar who made the necessary move to break the deadlock.

"Mr Jasper, I believe. We have never met, sir, but I seem to know you, nevertheless. Miss Bud and I arranged to meet here today, and so I consider this the moment, sir, when we bid each other arrivederci."

The Italian phrase was not lost on John Jasper. If an insult and a challenge could have been delivered with more grace, it is difficult to imagine how it might have been done.

The choirmaster inclined his head without letting his eyes leave the other man's; looking up at the sailor from under his thick brows and framed by his *thick, lustrous … black hair and whisker*, the eyes appeared almost devilish. With a slight smile, he raised his hat to Rosa and sauntered off through Russell Square Gardens as though a stroll and a few pleasantries were all he had in mind.

Watching his well-groomed back disappear, Rosa's old fear returned. She felt faint, without actually passing out, and leaned heavily against the lieutenant, whose arm encircled her as naturally as if it had done so daily – as, indeed, it had since the summer. His smile told her all she needed to know. This, after all, was the man in whom she had confided her deepest fears and entrusted her fondest love.

"I think a nice cup of tea will settle us down," said Lt Tartar, and without taking 'no' for an answer he curled her arm through his and set off for the small, nearby tearoom where he and she – together, at the time, with Miss Twinkleton – had enjoyed an afternoon together.

*

John Jasper, once he knew himself to be out of their sight, sped south as fast as his legs would carry him. A walk of almost half-an-hour took him but fifteen minutes, such was the anger in his step. At last, he came to his destination, Waterloo Bridge, the Bridge of Sighs; he leaned over the parapet and looked down into the waters, at the turgid flow of the river. When he had been here before, gas lights had illuminated the surface: now, it was the early afternoon sun, but even its brilliance was no more successful in piercing the gloomy depths. Whatever lay beneath remained hidden from the human eye and human consciousness.

He stared for a long time into the murkiness, aware that once again he had been confounded. He remembered a collapse when realisation of the meaning of the broken betrothal came home. He remembered meeting another rival on this very bridge one-night last summer, a night that seemed so long, long, ago. There was no retracing of steps, no going back over the long journey made; stepped in so far that, should he wade no more, returning was as tedious as go o'er.

Chapter 18
Mr Grewgious Takes A Walk

Hiram Grewgious was annoyed with himself on two accounts: his reticence when that confounded detective had tried to interview him the first time and his gullibility when the same man had twisted his thinking the second. More than either of these concerns about his own involvement in what had now proved to be a sorry and dangerous state of affairs, however, was his concern for his guardian, Rosa Bud.

She had returned with her lieutenant and explained in rather more detail than he wanted to take in at one sitting what had transpired in the gardens at Russell Square. Listening to her revelations, his concerns regarding John Jasper had been revived and he found himself brooding upon the events of last Christmas and, more latterly, last summer. Perhaps – but there was no point in 'perhapsing'. Hiram Grewgious was not a man to 'perhaps'. He preferred a list of actions to be undertaken.

Always, when in such a state, the *Angular man of business* for whom *business was business ever* decided to take a walk. It was not cold, not yet, despite the autumn fogs bringing with them a dampness and a chill, but he, nevertheless, wrapped himself up well with a muffler and gloves.

To some extent, the fog suited him: he liked to walk slowly, and the fog imposed such a choice. *He stepped gingerly along* Holborn, past Newgate Prison, making towards St Paul's, *feeling his way beside the walls, windows and doors*, whenever he could. On the highway, *horses were splashed to their very blinkers*; on the pavement, *foot passengers jostled one another ... in a general infection of ill-temper ... losing their foothold at street corners.* Occasionally, he found himself choking in the *smoke lowering down from chimney pots, making a soft black drizzle, with flakes of soot in it as big as full-grown snowflakes*, as though, Mr Grewgious thought, they had *gone into mourning ... for the death of the sun.* It was then he wished he had remembered to bring his umbrella, but no matter: the walking, despite the conditions, was clearing his head.

At St Paul's he turned slightly back and found himself heading towards Fleet Street, stopping on Ludgate Hill, as though impelled to do so by some force outside his sphere of influence. Mr Grewgious did not like such forces: a measure of control was necessary in this world if chaos was not to ensue, and the Law saw to it that such measures were imposed.

But there he was: outside the coffee house where the detective had brought him "for a friendly chat in comfortable surroundings" last summer when he had come down from Cloisterham.

He, Hiram Grewgious, had not been taken in by the detective's manner, of course. The man had known full well that 'comfortable' for him would have been his chambers in Staples Inn; but the man had simply taken his arm, as though placing him under arrest, and sped him away, chattering all the while in that fashion the detective no doubt felt to be amiable but which he found irritating. They had arrived at the coffee house on the north side of Ludgate Hill, where the solicitor found *cosy mahogany boxes and sandy floors in dark-panelled rooms with a vast range of newspapers.* It had, indeed, been comfortable; and settled with a brandy-and-water, which seemed to be the detective's favourite beverage, they had conversed quite cosily, although later, once he had been returned to his chambers, Mr Grewgious had felt 'wrung-out'.

Mr Grewgious now found himself well-settled for a second time in the same establishment – on this occasion needing to be wrung-out after his walk in the fog – because the waiter who had served them before seemed to recognise the solicitor and placed him immediately in the same booth he had shared with the detective.

Once his coffee and a selection of biscuits, which he had not asked for, were placed before him, Mr Grewgious *took a pocket-book from his coat-pocket, and stump of black-lead pencil from his waistcoat pocket* and proceeded to make *a guiding memorandum* to organise his thoughts.

The ring was the first of these.

He hadn't wanted to tell the detective about this on the man's first visit: it was a deeply personal matter he had no wish to share with any stranger, let alone a policeman; but it seemed that Bazzard had let the cat out of the bag – perhaps, on consideration, for the best reasons – and on the detective's second visit a full explanation had been required.

The ring once belonged to Rosa's mother – a lady whom he had loved but lost to another: a friend, but that made the loss no less hard to bear – and which had been entrusted to him following her death. It had been *removed from her dead hand, in his presence, with such distracted grief as he hoped it may never be his lot to contemplate again. Hard man as he was, he was not hard enough for that.* The *rose of diamonds and rubies delicately set in gold* shone brightly *and yet the eyes that were so much brighter, and that looked so often upon them with a light and proud heart, had been ashes, and dust among dust, some years! If he had any imagination (which it is needless to say he had not), he might imagine that the lasting beauty of those stones was almost cruel.*

The ring had been given to the young lady who was drowned so early in her beautiful and happy career, by her husband, when they had first plighted their faith to one another. It was he who had removed it from her unconscious hand, and it was he who, when his death drew very near, placed it in Mr Grewgious's. *The trust in which he had received it, was, that, Edwin and Rosa growing to manhood and womanhood, and their betrothal prospering and coming* to *maturity*, he, Grewgious, *should give it to Edwin to place upon her finger. Failing those desired results, it was to remain in his possession.*

He had warned the young man, sternly, that *placing it on her finger would be the solemn seal upon his strict fidelity to the living and the dead ... If anything should be amiss, if anything should be even slightly wrong, between them* he had charged Edwin *to bring that ring back to him.*

The detective had been mightily impressed with this story – despite Mr Grewgious having missed out the details of his own feelings for Rosa's mother – and had sat in silence for some time: but not, unfortunately, for long. Having adjusted his pre-conceptions to accommodate the story of the ring, the detective had pressed on with what seemed more like an interrogation than a "friendly chat", obliging Mr Grewgious to give an account of the choirmaster's behaviour on that memorable occasion soon after Edwin disappeared.

Mr Grewgious, taking a swig of his coffee and then replenishing the cup from the pot, made the second note in his memoranda: *The Collapse.*

Why had he been so reticent on that first occasion to tell the detective of Jasper's reaction to the news that Edwin and Rosa had, mutually, called off their betrothal? Perhaps if ... But, then, the world was too full of 'ifs' and 'buts'.

The fact was that Jasper had reacted in a quite extraordinary manner upon hearing the news. He recalled his exact words to the choirmaster: '*After some innocent and generous talk, they agreed to dissolve their existing, and their intended, relations, for ever and ever.*' Jasper had risen from his easy chair, *open-mouthed* and as ghastly a figure as one might suppose a ghost to present. He had lifted his *outspread hands towards his head, thrown back the head, clutched at his hair* and turned towards the solicitor with *a writhing action.* Mr Grewgious had never witnessed such a sight. He *heard a terrible shriek, and saw no ghastly figure, sitting or standing; saw nothing but a heap of torn and miry clothes upon the floor.* He had not changed his action even then. He remembered opening and shutting the palms of his hands and looking down at the bundle, *a limp, loose suit of clothes as if the man had gone out of them.*

The detective had also shown a great interest in this occurrence – an interest and a disapproval, Mr Grewgious thought, judging from the frown he had received.

Remembering his reaction at the time and the news that had so reduced Jasper in his opinion, Hiram Grewgious made his third note: *Rosa.*

There had been a possible reticence about her betrothal on his ward's part when he had travelled to Cloisterham in early December of last year to tell her of the circumstances surrounding her proposed marriage and her father's will; and he had, in his *awkward and hesitating manner,* not given her concerns the attention they deserved. He recalled her words: '*It was not bound upon Eddy, and it was not bound upon me, by any forfeit, in case …*'. He, Hiram Grewgious, supposedly her guardian and solicitor, had not sensed the question in her appeal. Had he not wanted to hear the question? He had hurried on to assure her, it is true, but perhaps – that word again! – he would have done better to listen to the young woman; perhaps it would have been kinder to let her open her heart? Mr Grewgious thought himself *a particularly Unnatural man, born advanced in life, a chip and a dry one.* Perhaps if he had listened earlier none of what seems to have transpired would have done so?

Back to the detective again. Perhaps the man's persistence was more than just an irritating trait of his personality? Mr Grewgious thought him particularly persistent.

Note number four: *Bazzard.*

The detective had pierced Bazzard's disguise but had the temerity to suggest – insist was the more accurate word – that he should remain in Cloisterham to fulfil the purpose Mr Grewgious had sent him to accomplish; to keep an eye on Mr Jasper's comings and goings and generally "nose around". It wasn't a phrase of which Mr Grewgious approved, but he had given in to the suggestion at the detective's insistence – yes, that was the word. Bazzard's absence was no bad thing, of course. Mr Grewgious had taken him on out of kindness. The son of a turkey farmer in Norfolk, Bazzard had ambitions to write a play – something his father could not countenance – and Bazzard, on an occasion when he brought his father's rent to London and to Mr Grewgious, had appealed for his help. Mr Grewgious, to save the young man from starvation, had taken him on as his clerk. This kept the wolf from the door but left Bazzard with a feeling of degradation. Mr Grewgious was prone to tread warily where the clerk was concerned, and it was, in some ways, a relief he was now otherwise engaged. But that knowledge did not take away the sense that the detective had manipulated him and, moreover, had not been entirely open in his reasons for wishing Bazzard, as Dick Datchery, to remain in place.

And Jasper had returned to haunt his ward. Did the detective – now off the case – need to know this? Mr Grewgious, somewhat reluctantly, thought he might appreciate the news.

He remembered Rosa falling upon his neck, tears in her eyes, after she had taken flight from Jasper in the summer. He had been in his room but had not heard her tap on the door, and so she had turned the door-handle and entered. He had been *on his window seat at an open window, with a lamp placed far from him on a table in the corner.* When he turned and saw her, Rosa had been in the twilight of the room;

"*My child*", he had said, "*my child! I thought you were your mother!*"

*

His cogitations may have, hopefully, cleared the solicitor's mind regarding his part in the drama that was unfolding, unbidden, around him and invading the lives of those he loved and cherished. When he left the coffee house, he was firm in his decision that he would, the following morning, make haste to Great Scotland Yard, by Trafalgar Square, where he hoped to find Detective Sergeant Warden.

He was not to know that the detective was already au fait with John Jasper's visit to Russell Square. While Mr Grewgious enjoyed his coffee, the detective was sitting in a cell at St Giles police station watching a boy, dressed in rags, with a jagged gap in what remained of his front teeth and a habit of contradicting what anyone said with the phrase 'Yer Lie!', sitting on his bed enjoying a nice cup of char and a bit of bread and dripping for his breakfast.

"I did what you said - if ever you're lost in the city, son, make your way here to the police station," said Deputy with a wink at the detective.

"The idea was that you wouldn't find yourself lost, my boy."

"I follered him on the next train. I knew where he'd go. It was easy."

"Who gave you the money."

"Yer Lie! No one, but I follered him everywhere. He didn't escape me!"

Samuel Warden thought that the man the boy spoke of had escaped everyone, including himself.

Chapter 19
Helena Landless Accepts a Challenge

The decision to make her own way in life had been an easy one for Helena Landless; and driven, intuitively, back to Cloisterham, where she sensed she would find justice for her brother, she had found both lodgings and work.

Work had proved the least complicated of the two endeavours. It was a fancy she had been harbouring for how long she could not be sure, but the idea came to her as she and her friends sat on the little bench beneath the Bridge of Sighs.

The previous autumn – the autumn prior to Edwin Drood's disappearance and her brother's banishment – soon after she came to know Rosa, Miss Twinkleton had taken the young ladies of her seminary on a visit to a London theatre, which Miss Twinkleton, in her *scholastic state of existence*, considered to be a necessary requirement of their education. The visit had been undertaken late in the season to take advantage of the Christmas plays that were fashionable, and so Helena had experienced one of these – replete with snow, bells, goblins and hauntings – at the Adelphi. It had been a shattering experience for a girl brought up in Ceylon by a *grinding stepfather* who had *stinted* on the education of both she and her brother and denied them *the commonest pleasures of childhood*.

Her passionate nature had been drawn into the world of the drama, a world that reflected and sharpened her own view of life; and those later visits when she moved to be with her brother in London, in the company of Rosa and Lt Tartar, had honed her knowledge of herself, her desires and her aptitudes.

When she approached the company at Cloisterham's Lyceum Theatre, they jumped at the opportunity, the company manager was delighted.

"My dear," he said, "you'll be an asset to the profession, you've the Spanish lady in your face, the duchess in your walk and Aladdin's genie in your colour. Why, I've never seen such whites of eyes before on any stage; and there'll be savings in the make-up."

"Will I be able to earn to earn a living by the stage?" Helena had asked.

"Earn a living!" exclaimed the manager, who she later learned was known by everyone simply as Maestro, a nickname that had certain alliterative qualities when put alongside his surname, Muggins, which he was anything but. "Earn a living!" he repeated, a habit crafted on the stage, *"You'll live like a princess – a pound a week and double when we have a run of good houses."*

With joy in her heart, Helena had accepted the offer and Maestro Muggins gave her his hand upon the bargain.

Lodgings had proved a more complex manoeuvre, although the sense of her taking on her brother's old room at Minor Canon Corner had been obvious from the outset.

The problem – if such a word should be applied to an old lady – had been Mrs Crisparkle. And, to be fair, Helena herself. Both ladies were of a rather decisive nature. Once the mind of such a lady is made up, it usually proves difficult to change. Helena had reservations about living in a house where her brother had been made to feel less than welcome by the doyen of the place. Mrs Crisparkle had reservations about the younger woman's intentions towards her only living, beloved son and her intentions, as a woman, to earn a living, let alone in the theatrical world.

The Rev Crisparkle had navigated his ship between this Scylla and Charybdis with a skill that his sailor friend, Lt Tartar, would have admired.

"Ma," he had said to the China Shepherdess on first broaching the idea, "don't you think we should not be too hasty in jumping to conclusions about Miss Landless? After all, her brother – to whom you took what I consider (and said so at the time) to have been an ill-founded dislike – has now passed from this world in what we must agree are tragic circumstances. Would it not be Christian of us to extend a welcoming hand to his sister who is alone, and friendless? *Let us discuss it, Ma.*"

"*I have no objection to discuss it, Sept. I trust, my dear, I am always open to discussion,*" replied the canon's mother, without adding, '*and I should like to see the discussion that would change my mind*'. "Mr Neville Landless *did great discredit to this house and showed great disrespect to this family.*"

"We will not pursue that point again, Ma – and agree to differ on the matter – but may, perhaps, discuss the situation of his sister who is of a different disposition. We must not ascribe the imperfections of the young man upon his twin."

"Peas in a pod, Sept."

"Ma, we are discussing people, and not vegetables. Miss Landless has emerged from the *disadvantages of her miserable life* much better than her brother. Neville himself described her qualities, when likened to his, as being those of the *Cathedral tower* compared to those of the domestic *chimney.*"

"No doubt he did, my dear," replied Mrs Crisparkle: a comment that offered no inroads into her stubbornness.

"To be candid, Ma, I feel that offering shelter and succour to Miss Landless is beholden upon me in the *best discharge of my duty according to my lights.*"

"*My dear Sept, I am sure of that,*" replied the canon's mother, feeling both blown off course by his determination and yet to have steered a true one by her son who showed himself to be a chip off the old block.

"I believe, Ma, I can recall you asking me what Mr Neville *would be without his sister?* You spoke of her capacity to influence him."

"I do recall such a comment, Sept."

"Then give Helena *a fair share of your praise*, Ma, and let us welcome her into our home," replied the Rev Crisparkle in what he felt to be a coup de grace.

The old lady had sighed and *immediately walked across the room and kissed him.*

"Of course, my dear Sept," she said, as though the matter had been decided by her long before their discussion began.

Helena's actual arrival had produced a day or so of tension as the two women contrived to establish their relative stations at Minor Canon Corner. It might be said, by those who enjoy domestic conflicts and see such things in terms of winners and losers, that the older lady won, since it was she who saw the other off to bed each night before deigning to retire herself; but this would be a small-minded view.

It was, after all, Mrs Crisparkle's house: she held the strings of the purse and the key of the door. Helena was a guest and, by and large, a welcome one. Mrs Crisparkle saw this not only in the young lady's conversation but also in the extra spring of her son's step when he set off for the cathedral and the manner in which the girl from Ceylon was welcomed by the congregation – at least, most of them.

Helen, herself, decided to play a waiting game and enjoy her new-found independence. Since her arrival in early September, the young actress's time was taken up largely by her work at the theatre.

"It's the high drama we look for in you, my dear," the Maestro had explained on her first morning, "You don't have the deportment for low comedy, which we can leave safely in the hands of my dear wife."

Mrs Muggins was a rotund woman, some ten years younger than her husband, who had been reared in a theatrical family and felt more at home on the stage than on the street. To Helena, she always seemed dressed ready for a part rather than a foray into the real life of the town. On their first meeting, Bella Muggins appeared as though dressed for the role of a dairy maid, complete with a blue-and-white striped dress supported by numerous petticoats, a sparkling white apron and a bonnet tied loosely under her chin that seemed intended to clamp down a mass of fair, curly hair but promised at any moment to fall into the milking pail. Like her husband, she could not have been more welcoming to the young woman.

"My dear," she said, "Welcome with open arms to our little company. Beautiful, quite beautiful. If you were a little paler, dear, you would do admirably as Juliet, but a touch of powder here and there and we might ..."

She never completed the sentence, which Helena discovered was a habit of hers, but clasped the young woman in her arms and lifted her off her feet in what can best be described as a bear hug.

On release, Helena took the chance to look about her and to take in her new world: dark walls, heavy curtains, the smell of paint and turpentine and lamp-oil, rows of seats that vanished in the distance, scenery that looked dull and used like clothes one had been obliged to wear out, posters cast carelessly aside, dusty floors, ropes and cables that led she knew not where, rack upon rack of crushed costumes and shelf upon shelf of what she later learned were called 'props'.

"Magic, my dear," said Bella Muggins, embracing her once again, "All transformed by the magic of the art."

It was an art Helena learned rapidly: within the week she found herself performing the role of a Spanish aristocrat in *The Countess of Madrid*, a tragedy by an unknown Spanish playwright that involved a great many stabbings, poisonings and courtly intrigue before Helena's character found her true love, only to lose him to a broken heart in the final scene when he learns that his son has been killed defending the family's honour.

Her baptism of fire continued when the Maestro discovered she spoke French. She had been catching her breath between rehearsals for the second week's play and conversing with the young man in the cross garters who Samuel met, when Mr Muggins overheard their conversation.

"I am largely self-taught," Helena began to explain, "My step-father spent as little as possible on our education."

"Self-taught, self-taught – why that's the best way. It gives a natural tone to the spoken word. Here – wait here!"

He shot off in the direction of the Green Room, returning after a few minutes with a grubby copy of a play entitled, *Le dilemme du meurtrier*.

"*There, just turn that into English, and put your name on the title page*. On second thoughts, put mine. It isn't usual to find a lady's name on a playbill and it may put off the clientele."

The following morning no sooner had Helena arrived at the theatre than the cross-gartered young man, Emile Bertrand, approached her.

"Have you read the French piece? Anything in it for me?"

"It's a tragedy," replied Helena. "There is the son."

"What does he do?"

"He kills his father after the father has murdered his daughter."

"Is it a large part?"

"He comes on in the final scene," explained Helena.

"Oh," replied Emile, somewhat mortified Helena felt, since it seemed likely he would get the part but spend most of his time in the Green Room.

The Maestro, on the other hand, was delighted.

"It's a delicate piece, dear, a delicate piece, and the public will love it. There's novelty, you see, with the father killing the daughter to save her honour, and justice, when the son does the same to him. It balances things out nicely in the mind of the audience. People do like fair play. And there's a nicely rounded role for Mrs Muggins as the poor girl's mother. She does sobbing well, does my Bella. We'll have the audience on the edge of their seats. We'll get the bills posted around town and bring them in for the week after next."

"I've only read it, Mr Muggins. I don't think I can have it ready for rehearsals next week."

"*Pooh, pooh,*" said the Maestro, and that was all he said.

The other members of the company were supportive but unbothered. Mr Granger, who specialised in older men of a grumpy disposition, explained that "The Maestro will fill any gaps with stage business". Mr Crouching, who usually played amiable buffoons that turned up trumps in the end, advised that it remained simple with "No speeches longer than half-a-page but plenty of repartee". Mrs Gove, elderly ladies with an edge, suggested "The use of exclamation marks as often as possible". Miss Wayling, young women put upon and often seduced, "Delicacy in the romantic scenes" and Emile wondered whether a prologue might be written in for him.

But the general consensus was that 'things would sort themselves out on the night if cod-pieces and bodices were checked before going on stage'.

It was another world to Helena, so different from the constraints of her childhood, so out of tune with that of the cathedral and the serious churchman with whom she realised she had fallen in love; but the strange thing was that the more immersed she became in the world of the theatre, the more deeply ran her feelings for Septimus Crisparkle and her hope for a future she could not yet imagine. There had always been an element of the intuitive in her approach to life, and the theatre seemed to sharpen this faculty. She found herself living on her nerves, responding more with feeling than with thought in her private life.

"The theatre is a world," she said to Septimus, as they walked one night through the Monks' Vineyard, a favourite stroll of theirs and the one where Rosa and Edwin had decided to go their separate ways, "and the world is also a theatre."

"I'm not sure I know what you mean," he replied.

"No, neither do I, but I know it to be so."

Septimus Crisparkle squeezed the hand that rested across his left forearm and felt pleased with himself that somehow, without knowing why, he had gained the love of this woman and wondering whether he might prove a match for her oriental blood. She seemed to be living life more fully than he ever supposed possible following the death of her brother. He remembered those long, fruitless walks along the bank of the Thames, when they were both cloaked in sorrow. He remembered, however, her fierce determination and saw it, now, keener and with a cutting edge.

It was at this time, with autumn well advanced – berries ripened on the bushes, apples and pears on the trees – that Dick Datchery came into their lives and the detective made another, brief, appearance.

*

Samuel Warden had approached the playwright, Mr Bazzard, known in Cloisterham as Mr Datchery, before leaving Cloisterham towards the end of July, when summer was still in full swing.

He had suggested that Mr Bazzard might like to stay and fulfil his obligations to Mr Grewgious by keeping an eye on John Jasper and 'nosing around generally'. Mr Bazzard had disliked the phrase – it suggested something less than purposeful – but the idea of having two months at his disposal (and the detective had suggested this might be extended 'if things worked out' – another indelicate phrase, disliked by the playwright) appealed to him. It was a more dignified way for an artist to spend his time than slaving over wills, conveyances, receiverships and the like in a solicitor's office as a solicitor's clerk.

Moreover, the detective had taken on the task of persuading Mr Grewgious that this was an idea to be admired, something Mr Bazzard would have been loath to undertake on the grounds that it might sound like begging.

What had not appealed to him was the detective's suggestion that he should spend much of his time completing his play, *The Thorn of Anxiety*, and, worse still, that he might like to consider (meaning he should consider) making a few changes, if necessary, so that the play included a ghost scene or two, whereby 'the dead might become visible to the living'.

He remembered the detective's phrase with distaste. He had not written a ghost story but one along the classical line, involving philosophers, senators, forums and soldiers. The policeman had then gone on to suggest that 'a murder always whets the public's appetite, especially one involving love, as distinct from statesmanship'. What did he know about writing plays!

On the other hand, the detective said he had been in touch with the local theatre, suggesting that the local mayor might care to sponsor a play for the enlightenment of the townspeople over the festive season; and the local theatre manager, a vulgar man called Muggins, had welcomed the notion. Cloisterham was not London, and Mr Bazzard's play certainly deserved viewing in the metropolis but no one – as yet! – had been farsighted enough to bring it out. A provincial (not that he liked the word) premier might jolt them to their senses.

He had visited the theatre and met Muggins, and, worse still, Mrs Muggins, and he had not been impressed. His play deserved better than *bare walls, dusty scenes, mildewed clouds, heavily daubed draperies and dirty floors*; but the man was enthusiastic. There was no denying the fact. After a while, he had come to see Mr Bazzard's point of view and had talked of 'Appius Claudius' and 'Icilius' and 'Virginius' as though he knew them personally. Mr Bazzard had also been given a demonstration of combat, using the Roman short sword, by two boys who turned out to be Muggins's children.

All had seemed to be going as well as could be expected – even the *solemn donkey* of a mayor had turned up to ask how his – his! – play was going (and so the detective had been as good as his word) – until the girl turned up in September. She had not said much at first, and seemed as bemused as Mr Bazzard felt at times, but as October opened its doors to fresher winds off the Medway, she had approached him.

"Mr Warden has been to see me," she said, 'and has asked me to take an interest in your play."

It was true. Samuel Warden, hearing Helena had gone to Cloisterham for work following her brother's death, had arranged a day off-duty and travelled to the town, quietly. He had made straight for the theatre and taken Helena Landless aside. It had been a long and detailed discussion, and she knew he had drawn her into his confidence closer than anyone else and provided her with a challenge.

"You're an actress, Miss Landless. Never forget it: to beguile the time, look like the time. Others will play their part when the moment comes, but for now it is you and you alone. Even Bazzard – especially Bazzard – is to be kept in the dark."

She had seen immediately what the detective was hoping to achieve and had taken the playwright in hand. Her expression of 'interest' had been met with a snort, but she was an attractive young woman and he could see her in the part he had written.

"It is to be a Christmas play, Mr Datchery," said Helena, staying with his assumed name as they had agreed, during one of the sessions in which his work of genius was in the process of being re-drafted.

"A Christmas play! That's out of the question."

"They're very fashionable in London. Why, I hear that two years ago the Adelphi had two such plays running: *A Christmas Carol* in the February and *The Chimes* in November. We're ringing bells, Mr Datchery – out with the old and in with the new!"

For a moment, Mr Bazzard, Playwright, thought he heard the detective talking.

"We might even have snow," continued Helena, "I'm sure Mr Muggins …"

"Snow …?"

"Snow, bells, goblins and hauntings, although we may forgo the goblins, I think."

"There's no question of goblins, Miss Landless."

"No, you're right, no goblins but, perhaps a howl, the long, dismal, woeful howl of a dog – or, at least, the ghost of one."

Her excitement affected the other actors, sufficient in the case of Mr Granger for him to seek out where the title of the play had originated; Mr Granger, the son of a Norfolk Methodist, knew his Bible.

"Saint Paul's letter to the Christians in Corinth," he said, opening the battered volume he had received at his confirmation, "And lest I should be exalted above measure through the abundance of the revelations, there was given to me a thorn in the flesh, the messenger of Satan to buffet me, lest I should be exalted above measure."

"They knew the value of repetition did those who wrote the Bible," suggested the Maestro, who had joined the group around Mr Bazzard, "How are we doing, Richard? How goes the drama?"

Mr Bazzard, who shared his Christian name with his assumed character, had never been addressed by that name by anyone except his mother; he cast a dismayed look at the theatre manager, the look of one whose privacy had been invaded.

"Your case, Mr Datchery, the one you use to carry your papers, bears your name on the lid. And if I might say so, it is an extraordinarily appropriate case for the solicitor: battered and careworn but looking out for itself. We'll find a place for that in the play."

"There's no solicitor in my play."

"There will be, Richard. We shall make room for one. We cannot have that case ignored."

As October moved into November and the nights sharpened with an occasional frost, so Mr Bazzard's play took shape; not the shape he had intended but a "performable shape", as the Maestro expressed it. The friendly crowd dropped 'Mr Datchery' in favour of 'Richard' and then 'Dick'. Mr Bazzard, solicitor's clerk and playwright, and Mr Datchery, *idle buffer living upon his means*, had become one.

The action of the play moved from Rome to Verona, skipping several centuries but retaining what the Maestro called "the Italian flavour" and giving the company the chance to wear doublets and hose of which there was an ample supply in the Wardrobe. The Roman magistrate, played with a blend of sinister grumpiness by Mr Granger, had become an Italian count; the slave girl who he desired, played with "reticence, dear, reticence" by Miss Waling, had become an orphan, working as a seamstress, in love with Emile's young man, a part that elevated him from just one scene but brought about his early death when he was murdered by his own uncle, Mr Crouching, on the orders of the count who had a hold over him.

The revised play – now called *Return from the Dead* because "it's more likely to put posteriors on seats" but retaining, on Mr Datchery's insistence, its original name as a subtitle – gave scope for Mrs Muggins's to sob relentlessly as the young man's mother, Mrs Gove to attend to the young woman in the role of Nurse, Mr Muggins to appear, however briefly, as a lawyer with his case when matters needed tidying up and gave Helena Landless the role of Mysterious Stranger (a combination of apothecary, doctor and high priestess), a role that required her to address the audience directly and cast a spell over the proceedings.

The Maestro declared himself "delighted, but delighted" once the first rehearsal was underway in early December, as the nights drew in and the first snows fell upon Cloisterham, snows both artificial, in the theatre, and real, on the streets.

*

In London, Samuel Warden received news, through Helena's occasional letters, of the play's progress and was delighted. The time was approaching when others must play their part. If he remembered correctly, Lt Tartar had a yacht *lying somewhere down by Greenhithe*. If that was so, he might prove useful: Greenhithe was about halfway between London and Cloisterham. He would suggest they enjoyed another meal together at the Cheshire Cheese in Fleet Street and partake in another useful conversation.

Chapter 20

A Visit to the Theatre

Mr Crisparkle – at Mr Warden's suggestion on the day the detective spoke with Helena Landless at the theatre – had cultivated Mr Jasper's friendship throughout that autumn. It cannot be said to have been a close friendship because the Minor Canon still harboured doubts about the Choirmaster, but it was amiable enough under the circumstances, forgiveness being a keynote as far as clergyman of Septimus Crisparkle's persuasion were concerned.

Nothing at any time passed between them bearing reference to Edwin Drood. It is not likely that they ever met ... without the thoughts of each reverting to the subject – even now, with almost a year gone by. *It is not likely that they ever met, though so often, without a sensation on the part of each that the other was a perplexing secret to him. But neither ever broached the subject.*

False pretence not being in the Minor Canon's nature, he doubtless displayed openly that he would at any time have revived the subject, and even desired to discuss it. The determined reticence of Jasper, however, was not to be so approached. Impassive, moody, solitary, resolute ... he lived apart from human life. Constantly exercising an Art which brought him into mechanical harmony with others, and which could not have been pursued unless he and they had been in the nicest mechanical relations and unison, it is curious to consider that the spirit of the man was in moral accordance or interchange with nothing around him.

This indeed he had confided to the detective *on their first meeting,* and it was, perhaps this very remoteness from normal daily intercourse that the policeman wished to prevent, using the clergyman as his means. Accordingly, Mr Crisparkle took every opportunity to be convivial with the Choirmaster, even to the extent of accompanying him on several of his evenings with Mr Sapsea when the order of the day seemed to be the singing of patriotic songs.

He also coerced Mr Jasper into joining him on his long walks, taken at so brisk a pace that the Choirmaster, though a slightly younger man, was stretched to keep up with the Minor Canon. It was on one such walk that they came to Cloisterham Weir where the Rev Crisparkle had found Edwin's watch, watch chain and tie pin.

It was only when they stood by the rushing, tumbling waters as they cascaded over the posts and timbers that the clergyman stopped abruptly, realising where they were, shocked at his own insensitivity. The Choirmaster was the first to speak.

"Why have you brought me here?" he asked.

"My dear Jasper, I have no idea. I was drawn here, now, as on that first occasion," he said, hoping to allay the anger he saw in the other's face, "as though by a force beyond my understanding."

"I had hoped *nevermore to discuss this mystery with any living creature.* I am satisfied in my own mind that justice has been done and yet … and yet it has not been seen to be so. It is not enough that the wicked man should turn away from his wickedness and do that which is lawful and right, Crisparkle. It is not enough …"

He said no more but turned away from the Minor Canon and made his way back to Cloisterham, the other man trailing in his wake.

Sitting at his tea late that afternoon in the company of his mother and Helena Landless, Mr Crisparkle was less than his usual, cheerful self and it was Helena who commented on the fact, much to Mrs Crisparkle's annoyance – and yet, her satisfaction. No one, of course, would ever look after her beloved seventh son as she had done for the past thirty-five years but the young woman might – just might – prove to be almost, if only almost, suitable for the role.

The China Shepherdess had come to not only like but to admire the young woman. Naturally, her choice of the theatre as a means of occupying her time, while she sought for a husband, was not appropriate to the future wife of a clergyman, but that deficiency would be addressed when the time came. Mrs Crisparkle had seen none of the savage temper she witnessed in the brother and the young woman had the good taste never to mention him in her presence. She seemed calm, self-possessed and quiet, all three suitable attributes for a clergyman's wife; moreover, it was clear – certainly to a woman – that she loved Septimus, loved him dearly but with a proper discretion. She had come across them once whilst out walking and they had appeared close, but not too close, walking side by side, almost touching but only doing so when her son helped his – dare she use the word 'intended'? – through a gateway or down the steps that led form the Monks' Vineyard, a place that seemed to be one of their chosen walks.

"I walked with Jasper this afternoon," said the Minor Canon in response to Helena's expression of concern that he was unduly quiet, "and he seems to have sunk back into himself again. Perhaps it is to be expected: the time approaches when, a year ago, his beloved nephew disappeared. I fear the festivities of Christmastide will always hold a sour taste for our Choirmaster."

He never mentioned the weir lest it ruffled the composure of his mother, but later that evening, as he walked Helena to the theatre, where Mr Bazzard's Christmas play was approaching its dress rehearsal stage – something the Playwright had insisted upon much to the annoyance of Mr Muggins – he told her of his visit that afternoon to the place where he had found Edwin's jewellery.

"The time is not far off, Septimus," replied Helena, using his name with a familiarity that he found sent the traditional tingles along his spine, "when your little party will attend our play. If the Maestro is to be believed, Mr Sapsea accounts all his future friendships from such an attendance. Perhaps your visit will lift Mr Jasper's spirits."

There was a certain tone in her final comment that set the Minor Canon's nerves on edge: a sharpness he did not like to associate with the young woman he one day hoped to ask to be his wife. Mr Crisparkle was not one for arguments – or verbal disputes of any kind – but he could not resist pursuing the young woman's line of feeling.

"I was surprised," he said, "when, a few weeks ago, you asked to meet with Mr Jasper. He was not, I had thought, one of your favourite people."

It was a clumsy expression, but the clergyman was keen to avoid such words as 'dislike' or even 'loathe'.

"It was important I should meet and speak with him, Septimus. I felt there needed to be a harmony between us that was more than mechanical. We had acknowledged each other in the cathedral many times but not in such a way that an accord could be developed."

"It was very sensitive of you, my dear, to think in such a way about poor Jasper. He is a man with few friends and none of them close."

"Not even you, Septimus?"

"I fear not."

Mr Crisparkle left his beloved at the theatre door and turned back along the High Street, making his way towards Jasper's Gate House. It was that time of year when winter proper was not yet upon us and yet autumn was in a hurry to be gone: chilly and damp with mists that froze on the windows and evenings that pinched the cheeks with just a touch of frost, when dark clouds shrouded the sky and snow threatened to fall, a time when fires were lit in grates and the light they cast could be seen by passers-by flickering in the windows.

Septimus Crisparkle pulled his greatcoat about him and hurried home, passing under the arch of the Gate House without stopping as he had intended.

It was on such a night that his "little party" made its way to the Lyceum Theatre. The few flakes of snow that had promised a fall to the shoppers along Cloisterham High Street that afternoon failed to live up to their pledge; instead, a cold wind threatened, freezing its way onto the faces of those who had left their mufflers on the coat-stand and the hands of those who had left their gloves on the sideboard.

Helena had gone before and so Septimus Crisparkle walked with the Dean, while Mr Jasper lent his arm to Mrs Crisparkle, leading a collection of greater and lesser clergy accompanied by the cathedral faithful, which included Miss Twinkleton and Mrs Tisher and Mr and Mrs Tope. It was a distinguished party, the rook-like clothing of the clergy relieved by the warm, bright colours of their wives and their parishioners. It was not often that the two factions socialised in such a manner – indeed, the Dean remarked that it was the first time (much to his disgrace, he admitted) that he had actually visited this theatre – and there was a certain frisson of excitement in the air.

Mr Sapsea was waiting for them just inside the foyer when they arrived, eager to stamp his mark upon the occasion (HIS PLAY in HIS THEATRE in HIS CITY!): eager to stamp his mark and eager to forewarn his illustrious guests that the "audience was lively". He thought 'rough' but refrained from using a word that might mar the occasion with the truth and cast a slur on HIS PRODUCTION.

The "common people" of Cloisterham, as Mr Sapsea was wont to describe HIS CITIZENS, had an *innate love for dramatic entertainment in some form or other.* Mr Muggins knew their preferred tastes and served up a dish that satisfied their palates and left them asking for more; melodrama was high on their menu of favourites, melodrama occasionally spiced with a dash of morality designed to improve their daily lives – but only a dash, sprinkled rather than ladled on the main offering.

Mr Bazzard's play had given the Maestro some concerns in this respect, since it had been rather heavy on the spicing and rather light on the ingredients, but a few tweaks here and there – managed as effectively by the company's new young lady, Helena, as by himself – produced a dish that had proved to be an attraction of the season. It had pulled in an audience from far and wide; there was even talk of a post-Christmas extension.

Mr Muggins showed his "special guests" to their boxes, hurrying them past the doorways to the auditorium where the hoi polloi was already warming up, eager for the play to begin.

Looking down, Septimus Crisparkle saw that the theatre was full. He glanced across at John Jasper, whose presence Helena had insisted was essential, and saw the look of disapproval he had expected on the man's face: the Choirmaster was a man of *Alternate Musical Wednesdays* rather than the theatre. He looked uncomfortable and unsettled, a man about to make his dash for freedom as though he was a prisoner linked to a chain gang. The Minor Canon looked at the Dean and smiled, a gesture that was returned. The Dean's face bore a resigned expression indicating both his superiority to and tolerance of *the amusements of the people*. Mr Crisparkle was relieved: Mr Jasper would bow to the Dean's example.

Mr Muggins's prices were calculated carefully to cater for all: *the boxes a shilling, the pit sixpence, the gallery threepence. The gallery … was overflowing with occupants … faces rising one above another … to the very roof, and squeezed and jammed in, regardless of all discomforts. The company in the pit were … good-humoured,* whole families crammed together – husbands, wives, children and babies. The people of Cloisterham were gathered to see their mayor's play, unaware that he had sponsored the event.

Mr Crisparkle looked across and saw the **FAMOUS LONDON PLAYWRIGHT**, Mr Richard Datchery, (as the Maestro had expressed it on the posters) leaning across the front of his box, pushed there more by the other occupants jostling for a good view of the stage as by his own eagerness. Beside him, upright and angular, sat Mr Grewgious, resisting any pressure to bend him forward. The solicitor's face was a mask; it was impossible to read his thoughts, but the Minor Canon felt the night closing around him. This was to be the last performance before the world collapsed into the festive season: it was Christmas Eve.

There was a breathless moment as the curtain rose, and the cacophony of excitement died to a hush that was almost as deafening in its expectation. Septimus Crisparkle felt a tremor of fear for his Helena, exposed as she must be on the stage.

And it was she who came on first, the Mysterious Stranger who was to reveal all, a beautiful figure in a close-fitting gown that hugged her body and exaggerated her height with the hood of her cloak hiding her face so that she seemed almost supernatural. She moved among some bushes, bent and plucked, came forward to the edge of the stage and looked up, her eyes roving across the gallery, down to the pit and then up to the boxes. As they rested on the clerical box, she held out her arm and pointed and a few red drops fell to the ground. In her outstretched arm she held a thorn (large enough, the Maestro had ensured, to be seen from the rear of the gallery) and her hand was seen to be smeared in blood. She uttered only three words 'Sleep no more!' as she looked up at the clerical box where John Jasper sat. Somewhere backstage an owl screamed, a dog howled, and she was gone and the play proper, as far as the audience was concerned, was on its way.

Mr Granger's Count strode the stage, emphasising by his sneering tone and rough treatment of the servants that he was a villain. In the second scene, he roundly abused his Wife (played coweringly in a second role by Mrs Muggins) indicating that he was also a scoundrel. After some business with a whip, Mr Granger made his way into the town (a splendidly painted backdrop) ostensibly to order a new doublet, really to force himself upon Miss Waling's Seamstress. The third scene took the audience, now hissing favourably, to the Costumiers (where Mrs Muggins again presided, this time haughtily) appropriately adorned as 'Costumier to the Famous'. Here, the interest fell upon Emile's Young Man and Miss Waling's Orphan Seamstress. They were clearly in love; the balcony (insisted upon by the Maestro) gave ample evidence of this fact and Emile's passionate speeches, delivered first on his knees and then standing as the animation overcame him, left no room for doubt. Mr Granger, from the wings, witnessed this love-making and showed his contempt with an aside to the audience regarding 'spitting a body' and a 'rapier's point' that was lost on most of the audience but lifted the spirits of those who knew its origins. Several further scenes – wherein the Count upbraided Emile, attempted to force his desires on Miss Waling and consorted with Mrs Muggins as the Costumier – completed the first act.

The appetite of the audience – with the possible, although not definite, exception of the clerical boxes – was now whetted: they thought they knew what was going to happen, the excitement lay in how. The second act opened with a scene that left them in no doubt: the Count was seen badgering Mr Crouching, the young man's Uncle. He had some hold over the man – although its nature would not be revealed until the final act – and was in the business of blackmailing him into murdering Emile, thus releasing the orphan Seamstress to be wooed and won by the count.

Here, the play gathered some of the threads of Mr Datchery's original together; here there were not simply murderers but plotters. It suddenly had the smell of Rome about it and the names 'Appius' and 'Claudius' and 'Brutus' were whispered in one of the clerical boxes. The audience in the pit became unsettled. They had expected the Count, a recognisable villain, to murder the Young Man; they had not expected the deed to be done by the Young Man's own Uncle. A short act was the second – only five scenes – but one that turned the tide of the play and bore it fiercely towards its denouement.

Mr Datchery looked down upon the enraptured audience and passed a smug glance to Mr Grewgious. The solicitor read his thoughts as he had read them many times before: '*This blockhead is my master! A fellow who couldn't write a tragedy on pain of death, and whom will never have one dedicated to him with the most complimentary congratulations on the high position he has taken in the eyes of posterity*'. Mr Grewgious did not move or return the look: as one of the two people who had been taken into the detective's confidence (although not as completely as Helena) he was waiting.

Only Helena, as the Mysterious Stranger, knew what awaited him and the rest of the audience – and, more importantly, why. She had appeared briefly, as a hooded figure showing only one arm and a hand, bustling along a bench seeking among bottles of potions, during the third act, pausing only once to stare up at one of the boxes; but it was at the end of the penultimate one that she came into her own. The final scene of act four opened in what might have been a tomb. A few knowing glances were exchanged in the clerical boxes and the Dean's 'Romeo' was mouthed to Miss Twinkleton's 'Juliet'; but there were both to be surprised.

As the lid of the sarcophagus was pulled back, Emile emerged, a shrouded figure, his grave clothes covered in dust. Septimus Crisparkle felt his mother's hand upon his arm, glanced towards her, then back to the stage and down at the audience in the pit. Was the Young Man a ghost or was he risen from the dead? The question was in everyone's eyes; and then Helena's voice rang out: 'He was placed, living, in the tomb!' Since no one else was on stage at that moment, it was unsure to whom she was talking, unless it was the audience or the man who sat transfixed by her gaze in the clerical box. As Emile staggered from his grave and looked about him, the Mysterious Stranger reached out and the lights faded, only to come up again, a few moments that seemed like hours later, on the opening scene of act five: quiet and domesticated as a wedding feast was being prepared by Mrs Muggins in her role as the Young Woman's Nurse.

Act five was brief, three scenes only: the second being the wedding feast as Mr Granger's Count gets his way and weds Miss Waling's Young Woman, despite her protests, and the third allowing the Maestro to arrive, as the solicitor commissioned to tidy up the Young Woman's legal affairs, with Mr Datchery's battered and careworn case, and allowing Mr Muggins to share the curtain call.

But it was in the second scene, with the wedding breakfast in full swing, where the audience held its breath. Speeches were delivered, applause given, the wedding night anticipated, musicians played, guests danced, and Emile's Young Man appeared at the table, sitting in the bridegroom's place. Miss Waling started, gasping and holding her throat, her husband of a few hours, the Count, staggered back, and the Young Man's Uncle screamed. The guests looked on aghast. 'What have you done?' the Count yelled to the Uncle and he, the murderer, fell to his knees, fear painted all over his face, crying 'Does he rise again?' Mayhem followed, with the guests, fearing their host was mad, scattering and the Young Man approaching his Uncle who grovelled on the floor as he was handed the Mysterious Stranger's thorn. Swords were drawn and bodies left amid the ruins of the feast, lights faded, a backdrop fell as did the snow, in acknowledgement of the season, as Emile and Miss Waling found themselves in a street in Verona, winter upon them.

Had the Young Man returned from the dead? Was he a ghost or would the young couple live happily ever after? The final scene put the audience's mind to rest, as the Maestro intended. "Send them away happy, Richard," he had said to Mr Datchery, "and they'll come back again." It was Christmas, after all, a time for families to come together and be joyful. Taking her curtain calls – and there were five of them, such was the appreciation of the audience – Helena Landless threw back the hood of her cloak and looked up at John Jasper. She held his eye, as she had done with such care on her two previous appearances, and an accord was strengthened between them.

The unexplained always perplexes the thoughtful mind rather than one content that matters should be settled comfortably in everyone but the villain's favour. Walking home towards the cathedral, talk among the clerical party was of the thorn and its significance. Helena remained silent, knowing how annoyed Mr Datchery had been when his original epilogue had been cut to guarantee the happy ending, while the Dean wondered whether the thorn might appear in some sermon, later in the year certainly, after Christmas was past.

Having enjoyed their evening together the party dispersed their several ways, still chattering, Mr Crisparkle with his mother and Helena being the last to bid John Jasper good night as they made their way towards Minor Canon Corner, leaving the Choirmaster alone at his Gate House.

And so, he went up the postern stair.

He entered his rooms *softly with his key,* and found *his fire still burning.* From a *locked press* he took *a peculiar-looking pipe, which he filled – but not with tobacco – and, having adjusted the contents of the bowl, very carefully, with a little instrument*, he reached for a taper from a jug on the mantlepiece and lit his pipe. He inhaled deeply, walked across to his piano and sat on the stool. He was not a man who believed in ghosts, but the play was on his mind and he sat for some time, *a fixed and deep attention* marking his strong features.

He was relaxing under the effect of the opium when he heard a repeated tap at the window that overlooked the path to the cathedral, a tap such as fingernails might make when striking a hard surface. His own hand had made the sound many times on the piano lid when he sat playing with a tune. It came again: tap, tap and tap-tap-tap.

John Jasper walked to the window that overlooked the path to the cathedral precincts. He stood, looking down, his pipe cooling in his hand, for some time, and saw a figure emerge from under the archway of the Gate House. It was the very same greatcoat and top hat and boots – the very boots he had urged his nephew to pull off when he had arrived, wet and cold, back in Cloisterham to see his fiancé, so long ago now! John Jasper watched, unbelieving, his nerves shredded, as Edwin Drood made his quiet way towards the cathedral and its graveyard.

Chapter 21

A Cry is Heard

John Jasper tottered back from the window, an unnatural sweat breaking immediately from his hands, face and neck. He grasped control of himself as he almost fell against the piano and sat for what seemed ages on the stool before rushing over to the locked press to refill his pipe. He made for the fire, grabbed a taper and lit his pipe for a second time: better to give himself up to the spectres of the night than face those that waited for him in the precincts of the cathedral.

His mind must be conspiring against him; he had felt at the mercy of others all evening. The normal flow of his life had been disrupted. People had appeared who had no place in Cloisterham; the Landless woman several months ago, apparently recovered from the death of her scoundrel of a brother and, tonight, the solicitor, Grewgious, in the opposite box. Why had he appeared as though from nowhere, and why was he sitting with the playwright, Datchery?

He had the 'all-overs', as that woman in London called them. A pipe or two used to suffice. He would drift away, his dreams exotic, on a journey of pleasurable excitement, but sometimes it was the jitters that carried him along. Nothing to hope for, no compromise with his existence, drove him inwards to the demons in his heart. He drew deeply on the second pipe. He had rationed himself, at first – a pipe or two simply for the relief it gave – but now his habit had become a compulsion, his need a desperation.

John Jasper heard the gurgling sound he knew so well and then the *brief rattle* that told him the smoke was over; *the spirits of ten thousand demons stirred to life.* What was a ghost to him? And that apparition, the spirit of his darling boy, Ned? Nothing would convince him that Ned had returned. He would seek it out, this phantom. He had sought such spirits before after leaving the den in Shadwell. He had wandered the streets of the metropolis, noting the business and machinations of its citizens in the marketplace; he had visited art galleries and the opera houses, his mind absorbing vivid impressions of this otherworld, the impressions that inspired the artist. Coleridge had written his most masterful poetry when lifted by the drug: 'The souls did from their bodies fly – they fled to bliss or woe! And every soul it passed me by, Like the whizz of my crossbow!'

John Jasper chuckled to himself and then *burst into fits of laughter, placing his head down on his arms* that rested on the piano lid *to have his laugh out.* Souls! 'He shall save his soul alive': the words he had heard so many times came back to him. He shivered and, thinking of making his leave, realized he had not even removed his coat on arriving home, so keen had he been for that first pipe. He went a second time to the window that overlooked the cathedral precincts. Nothing moved out there. How come the tapping on the window? He would seek out the truth. He reached for his *large black scarf* and gloves, locked the door *softly with his key* and went down the postern stair. From a niche in the wall at the bottom he removed and lit the lantern he kept there once the nights grew darker and lit it.

Under the arch of the Gate House, only a slight fall of snow had drifted in, but it was enough to show a trail of footprints coming from the High Street and leading on to the cathedral. The winter night was cold and still. The new moon cast no light, but the faint dusting of snow picked up the glare thrown by John Jasper's lantern. Was it a shadow that flitted by or his imagination? He held the lantern high to spread the light it gave but saw nothing. A boy, perhaps? One of those savages from the Travellers' Twopenny? He cared not. He would not be conspired against by his perceptions or his fantasies; he would put his mind at rest. Tomorrow was Christmas Day and he looked forward to the usual cathedral services.

The Precincts were *never particularly well lighted* but tonight the snow gave some sense of his passage and the trail of footprints were clear. One person had walked this way, and not long before. He looked back; no one followed him. The walker had passed this side of the cathedral without halting; the footsteps were purposeful. At the corner of the west door, John Jasper paused again: this time to look up at the high elms that formed a line from the castle and bordered the old moat. Dark they were even against the dark sky, bearing the tattered nests of the rooks. Not a branch moved, so motionless and noiseless was the night.

He turned again and looked back at his home. Beyond it was the main street of Cloisterham and from there came the faint sounds of revellers, but they were faint and only served to accentuate the silence of the cathedral grounds. He suddenly remembered another night, a wilder one than this, when the streets were empty, the wind tore at the shutters and rattled the latches; but that was a long time ago, another world and another man.

Edwin would not have returned, would he? Once, he thought his nephew might have done so, on the night the solicitor told him of the broken engagement, the night he had collapsed in front of the man. Then, it had given him hope that his dear boy, distraught at the loss of his love, had gone abroad, perhaps to Egypt, where the engineering post awaited him. But he would have written after time had passed and would not have returned without letting him know – him, first of all, so close had they been.

He gazed back again and saw that the fire in his room was running low, judging by the faintness of its glow from the window, and then turned to follow the footsteps that led through the graves and tombs to the south of the cathedral. The prints were scattered here, not because the walker had stumbled but because it was grass underfoot and the tread was less clear to the eye. John Jasper followed closely, his eyes fixed firmly on the ground, although he knew where the footprints must lead, if they were to lead him anywhere. And he was right: the walker had stopped at the small door that opened onto the south quire transept and down to the crypt.

It was then he realised he had forgotten his keys, the ones that were *not much used* but had proved beneficial at times. Idly, without too much hope, before returning to his rooms, where – once settled – he knew he would not venture from again that night, John Jasper reached out for the latch, turned it and the door, apparently unlocked and awaiting him, opened, and he stepped into the blackness of the cathedral.

It was a place that chilled the marrow at the best of times: *gloomy shadows ... deepen in corners, damps ... rise from stone ... grey, murky and sepulchral*. At this moment, the worst of times as far as John Jasper was concerned, it seemed grimmer than ever as though the very silence was a knell summoning him.

The lantern shook in his hands as he closed the door behind him, and its light cast jerky shadows where none had existed. It was a place he knew well, and that should hold no fears for him, and yet it held many. He tried to remember those times when the choir had lifted his voice in song and praise, when he had *astonished his fellows by his melodious power*. He recalled Crisparkle commenting only last year – why this very day, Christmas Eve! – on his skill and harmony. "Beautiful! Delightful! You could not have so outdone yourself, I hope, without being wonderfully well.' He was honoured, then, with golden opinions from all sorts of people.

Now, he stood alone in the cathedral, the very place where it was thought by all who knew him that he had found his niche in life; but the very place that had driven him to *carve demons out of his own heart*, as once the monks had carved them *out of the stalls and seats and desks*.

He walked to the top of the steps that led down to the crypt. There were no footprints there, no trail to follow but he knew he must go that way: it beckoned to him. The steps were rugged, and he descended carefully, fearful of a fall, but knew not why he feared. Had he not been here before? The moonlight had *struck in at the groined windows* on that other occasion – *windows bare of glass, the broken frames* just visible where the snow settled on them.

He heard a fluttering sound and thought it must be a bird or two seeking shelter from the cold. John Jasper paused, held his lantern high and listened; but there was only the numbing cold and the silence. Nothing moved in the crypt; the only sound was that of his own breathing and the slight rasp of the lantern as it swung on its handle.

The crypt was vast, and he had been glad of that once, but now it seemed like the measureless time of eternity calling to him. He felt his way along the lanes between the heavy pillars that supported the roof and remembered Durdles tapping the walls, knowing who was buried where and how long it had been since their internment. The place was as untidy as ever: the dust heaps and earth mounds, the tools of the stonemason's trade, a few baskets cast aside. John Jasper was looking for the paved area, beneath which some of the dead were buried. He remembered the stone slabs; he remembered … he remembered how they had been lifted, but suddenly lost any sense of why he was here. What phantom of the night had summoned him? Was he called here to put his mind at rest or to discover what he knew in his heart must be hidden where only he might find it?

He pulled a shovel from one of the mounds of earth as he passed. He would need such a tool when the time came. When the time came! *'How did I come here!'* was his first thought as he stopped. *'Why did I come here!'* was his second. He stood, transfixed to the place, listening intently. The stone slab was at his feet and raise it he must. John Jasper placed the lantern to one side, eased the shovel under the slab and prised it upwards.

It was easy, then, to lift it to one side and place it beyond … beyond what? He could not frame the word, let alone allow it to pass his lips. Earth, but a year old, clung to the underside of the slab. He raised another and another until a patch of earth, the length and more of a human body was exposed at his feet.

A sharp smell assailed his nostrils and beneath and within it the smell of death. He knew what he must find there if he chose to clear the earth. He was certain, as certain could be, why the phantom had led him to this … grave! There, he had said it! Dare he move aside the soil? Dare he not! John Jasper knelt to his task, a task ordained for him as Lay Precentor and Choirmaster, as the appointed Guardian of Edwin Drood. He must admit, at last, the fact that his *dear boy is murdered … he was murdered that night* and that he was pledged to *nevermore discuss this mystery with any human creature … that he would fasten the crime of the murder of his dear dead boy upon the murderer and that he devoted himself to his destruction.* The words he had written in his diary and shared only with the Rev Crisparkle came back to him as John Jasper fell to his knees and began, handful by handful. to clear the soil from above what he now accepted must be the corpse of his nephew.

He had moved no more than a small mound when he heard the footsteps approaching: sensed rather than heard for the hush of the crypt dominated his mind. He struggled to his feet and reached for the lantern, his only light, his only security in this place of the dead. In its glare he saw the figure. It was the same one he had seen walk out from under the archway of the Gate House. But it couldn't be! Edwin Drood was dead! There was no doubt of that fact; it was a fact carved on his heart. Of all men alive, he – John Jasper – must know that to be true for he alone was the one who had suffered most when his ward disappeared; he was the one who had searched until exhaustion overcame him. Through the misery of this certainty he had lived for so many nights that the belief must be a fact.

The figure stopped within a few feet of the choirmaster and looked straight into his eyes. John Jasper raised the lantern and leaned forward. The ghost – if a ghost it was – stood with its left side towards him and with its left hand reaching inside its coat as though to retrieve some object the phantom held dear. There was a calmness about the figure, a stance, a bodily expression such as one might hold if, at last, a resolution had been attained. And there no mistaking the three-quarter length greatcoat and the hat whose brim cast a shadow over the face. John Jasper raised the lantern just a fraction higher, his courage lifted, to examine that face.

As he did so, the figure removed its hand from inside its coat, extended its arm and pointed to the grave. It was not so much the gesture as the memory of the gesture that terrified John Jasper: a memory he could not quite recall that irritated the man. The first effects of the opium were leaving him; exhilaration was turning to tiredness and tiredness was imbued with anger as the choirmaster attempted to keep control of himself.

The figure's outstretched arm did not falter, and much as he wanted to do so the choirmaster dare not look into the eyes of the phantom, eyes shielded still by the brim of the hat. He raised his lantern just so far and held it as steady as his shaking hand allowed; but this action only lit the arm further and he was forced to look downward to where the grave lay uncovered.

"Who are you?" he heard a voice shout out, and realised it was his own.

The sound released him from his immobility and the question was followed by a long, drawn-out cry that rent the air, a cry that was carried from the crypt as the choirmaster's neck muscles tightened even further and he gave vent to feelings stored and battened down for so long. The cry, no longer a ghost of one, tore through the fabric of the cathedral, echoing to its very roof.

Giving his wife's dog a final walk in the Cathedral Close before retiring, Cloisterham's mayor, Mr Sapsea, heard the cry and the little dog let out *a long, dismal, woeful howl, such as a dog gives when a person's dead*: a real howl, no longer the ghost of one. Mr Sapsea looked up, amazed and affronted. HIS CATHEDRAL had no business emitting such a sound at any time, let alone on the night of Christmas Eve. Mr Sapsea's sense of proprietorship as regards the cathedral was assaulted as keenly as his senses, and he made his way to the west door where he thought he might assert himself. Finding this locked, he pursued his anger around to the south side of the cathedral and the little door that led to the south quire aisle and the stairs of the crypt

Mr Durdles, too, was taken aback by the sound. As was his usual practice when celebrating the Lord's birth, he was doing what he considered *correct by the season, in giving it the welcome it had a right to expect* and was asleep on the winding staircase of the great tower. He had sought sanctuary there, having fully lubricated his prayer muscles, when he was *set upon by the town-boys ... at their worst.*

He woke with a start, clutched his bottle of brandy tightly, lest it should fall from his grasp when he was descending, and made his unsteady way to the foot of the stairs.

Opening the already unlocked door and leaning heavily against the wall, he peered across the south quire aisle towards the open door of the crypt and saw the choirmaster staggering up the rugged steps, a lantern swinging in one hand while the other grasped the iron rail to prevent himself from falling. It was a twice-ghastly sight: Durdles, only partly-conscious, his drunken face a mottled blend of yellow and purple, and Jasper, his greatcoat askew, the long black scarf dangling from his neck so that he almost tripped on it, his hands and clothes bearing the earthly marks of the grave, flushed and sweating, his tortured expression showing every signs of nausea and depression, looking wildly about him in the darkness.

"Where is my nephew?" he cried, ferociously.

"He ain't here," replied the stonemason, gruffly, his voice blurred with brandy.

John Jasper tumbled across the aisle, pounced on Durdles and, *seizing him with both hands by the throat*, shoved him violently against the wall. The stonemason clutched at the hands that choked him.

"The keys," cried Jasper, "The key to the gate that lets me pass to the staircase of the great tower."

Durdles fumbled among his pockets for the key confided to him, and Jasper, releasing his grip on the man's throat, snatched it, threw the stonemason violently to the floor and made his way up the steps *that emerged on the cathedral level to a passage at the side of the chancel.*

As he vanished, two men appeared from the shadows of the Crossing steps. The first – slight of build, but fast on his feet and quiet in his manner – moved swiftly to the open doorway of the tower; the other – broad of shoulder and robust in his movements – attended to the stonemason, lifting him from the ground and sitting him in a nearby pew.

"We must follow him – and quickly," said the first man, the detective, coming across to the other, "He must not be allowed to reach the top of the tower before us. It is imperative we stop him."

The second man seemed to hesitate, a concerned look on his face as he peered towards the door of the crypt with those *far-seeing blue eyes* that *watched the world without flinching.*

"I will go alone, then," said the detective, "Follow when you can."

But the sailor was spared his indecision when, at that moment, the small door through which John Jasper had entered the cathedral opened and the Minor Canon appeared with Helena Landless. A hurried consultation followed, which led to the detective and the sailor, the latter now leading, making their way up the staircase of the great tower and the Minor Canon retracing his steps to the graveyard, while Helena Landless walked towards the crypt.

Lt Tartar took the first few flights of steps in leaps and bounds, his sureness of foot enabling him to outpace the detective and gain on John Jasper soon after the choirmaster reached the iron gate. He had it unlocked and opened when the sailor grabbed hold of one of the bars and yanked it backwards bringing the choirmaster with it. But John Jasper was a man possessed of one ambition: that of bringing the murderer of his dear boy to justice. Colliding with the sailor, he struck out, catching Lt Tartar under the chin to send him spiralling down the stone steps. The sailor had the presence of mind, however, to snatch the keys from the choirmaster's grasp and he held onto these firmly as his back and legs took the brunt of the fall. When he came to rest, Samuel Warden lifted him from the ground and looked up at the choirmaster.

"Give yourself up, sir. It will be for the best."

"Not until I've found the man I seek," replied John Jasper, turning, running back up through the gate and slamming it shut.

"I have the keys," said Lt Tartar, breathless and bruised, "He cannot prevent us following him."

And they did, *up the winding staircase of the great tower, toilsomely, turning and turning, and lowering their heads to avoid the stairs above, or the rough stone pivot around which they twisted.* Samuel Warden had lit the lantern he carried *by drawing from the cold hard wall a spark of that mysterious fire which lurks in everything, and, guided by this speck, they clambered up amid the cobwebs and dust.*

Ahead, always just ahead but his flight signalled by the glare from his lantern, John Jasper ran and clambered. It was hard work and the opium, now inducing the desire for sleep, caused him to breathe heavily; he drew each precious gasp into his lungs with difficulty and a stabbing pain. He felt nauseous, his pulse was racing, and the sweat lay on his face and hands like drops of rain, but with no beneficial cooling power. As he ascended, the choirmaster began to tremble.

The way lay *through strange places. Twice or thrice they emerged into level low-arched galleries, whence they could look down into the nave* and the glare of their lanterns *showed the dim angels' heads upon the corbels of the roof, seeming to watch their progress. Anon, they turned into narrower and* steeper staircases, and the night air began to blow upon them, and the chirp of some startled jackdaw or frightened rook preceded the heavy beating of wings in a confined space, and the beating down of dust and straw upon their heads.

At last ... they looked down on Cloisterham and on its sanctuaries of the dead at the tower's base. John Jasper leaned against the parapet of the tower and eyed his pursuers as they emerged to face him.

"Of all others, I have avoided you," he cried, raising the lantern and shaking it towards the detective.

The light snowfall had settled and there was little but slush underfoot, and the going was unsteady as Samuel Warden moved slowly towards his quarry, the sailor close on his heels.

"I have pursued him this far," persisted the choirmaster, "You shall not stop me now. I will avenge my dear boy."

"We have much to talk about, Mr Jasper, Choirmaster, and I'm sure we can find a cosier place than this. Let's be comfortable."

John Jasper looked at the detective as though the man was a lunatic. The choirmaster had experienced visions like no other; *he had travelled where ten thousand scimitars flashed in the sunlight, and thrice ten thousand dancing-girls strew flowers ... followed by white elephants caparisoned in count- less gorgeous colours, and infinite in number and attendants.* Where had this man travelled and what visions could they share?

The cold on the roof of the tower hung about them and the light wind blew the odd flake of snow around their heads as the three men waited for each other to make a move – any move at all. Only their lanterns relieved the dark of the night.

"He must not be allowed to escape," said the choirmaster, trembling as the shakes overcame him, "I have come so far. He cannot escape me."

Lt Tartar stepped to one side of the detective, ready to rush forward should the choirmaster do what he knew the detective feared and throw himself from the tower in pursuit of the very devil who haunted his sleep and plagued his days. A sudden rush and he could grab the choirmaster, but he had several feet to cover and the madman – for that is how the lieutenant saw the other – would turn and be gone, off the tower and into the air.

John Jasper looked wildly about him as though bewildered that the man he sought was nowhere to be seen. He rushed along one side of the tower and looked over. His quarry was not there. Above him rose the spire of the cathedral. He gazed up as though he thought the criminal might be climbing, ever towards Heaven: but nothing. Behind him, the two who pursued his search for justice approached, and the choirmaster, Edwin's guardian, climbed onto the parapet.

Lt Tartar was on him before he could cast a second leg over and hauled him back. They struggled, but the lieutenant, although the stronger man by far, was no match for the desperate choirmaster. John Jasper shoved the sailor from him for a second time and ran on.

"*Delusive hopes … I give to the winds*," he cried.

They were on the north side of the tower, now, above the 'Devil's door' where the evil spirit that lies within the child might be driven out at baptism.; but Jasper's evil spirit was not so driven. He pressed on to the west side of the tower, heading for the south where they had emerged on the roof and where the detective would be waiting. Lt Tartar reached him for a third time, pulled him to the ground and set his knee onto the choirmaster's chest. *They rolled on the ground together* in the slush of the fallen snow, the sailor *heedless of the blows that showered upon him, wrenching his hands tighter and tighter about the* choirmaster's greatcoat until the man lay quiet, apparently beaten and subdued. The sailor, having brought many a drunken man to order, did not loosen his grip but called to the detective.

The shout roused John Jasper, who launched himself into another frenzied assault on the sailor, twisting from under him and pressing his knee into Lt Tartar's throat. Unable to breath, the sailor loosened his hold and reached for the knee that choked him. The choirmaster delivered a blow to his opponent's head, leapt clear and made for the parapet.

Over which, at that moment, a head and hands appeared: it was the Minor Canon, the Muscular Christian *whose trots* so often *ended in a charge at his favourite fragment of ruin, carried at storm, without a pause for breath.* Usually it was the castle walls that tested his skills, but tonight it was the arches and columns, the blind arcades, the carved stonework, the corbels and gargoyles, the ornamented canopies, the niches and recesses, the pediments and pilasters, the very rooftiles of the cathedral and, finally, the parapet of the tower. He had eyed them often, always needing a reason to test himself further; tonight, his moment had come.

He emerged not far from John Jasper, out of breath and with his hands scraped to bleeding. The choirmaster floundered, seemingly mistaking him for someone else in the dark.

"You," he gasped, "How can you climb back? I will have you this time."

He charged at the clergyman, but Mr Crisparkle's boxing days served him in good stead. He dodged, weaved, and *propped* Jasper *by the elbow with a strong hand (in a strictly scientific manner, worthy of his morning trainings).* Lt Tartar retrieved the lamp, which had fallen in the struggle, leaving it only necessary for Detective Sergeant Warden to have a quiet word concerning the orderly manner in which the purpose of the evening had been accomplished.

Having, once more, gained the south quire aisle, the foursome found Helena comforting Rosa, who had now discarded the attire she wore as 'Edwin' and Mr Sapsea, wondering why HIS CHOIRMASTER seemed so subdued, so unlike himself, so 'un-English' in his deportment. In truth, the mayor's observations – freed from their usual concerns with his own importance – were accurate: John Jasper was no longer himself.

The four young people made their way to their various places of residence: Lt Tartar and Rosa Bud to his yacht moored off the marina at Cloisterham – where, it should be stressed, she enjoyed a cabin of her own – and Mr Crisparkle and Helena to 1, Minor Canon Corner.

On his way with Mr Jasper to Cloisterham gaol, Mr Warden was joined by a young boy with jagged teeth, wondering whether he "had done right". He had; his years of stone throwing perfected to such a degree that he could hurl gravel in such a way as to tap, tap and tap-tap-tap on a window without breaking it, giving anyone inside the idea that it was a hand tapping.

"You were instrumental, my son, in bringing the evening to a satisfactory conclusion," said the detective, "But for you, Mr Jasper would not have found what he was looking for and the Rev Crisparkle would not have arrived in time to assist him. Take this shilling, by way of my thanks – just for the moment – and trot off back to the cathedral, where Mr Durdles should have finished locking up. I'm sure he would wish you to stone him home tonight."

Deputy made no objection to the term 'my son', and shot off chanting to himself:

"Widdy widdy wen!

I – ket – ches – Im – out – ar – ter – ten …"

It had been a long day for all concerned, a long day that followed many months of planning. Despite what he knew must lie ahead, Samuel Warden felt quite pleased with himself as he walked arm in arm with John Jasper under the Gate House arch and so on to the High Street; and he felt entitled to hum his favourite carol, 'In the bleak midwinter'. Hearing the sound, on key but lacking tone, John Jasper joined in singing the words; never had he *sung with such skill and harmony*, astonishing the detective with his *melodious power*.

Chapter 22

John Jasper Gets His Man

Christmas Day in Cloisterham and the choirmaster indisposed. The Dean trusts that he will soon recover from whatever ails him, and Mr Crisparkle, who is at the early morning service with Helena and Mrs Crisparkle, assures him that matters are in hand.

Always a joyous morning, the one morning of the Christian year when the whole congregation seem to be in good voice as they welcome the Lord into the world. The choir miss Mr Jasper's lead – his fine, robust voice could always be relied upon to carry the anthem – but nevertheless they sing Creation's story and hope for brighter visions to beam afar in the coming year.

It is a bright, crisp day. The sun shines from a blue sky and the whole world seems ready to give back the song that once the angels sang, as the worshippers gather outside the old cathedral to wish each other the best of the season.

Miss Twinkleton and Mrs Tisher attend as usual before retiring to the Nuns' House for a quiet day filled with romantic memories of Christmases past and a *certain season at Tunbridge Wells*; the former lady is pleased to see her one-time pupil, Rosa Bud, at the service and her heart flutters when she sees the young woman's hand on the arm of Lt Tartar..

Mr Sapsea graces his place of worship with his presence; it will be a lonely Christmas for him without his wife, now passed on these two years, but he will visit her tomb in the afternoon so that he may remember the times she was able to look up to him.

Mr and Mrs Tope are in a bit of a hurry but not so much that they fail to pay the respects due to the season; besides, Mrs Tope was up early, and the important event of the day is in hand. She passes a few words with Mr Warden, who attends with Mr Grewgious and Mr Datchery and sits quietly at the back. She notices her three gentlemen part company when they leave: Mr Grewgious and Mr Datchery taking what has all the appearances of a solemn walk to the Esplanade and Mr Warden what she describes to Mr Tope as "a hurried stroll somewhere else". Mr Tope is unable to enlighten her as to where and they walked home in marital silence.

Mr Warden is in point of fact looking for Mr Durdles; there are certain matters to discuss of a forensic nature regarding the crypt and the detective is eager to commandeer (or at least restrain) the keys he borrowed the previous night. The investigation is well in hand but has far to go, and the detective is only too aware of the truth of his mother's well-worn aphorism regarding a cup and a lip. Moreover, Durdles's house is close to the Travellers' Twopenny, where he might find the young savage, Deputy: a savage Mr Warden is eager to tame for the boy's own sake as well as that of society.

Their greetings exchanged, the congregation eventually disperses, in dribs and drabs and families, for time is hastening on and Christmas dinner is yet to be brought to fruition.

Mrs Crisparkle is excited in the extreme: so many times, she has shared her day alone with Septimus but now she has Helena and, also, Lt Tartar and Rosa Bud. It will make a fine gathering. The lieutenant's man, Lobley, has been invited but – as the lieutenant explained – Lobley is a man of the sea: happy in his own company and the company of his ship but awkward on land; indeed, so used is he to the roll of the sea that Mr Lobley has the tendency to sway and sometimes tumble when ashore.

The China Shepherdess bustles about, in her element and wishing for no help in the preparation of her repast. Two geese roasted, one larded, hold pride of place on Mrs Crisparkle's table, accompanied by a chine of beef and a grand salad, preceded by stewed broth of mutton marrow bones, and followed by plum pudding and custard. It is, by the standards of the day, a modest feast, but Mr Crisparkle's father had insisted it be so, bearing in mind the nature of his calling; and Mrs Crisparkle has always adhered to her husband's wishes even after his passing. Since that day, however, the Christmas cracker has made its appearance and her guests fall about laughing as the crackers explode and the bonbons fall out.

Mr Warden, having concluded his visit to Mr Durdles, who is still sleeping off the celebrations of the night before, is seated at Mrs Tope's table with Deputy. The detective declined the offer to join the festivities at Minor Canon Corner in favour of sharing a Christmas meal with Mr and Mrs Tope and her other guests, Mr Grewgious and Mr Datchery. The detective has several reasons for this decision, not least of these being a further attempt to civilize the young savage, one that he considers somewhat less than 'noble'.

How the policeman received the invitation, Mrs Tope is unsure (she couldn't remember asking him) but he is good company and appreciative of her culinary efforts.

The invitation seemed to come about when she discovered that Mr Grewgious is in the habit of spending Christmas day with Mr Datchery, in his former guise as Mr Bazzard, who – it turns out – is no other than the solicitor's clerk and the son of a Norfolk farmer who always sends a turkey to the solicitor for the festive season. They are accustomed to having it boiled with a celery sauce but fall in readily with Mrs Tope's suggestion that it be roasted and stuck with olives; after all, it is not every year a turkey adorns Mrs Tope's table and that alone will provide a conversation piece for many months to come.

She is pleased to see her guests tucking in, especially the boy who seems never to have eaten in his life before and is able to fulfil the task without recourse to cutlery. The pottage of capon goes down a treat and nothing is left of her steak pie or boiled partridge by the time they reach the mince pies (a speciality of her house) and custard.

It is as they sit, replete to bursting, that Mr Grewgious speaks for the first time since sitting down to eat, for he considers himself a man of *no conversational powers whatever*.

"And now," he says, "I drink to our gracious hostess, Mrs Tope. I think I can say, without offending Mr Bazzard, that this meal is the finest we have enjoyed together. Gentlemen, I devote a bumper to Mrs Tope."

"I follow you, sir," says Mr Bazzard, "and I pledge you!"

"Mrs Tope!" replies Samuel, looking at Deputy, who responds likewise, much to the detective's pleasure. "And if I might pledge a second toast," he continues, "to Mr Bazzard, whose play we enjoyed so much last night, and who has been so instrumental in securing the success of our time in Cloisterham. I devote a bumper to Mr Bazzard."

"Mr Bazzard!" is the cry of all to the resident playwright who seems pleased enough and is no doubt wondering whether somebody in the city might hear of his masterpiece and consider *bringing it out*.

In the silence that falls, Mrs Tope comments that she misses Mr Jasper, who she has always seen to at Christmas, but understands that he is out of sorts. She will be only too pleased to put up a plate for him, when Mr Warden offers to tempt his appetite.

On his arrival at Cloisterham gaol, the dish nicely covered with a gingham cloth and still warm from being over Mrs Tope's stove, the detective finds the choirmaster has no appetite at all.

The Duty-Inspector is reluctant to inform Mr Warden that the prisoner has refused all food, including the special Christmas breakfast (a made dish of chicken in puff pastry) and appears to be somewhere between life and death. Dazed and unresponsive, John Jasper sits on his bench, in a state Samuel thinks he has heard described as cataleptic.

The following morning, Boxing Day early, the detective, discreet as ever, commissions Joe's omnibus and accompanies the choirmaster to Maidstone gaol, where Mr Jasper is to stay for a time. He goes very quietly, looking back at his Gate House as though never expecting to see it again.

During this time, he is visited often by the Rev Crisparkle and Helena: the clergyman because of his vocation, Helena to strengthen her accord with the choirmaster, hopefully.

To Helena, the very place is terrifying and becomes more so, rather than less, on each visit: *the low, massive doors … looking as if they were made for the express purpose of letting people in, and never letting them out again; the dark building on one side of the yard, in which is kept the gibbet with all its dreadful apparatus; the thick door, plated with iron and mounted with spikes; the small, grated windows; the dismal cells.*

On arrival, each time, they are ushered into a small office where they wait until the officer who is to chaperone them can be found. He then leads them into another room, even smaller, which contains no furniture other than a little desk on which resides a visitors' book they are obliged to sign. From this they pass through a *heavy oaken gate, bound with iron* and *studded with nails … guarded by a turnkey*. This door opens onto a *flight of narrow steps* that terminate *in a narrow and dismal stone passage* and leads to *the different yards, through a number of tortuous and intricate windings, guarded in their turn by huge gates and gratings, whose appearance is sufficient to dispel the slightest hope of escape. Every gate that is unlocked for them to pass through is locked again as soon as* they *have passed* until, eventually, they arrive at the cell set aside for John Jasper, while he awaits his trial.

The choirmaster's cell reminds the Rev Crisparkle of a monk's he once visited; the word 'spartan' comes to mind. It is equipped with gaslight and a chamber pot. On the one shelf are a number of books, including the Bible, together with a plate, a tin mug, a wooden spoon. There is a chair and a little table on which rests a pen, inkpot and paper. His bedding is rolled neatly at the head of the bench on which he sleeps. Helena expects him to be dressed in the prison garb she has seen the other inmates wearing, but no – John Jasper wears his own clothes and looks every inch the clergyman.

They learn that during the months he waits for his trial, he is allowed one bath a week and is able to exercise once a day in one of the several yards assigned for that purpose, walking quietly round, six feet behind the prisoner in front of him to whom he is forbidden to speak. Each day, he is allowed to visit the chapel, which he finds brings him great solace. His morning ablutions and cleaning his cell occupy some of his time; meals help to arrange the hours of the day. Through a small, barred window he is able to see the sky, and this brings him great comfort. Religious music has always been a great joy and he sings the cathedral services in their proper order each day.

John Jasper is very calm, almost serene, during the three months he waits for his trial. His self-composure is unsettling to the young woman who believes he is responsible for her brother's death as well as the murder of her friend's ex-fiancé; and he carries this tranquillity into the courtroom, a man certain of the outcome of his inquisition.

*

Winter passes into spring and the rough winds of March buffet the crowds who gather in the courtroom where the choirmaster's fate is to be decided. In a room of dishevelled people, he is the imperturbable presence: unruffled, unexcited, unmoved. The newspapers are in complete agreement on this point, and day after day, as the trial progresses, they continue to be amazed and to amaze their readers.

John Jasper stands smiling at the evidence as it is arraigned against him, wondering how the jury can believe such things of him, a Choirmaster and Lay Precentor. He is puzzled how anyone can believe the ramblings of the stonemason, Durdles, a man whose grasp of language is primitive and whose memory is befuddled by drink. He is perplexed as to why the words of the young woman, Rosa Bud, who is evidently no more than an excited and highly-strung child, can move the jury. Certainly, the detective, Mr Warden, presents his evidence in a workman-like manner, calmly and steadily, clue by clue from small beginnings to its final resolution; but he is a policeman, no more, a functionary of the state. He bestows a grateful look on the sailor, Lt Tartar, when the man describes how, on that fateful night, he prevented the 'prisoner' (how the choirmaster hates that word!) throwing himself off the cathedral tower; surely it is understood that he was distressed beyond measure and devoted to finding the killer of his dear boy. He is grateful to the Rev Crisparkle for confirming his determination in this matter. He is dubious as to why the solicitor, Grewgious, is called merely to ascertain that he, John Jasper, collapsed on hearing the news of the broken engagement. And the ring? He knew nothing of the ring. He appreciates that the other woman, the determined one, Miss Landless, with whom he has built an understanding over the months in prison, is not – will not? – be called to testify. She is intelligent and understands the times and tides of life; she who has more cause to do so than most.

He grants the public gallery a smile and there is a sympathetic reaction from them. He has always doubted the sensibilities of the people but for him they have come up trumps. His demeanour is proof enough, if proof is required, that he is a man who would naturally detest the crime of which he is accused. He is sanguine. His counsellor is sanguine and expects nothing less than an acquittal. He knows the newspapers speak well of him; he has read their comments *'collected and resolute in his demeanour'*, *'rather mild and conciliatory in his address'*, visited by *'friends whom he receives with cheerfulness'*, *'increasing in confidence as the day which is to decide his fate draws near'*. He understands that the bookmakers have odds in his favour. He has only to believe in himself and others will sense the sincerity of that belief; he has only to retain and disseminate his dignity for all to experience. He knows he is innocent of the charges against him and the court will come to understand that as well.

One man in the courtroom, and one man alone, notices that John Jasper is not quite as composed as others may suppose; but he is a detective and one may dismiss him as occupationally sceptical. Detective Sergeant Warden observes that at times the prisoner is *pulling on and off his glove, that his hand is … passing over and over his face, that he is … writing and scattering notes,* which he hands to his counsel, that he arranges and re-arranges the papers in front of him, that his address to the court is in the style of a well-known actor (rather than as himself) and expresses the joy he will feel in being able to resume his duties at the cathedral. Only small points and perhaps of no importance.

*

A month has passed since the trial and the verdict; and the cell now visited by the Rev Crisparkle and his fiancée, Miss Landless, is of a different stamp. There are three such cells reached by a *narrow and obscure staircase leading to a dark passage, in which a charcoal stove casts a lurid light over the objects in its immediate vicinity, and diffuses something like warmth around.* It is on *the left-hand side of this passage, the massive door of every cell … opens, and from it alone can they be approached.*

The cell *is a stone dungeon, eight feet long by six feet wide, with a bench at the further end, under which are a common horse-rug, a Bible, and a prayer book. An iron candlestick is fixed into the wall at the side; and a small high window in the back admits as much air and light as can struggle in between a double row of heavy, crossed iron bars.* The room contains no other furniture of any description, but the warder provides two chairs for the prisoner's guests.

For it is not the choirmaster who sits on the bench, but the prisoner. His present guests have visited him many times during the past month, and he has been grateful for they will know he succeeded in his quest to hunt down the murderer. The young woman, in particular, has been in accord with his explanations, and seen events as he sees them. Her eyes never left him when he spoke, and several times she has made strange passes with the points of her fingers at a short distance from him, from his face down his arms, body and legs. This has relaxed him into telling his story, and a strange story it is.

"I knew from the first time I laid eyes upon him that he wished my dear boy ill. Oh, had it not been so! But there was no calling him back, once his mind was settled on this evil scheme. He was a wicked man and he had the *cause and will and strength and means* to further his wickedness. His preparations were fastidious, and he had brooded upon them for many a long night, far into the hours of darkness; dwelt upon them until they obsessed every waking hour. And he waited. Oh, he knew how to wait until the chance came! And it came with a rival for his true love's hand.

The rival was of no consequence but the deed he had planned for so carefully could now be accomplished and another gilded to bear the guilt. It was a wild night when the rivals sought out the storm – a boisterous gale. *Strong blasts of wind blowing out the lamps* served his purpose. He revelled in the confusion of the night. The trees themselves tossed and creaked and seemed *in peril of being torn out of the earth*. He was as wild as the storm., but he waited patiently, the devil, he waited so patiently until my dear boy returned – and alone! The other had gone his own way. The very devils were smiling upon him that night!

Returning from the river, they had parted, each to his way home. He knew my dear boy had to walk back past the graveyard, by the southern door he knew so well. The cathedral precincts are always dark at night. *Time and place were both at hand!* It was easy to waylay him, twist the long, black scarf he kept for the purpose about my dear boy's neck and tighten it until he could breathe no more. The body lay at his feet. *No struggle, no consciousness of peril, no entreaty.* It was over! It had been *too short and easy. To think how many times he went on the journey, and never saw the road!*

It was only a step or two to reach the door of the south transept and the crypt; but the journey was yet perilous. He had imagined it so many times, *always in the same way.* The crypt! How he had come to love the crypt. It had become as home to him. The crypt!

Ever since the night he explored the possibilities of the cathedral as a suitable tomb, he had dreamed of the crypt. The stonemason's yard – although a long haul for his purpose if he was to reach it by the High Street or the Monks' Vineyard – was but a short distance if he took the route that went directly by the Deanery and so to the precincts of the cathedral.

And a short distance he needed for he had seen the mound of quicklime in the stonemason's yard. And he had sweated that night, but to purpose. Barrowload after barrowload, five in all, he bore to the crypt, where it waited for its victim among the mounds of earth.

It was easy, then, to raise the slabs on the site he had selected, remove the earth, drop in the body, cover it with the quicklime that would decompose it quickly ... It was a journey he had made and a task he had undertaken *hundreds of thousands of times* in his own mind, a *difficult and dangerous journey ... a hazardous and perilous one ... where a slip would be destruction* ... He looked down at his night's work, at what was lying there at his feet in the bottom of the grave ... and, finally, he replaced enough soil and the slabs.

And there was nothing to be seen. He was gone from the face of the Earth forever! It was over so soon ... so soon ... it barely seemed worth the doing, it was so unreal."

He has told this tale many times in the month he waits, his sin ever before him; and each time the young woman, as he completes the story, asks:

"And the rival? What became of him?"

"The journey's made. It's over."

He will say no more, as though he resents the question, and a faint smile plays about his lips; but this morning, this last morning, *an overwhelming sense of his helplessness,* his hopelessness, *rushes upon him, he is lost and stupefied, and has neither thoughts to turn to, nor power to call upon the Almighty Being, from whom alone he can seek mercy and forgiveness, and before whom his repentance can alone prevail.*

"Waylaid he was and fought upon the parapet and lies at the bottom there in the murky, hidden depths," he replies, as though a burden has slipped from his shoulders.

Helena can bear no more, and leaves the cell, but her fiancé remains.

"John," he says, calling him for the first time, in all the time they have known each other, by his Christian name, "When the wicked man turneth away from his wickedness that he hath committed, and doeth that which is lawful and right, he shall save his soul alive."

The prisoner has heard the words many times, but it is only now that their true meaning comes home to roost. He turns to the clergyman.

"His sin is ever before him," replies the prisoner.

Of those he knew, only two witness his last moments. The Rev Crisparkle and Detective Sergeant Warden watch him mount the gallows: *the black stage, the crossbeam, the rope, and all the hideous apparatus of death.* And then he is nothing but *a limp, loose suit of clothes as if the man had gone out of them.*

Chapter 23
Samuel Warden Attends a Wedding

"The case went well, Sam," said Detective Inspector Charles Field, who sat watching his sergeant from across the broad, leather-topped desk, "You should be pleased with yourself ... *and* it will do you no harm in the eyes of those above," he continued, pointing at the ceiling as though the office of Sir Richard Mayne, who had established the elite force known as the Detective Police, might be found there. As he spoke, the senior detective tapped his nose with a fat forefinger, a habit of his that the younger officers found amusing.

"The real work was eventually carried out by the civilians, sir," replied Samuel, "They all conducted themselves with intelligence and courage – not least Miss Bud, who volunteered – nay, insisted – on playing the role of Mr Drood. She said she was about his height and size and knew the way he walked. It was essential that Jasper believed his victim had returned from the dead. We anticipated Mr Bazzard's play might shake him up a bit – rattle the nerves, you know. He had to lead us to the grave."

"And himself to the scaffold," said Detective Inspector Field, with what one might describe as 'gallows humour', "Did he repent, do you know?"

"I think not, sir. You can't judge men like him by normal standards. They are, as one of our writers has expressed it, 'a horrible wonder apart'."

"Quite." replied the inspector in his husky voice, his moist eyes watering, "There's always a moment in any investigation when the light begins to shine through the murkiness, isn't there, Sam? When was yours?"

"It was in trying to account for the unaccountable, sir. From the beginning, it was clear that Mr Drood had either been murdered or had chosen to disappear for reasons of his own. There were grounds enough, from Miss Bud's account, to believe he was sufficiently upset to have, simply, gone off. I held this in mind for a long time – indeed, sir, I allowed myself to be led astray by this belief quite late in the investigation ..."

"None of us are perfect, Sam."

"No, sir. Had the solicitor, Mr Grewgious, been open in his explanations – explanations regarding the ring – I would have dismissed the idea, since I felt that Mr Drood would not be the kind of man to abscond with something so valuable. But he was not!"

"The legal profession is not among our favourites, Sam."

"No, sir. The only other explanation was that Mr Drood had been murdered. There were only two people who had a motive for this: Mr Jasper through thwarted desire, and Mr Landless through ill temper. I dismissed Mr Landless early on – although holding on to the possibility – because of his sister's implacable faith in him ..."

"Intuition, Sam?"

"I'm afraid so, sir. Once my attention moved in Mr Jasper's direction – again, this would have occurred sooner had Mr Grewgious made me aware of Jasper's reaction when he was told of the broken engagement – I attempted to track his movements.

The expedition with the stonemason, Durdles, was key among these. Why had the choirmaster taken so much interest in the cathedral precincts? Mr Durdles took me over the route he had taken with Mr Jasper – twice! – but still nothing was clear to me. He was a clever man was Mr Jasper!

I came to the conclusion that we needed to flush him out. Hence, the play! I encouraged Mr Crisparkle to befriend him. I confided in Miss Landless what I had in mind and she – together with the actor manager, Mr Muggins – adapted Mr Bazzard's play to our purpose. I think the rest is in my report, sir."

"The ring was the clinching factor in identifying the body?"

"Yes, sir. Once we found Mr Drood's grave, we were able to piece together the remaining pattern of events on the night of Jasper's unaccountable expedition with Mr Durdles and on the night of the murder," replied Sam, "Mr Jasper was unaware of the ring and disposed of those other items that would have identified Mr Drood – had the body ever been discovered – by tossing them into the weir, where the Rev Crisparkle found them."

"Where Mr Jasper intended them to be found in order to incriminate Mr Landless?"

"Yes, sir. The Rev Crisparkle never knew why he was drawn to the weir. He said that his *first consciousness of being here was the sound of the water*. I think he was drawn there under Mr Jasper's influence. The man had a mesmeric power over others. We had evidence of that from Miss Bud, and I saw similar powers in Miss Landless both at the theatre and in Mr Jasper's cell."

"Animal magnetism it's called, Sam, and quite fashionable in certain circles."

"No doubt, sir," replied the other, dryly, and then added, "As a matter of interest, sir, it's worth noting that Mr Jasper was wrong with regards to the quicklime."

"So, I understand. On certain parts of the corpse it has a preservative effect?"

"You may recall, sir, there was a case some time ago when the murderer attempted to dispose of his victim in such a manner?"

"Yes, yes. He was identified by his teeth, I believe?"

"Quite so, sir."

"Thank you, Sam. You've done us proud."

"In that case, sir, might I request a few days' leave?"

"For what purpose?"

"I have a wedding to attend, sir."

*

Spring is now in full bud and bloom, and Easter is upon us, late this year so that the lambs born in February are large enough to leap, if not to the tabor's sound then in the sheer joy of being alive. The blackthorn is in full blossom, marsh-marigolds are in bloom and the larch is spreading its young green leaves.

In quiet spots along the Medway, moorhens build their rough nests of reeds and twigs; a willow warbler sings on a branch.

Samuel notices these things because he is a country boy who has come to town. He notices the activities of the skylarks in particular; they have been around for a while but are only now turning their attention to nest-building, ready for the rearing of their young.

It is a fitting image for Samuel as he attends his wedding, a double in fact, that of Lt Tartar to Miss Rosa Bud and the Rev Crisparkle to Miss Helena Landless. The Dean and one or two other senior clergy were not over-excited with this idea, the event being so close to Easter and being unusual, but persistence prevailed, the China Shepherdess being not as delicate as she appeared. It is a glorious day, as befits the wedding of two couples for whom everyone in Cloisterham have high hopes. Their vows taken, they emerge from the west door of the cathedral to cheering and applause.

The photographer (suggested by Lt Tartar since he is a man of his time and those *far-seeing blue eyes* anticipate the potential of the new art form) is waiting. The young couples are backed, and then fronted, by Mr Muggins's Theatre Company, all keen to be 'in the picture'. Their dress, selected from Wardrobe, may be a trifle eccentric for the tastes of the clergy and Mr Sapsea, who has honoured the occasion with his presence so that both young couples may look up to him in the manner of his wife, and if not then they are best to 'with a blush, retire'. Mr and Mrs Tope, however, are over the proverbial moon: the former being a natural showman and, since their visit last Christmas, rather a theatre addict, and the latter, a lover of occasions – any occasion! Miss Twinkleton, with Mrs Tisher at her side, are dressed elegantly as befits the day: their curls smartened, their eyes brightened and their step sprightly. Miss Twinkleton is keen for it to be known that both brides (she blushes as she says the word) are splendid examples of what is achieved daily at her seminary for young ladies.

She will repeat her admiration often in the years to come as 'her' Mrs Crisparkle brings forth not one or two but seven children into the world: all little Crisparkles adorning the town of Cloisterham. They will be visited often by the children of her other young lady, who now lives in London, where she has found a pleasant house in Doughty Street: Lt Tartar having decided that he must find a more suitable residence than Staples Inn for his growing family but leaving his beloved yacht in the care of his man, Lobley.

She is not to know the secrets of other hearts, of course, and is unaware of what a stalwart the Rev Crisparkle is, every day, to his wife. Helena settles in well at Minor Canon Corner and she and the elder Mrs Crisparkle rub along as well as might be expected of daughter-in-law and mother-in-law. To be fair on the China Shepherdess, she is devoted to her grandchildren, giving them the love that nurtures beyond childhood as she was not able to do with her own children. But, for Helena there will always be an emptiness in her heart: she is now a lone twin, and the love she gives to her husband and the love she receives from him cannot replace the brother who fought evil on the Bridge of Sighs and fell to his death doing so. Still, she seeks joy in her consolations: her husband, her children and her beloved theatre of which she will be an active member and eventually patron until it closes down almost forty years later.

To the relief of all, Helena and Neville's guardian, Mr Honeythunder, is not at the weddings and is seen no more. He was not invited, but there was always a fear he might turn up on the day, his voice booming across the cathedral, crushing the melody from the hymns as he crushes the generosity from philanthropy.

Mr Grewgious was, sitting in a rather angular position at the back, a position as much imposed by the pew as by his own disposition: but without Mr Bazzard who is in one of his sombre moods. Mr Grewgious, however, is more than pleased to be at the wedding of his ward. After the counsel for the prosecution had no more use for it, Rosa's mother's ring had been returned to him. Truth to tell, he had been tempted to keep it, leaving it to Rosa in his will – after all, he had lost her mother to another, and the ring was a reminder of what might have been – but it seemed fitting, as part of the trust placed in him, that Rosa should wear it, and she does on the ring finger of her right hand.

Mr Grewgious and Mr Bazzard continue in chambers as solicitor and solicitor's clerk; after all, Mr Grewgious cannot have the younger man starving for lack of recognition, and Mr Bazzard's success in Cloisterham has not been matched by anything similar in the city. As a consolation, he has joined the Syncretic Society, whose members *'wrote plays which theatrical managers refused to produce'* and who dedicated their plays to each other. Mr Muggins's invitation to become resident playwright at the Lyceum was not taken up by Mr Bazzard.

Samuel has other reasons for being in Cloisterham at this time: to be precise, one reason, Deputy. He is concerned that the boy does not drift to the city as he grows older; the city of London is no place for a child, and Samuel goes to see the boy, who has watched the weddings from a place on the wall surrounding the castle moat, once the other guests have departed.

Samuel is bound for Wherstead, the little village near Ipswich where he was born and where his mother and father still reside. Sam's father is a railwayman, but his uncle is the village blacksmith and Sam already knows he is willing to take on an apprentice, provided someone will provide the boy's indentures; Samuel will.

"You'll learn a skill, son, that will serve you as food and drink, clothes and shelter for the rest of your life. Besides, you'll be in the company of quiet, loving people – my mother and father – who will look after you as though you were their own child."

"I'll have a mother?"

"And a father."

"I wouldn't know what to do with either," replied the boy, in a return to his surly voice, "This is my home. It's the only one I've known."

"Stoning Durdles and maiming sheep is no way to live, son."

"But I know Durdles and I know the Travellers' Twopenny."

There is nothing Samuel can say to refute this comment. He knows what the boy meant: he had experienced the same fear when joining the force, and sometimes still yearns for a quiet life in the country. Maybe it is expecting too much to take the town out of the boy.

"I hadn't planned on staying the night," he says, "but I'm sure my landlady at the Royal Victoria and Bull will find me a room. I have a few calls to make. Will you meet me tomorrow: same time, same place? A man needs a trade, son, or a craft to call his own."

With Deputy's agreement as certain as anything in the boy's life has ever been, Samuel visits, firstly, Durdles and, secondly, the Rev Crisparkle, who he waylays before the clergyman has the chance to set off for his brief honeymoon.

Rev Crisparkle agrees and Durdles listens and nods, eyeing the detective with some asperity at the suggestion he might not be up to the task.

"Durdles knows," he said, doggedly, "no man better. Ask 'ere a man in Cloisterham whether Durdles knows his work.

When Durdles puts a touch or a finish upon his work, no matter where, inside or outside, Durdles likes to look at his work all round, and see that his work is a doing him credit."

And he did, and Deputy became as fine a stonemason as his master, in his early days and without the drink, had ever been; and Samuel Warden, reflecting on his time in Cloisterham, considered that his securing an orphan a trade far outdistanced in importance his apprehension of a villain by the name of John Jasper.

Author's End Note and Acknowledgements

The temptation to think through an ending to *The Mystery of Edwin Drood* is strong. Apart from the desire to restore order and the dislike of an unsolved mystery, there is also the fascination to wonder how Dickens would have resolved his story.

Most attempts to address this fascination, whether in play or novel form, have begun by following Dickens's own first part and then working through to a resolution. This approach is fraught with problems, not the least being the challenge of imitating Dickens's style.

It seemed to me that a more straightforward way would be to send a detective to Cloisterham at more or less the point where Dickens's fragment ends, which is six months after Edwin disappears. I had come across his admiration for what were then called the Detective Police when reading his journalism and decided that one of these gentleman might make the journey and investigate the mystery by looking at the available evidence in his quest for an answer.

The detective story flourished in Victorian times. From Poe's Auguste Dupin in the 1840s to Conan Doyle's Sherlock Holmes at the turn of the century, detective stories thrived. Notable among these was Wilkie Collins's *The Moonstone* (1868), which gave us Sergeant Cuff of the Detective Police, although Dickens had already introduced Inspector Bucket from the same organisation in *Bleak House* (1853).

The work of the Detective Police, a force formed in 1842, was marked by its emphasis on evidence rather than chance, prejudice or conjecture. Dickens writes '*the Detective Force ... is so well-chosen and trained, proceeds so systematically and quietly, does its business in such a workmanlike manner and is always so steadily and calmly engaged*'. He goes on to say that the officers are '*famous for steadily pursuing the inductive process, and, from small beginnings, working on from clue to clue*' (*Detective Police: Household Words, 27 July and 10 August 1850*).

I decided that my protagonist, Detective Sergeant Samuel Warden, would attempt his investigation in a similar manner, and this has also been my approach to the story. I have been aided in my research by the books listed below and I hereby acknowledge a debt of deep gratitude to the authors and editors involved.

From my reading I made two key decisions. Firstly, some questions raised by the nature of the unfinished fragment were unanswerable and speculation was misleading; secondly, there was clear evidence of Dickens's intentions in other matters.

The unanswerable questions were Datchery's identity, the origins of the Landlesses, Jasper's family history (including his possible relationship to Princess Puffer), the purpose of Princess Puffer's visit to Cloisterham on the Christmas Eve that Edwin disappears, the role of Deputy (if any) in the final resolution, the meaning of Durdle's memory of the scream a year before Edwin's disappearance, how and by whom the person responsible for Edwin's disappearance will be brought to account.

Clear evidence does exist, however, for certain of Dickens's intentions, if one is to believe the comments of his illustrators, the words of his family and friends and his own working notes; and there seems no reason why one shouldn't. The story concerns the murder of a nephew by his uncle, the murderer was to review the crime (while in the condemned cell) as though it had been committed by another, the engagement ring was to play a vital role in identifying not only the murderer but the location of the crime, the uncle was to urge on the search for Edwin and the pursuit of his murderer and the murder was to be by strangulation.

It also seems likely from what John Forster had to say that important roles were to be played by other characters, notably Rosa Bud, Septimus Crisparkle, Helena Landless and Lieutenant Tartar. Dickens endows each of these characters with special qualities likely to be useful in the pursuit of justice: Rosa's initiative, Crisparkle's 'muscular Christianity', Helena's strange powers and Tartar's athleticism.

Researchers are generally agreed that Dickens intended Rosa to marry Tartar, Crisparkle to marry Helena and that Neville was one of those Dickens characters marked for death.

Two of the unanswerable questions, however, had to be addressed: the identity of Datchery and how and by whom the person responsible for Edwin's disappearance was to be brought to account. In the first, I was aided by Wendy Jacobson in her wonderful book, *The Companion to Edwin Drood*, where she points out that Bazzard *'is the only* (existing) *character available for disguise as the stranger in Cloisterham'* (page 151 of the *Companion*). She also points out that Datchery might be *'simply himself'*: a new character, perhaps a detective?

I didn't want to make this assumption. Besides, Bazzard as the only existing character possible suited my purposes with regard to how the person responsible for Edwin's disappearance was to be brought to account. Thanks to Simon Callow's *Charles Dickens and the Great Theatre of the World*, the idea occurred to me that Dickens may have already given us an indication of this in his fragment.

In approaching the story, I also kept in mind Dickens's comments that the novel was to contain *'a very curious and new idea ... a very strong one, though difficult to* work' and his daughter Katey's belief that *'it was (never) on the Mystery alone that he relied for interest and originality of his idea'* but that *'he was as deeply fascinated and absorbed in the study of the criminal ... as in the dark and sinister crime'*. Lady

Pakenham's comments support this view: that the *very curious and new idea* was to be '*the pursuit and destruction of the criminal by himself* '.

Lastly, I have made no attempt to re-write Dickens's words and have kept his and mine very separate: those of the 'Inimitable' in *italic* font, mine are in normal.

Acknowledgments

Novels by Charles Dickens
The Mystery of Edwin Drood/ Introduction by David Paroissien; Penguin Classics 2002
The Mystery of Edwin Drood and Other Stories/ Introduction by Peter Preston; Wordsworth Classics 2005
Our Mutual Friend; Penguin Classics1997
The Adventures of Nicholas Nickleby; Penguin Classics 1999

Novels and Short Stories by Other Authors
The Moonstone by Wilkie Collins; Wordsworth Classics 1993
Victorian Detective Stories/ Introduced by Michael Cox; Oxford University Press 1993
The Woman in White by Wilkie Collins; Oxford World's Classics 2008
The Mystery of Edwin Drood by Charles Dickens and Leon Garfield; Random House 2015

Other Writing by Charles Dickens
Sketches by Boz; Penguin Classics 1995
Selected Journalism 1850-1870/ Introduction by David Pasco; Penguin Classics 1997
Dickens' Journalism 1834-51/ Edited by Michael Slater; J M Dent 1997

Writings about the Works of Charles Dickens
The Companion to The Mystery of Edwin Drood by Wendy Jacobson; Allen and Unwin 1986
The Companion to Our Mutual Friend by Michael Cotsell; Allen and Unwin 1986

Dickens and Crime by Phillip Collins/ 3rd Edition; St Martin's Press 1994
Charles Dickens and the Great Theatre of the World by Simon Callow; Harper Press 2012

Writings about *The Mystery of Edwin Drood*
Puzzle of Dickens's Last Plot by Andrew Lang; Kessinger Publishing 1905
Clues to Dickens' Mystery of Edwin Drood by J Cuming Walters; Chapman and Hall 1905
About Edwin Drood by Henry Jackson; Cambridge University Press 1911
The Decoding of Edwin Drood by Charles Forsyte; Charles Scribner and Sons 1980
The Murder of Edwin Drood ... by John Jasper by Percy Carden; Forgotten Books 2015

Background Reading
The London Underworld in the Victorian Period by Henry Mayhew and Others;
Dover Publications 2005
Victorian London by Liza Picard; Phoenix 2006
The Suspicions of Mr Whicher by Kate Summerscale; Bloomsbury 2009
Haunted Rochester by Neil Arnold and Kevin Payne; The History Press 2011
Dickens's Victorian London 1839-1901 by Alex Werner and Tony Williams; Ebury Press 2011
The Victorian City by Judith Flanders; Atlantic books 2012
The Victorian Detective by Alan Moss and Keith Skinner; Shire Publications 2013
Of Street Piemen by Henry Mayhew; Penguin Classics 2015

Articles from *The Dickensian*
Dead or Alive? by Steven Connor; 1993
Dating Edwin Drood by Ray Dubberke; 1992

Mr Crisparkle, Neville Landless and Magnetic Sympathy by Arthur J Cox; 2000
Drood and the Beanstalk by Charles Faulkner; 1984
Disappearances by Robert Tracy; 2000
The Singler Stories of Inspector Field by W Long
Inspector Bucket Visits the Princess Puffer by Phillip Collins; 1964
Some Observations on Collins's Sketches by Robert Raven; 1984
The 'Gritty Stages' – Psychological Time by Nancy Schaumburger; 1990
Last Words on the Drood Mystery by Willoughby Matchett and Others; 1908

Other Writings
A Charles Dickens Walk in Rochester by Richard Jones
Rochester Cathedral by Canon Jonathan Meyrick and Others
And
Rochester: City of Charles Dickens/ DVD by Graham Salter 2012

Sketch Map of Cloisterham with Detail of Cathedral from DS Warden's Notebook

1. Durdles's Yard
2. Cathedral
3. Mr Jasper's Gate House
4. Rev Crisparkle's House
5. The Esplanade
6. High Street
7. Miss Twinkleton's Seminary
8. The Deanery
9. The Monk's Vineyard
10. The Medway
11. Old City Wall
12. The Crypt
13. Lyceum Theatre
14. Royal Victoria and Bull
15. Travellers' Twopenny
16. Mrs Topes House (Mr Datchery)

1. Burial Ground
2. North transept
3. South Transept
4 S Quire Door
5 Crypt
6 Deanery